THE SOVIET ASSASSIN

ALLAN LEVERONE

Prologue

January 27, 1988
9:25 a.m.
KGB Headquarters
Lubyanka Square, Moscow
Russia, USSR

KGB Foreign Operations Director Fedya Ilyich crushed his cigar into a brass ashtray with one ham-fisted swipe and glared at his counterpart, Internal Security Director Slava Yakovich.

"There is something I feel you are not understanding, Slava." Ilyich was trying his best to keep his voice calm but could feel his blood pressure rising.

"And what might that be?"

"It is not as easy as you seem to believe to recruit and train assassins. When we have one we believe in, we like to keep him and utilize him to the utmost extent possible."

"But there is—"

"I have not finished speaking, Slava," Ilyich interrupted. He pause to light another cigar as Yakovich waited, closed-mouthed but clearly impatient to speak.

Too bad for you, Ilyich thought. *I am your superior, and you will speak when I tell you to speak.* He'd considered simply implementing his plan without consulting the internal security

1

director, but knew that to do so would be to invite trouble down the road.

And Fedya Ilyitch was not interested in courting trouble, down the road or anywhere else.

"As I was saying," Ilyich continued, "the man you know as Piotr Speransky is the best assassin we have in our stable at the current time."

"I understand he is a competent killer." Yakovich spoke drily, in the tone of a man who considered himself above discussions regarding people who murdered other people for a living.

"No, Slava, I do not think you understand. Speransky is not just a 'competent killer.' He is the finest assassin in our arsenal at present and, I believe, one of the best in the long history of the Soviet intelligence services. I am not interested in losing a man such as this over one mistake."

"But it was not just one mistake," Yakovich said. "Speranksy revealed intelligence that permitted a lone CIA operative to execute one of our most accomplished chemical and biological weapons scientists. And not only was Comrade Marinov murdered, he was shot down right here on the streets of Moscow!"

"I am well aware of Speransky's transgression, Slava."

"Then you know I simply cannot overlook it in my role as director of internal security. Our people must be held accountable to a standard of excellence. If they are not held accountable when they fail, we inevitably start down a slippery slope."

"Explain your slippery slope."

"It is simple. If we do not hold Comrade Speransky accountable, we risk devolving into an organization where covert operatives are free to perform sloppy assignments with impunity. This cannot be allowed to happen. There must be consequences for failure, Fedya, and they must be severe."

"Of course there must be consequences," Ilyich agreed. "I am not suggesting a sweeping overhaul of internal policy. I am suggesting nothing of the sort. A typical operative who fails in the manner Speransky did will still face either a lifetime in prison or a pair of Makarov slugs in the skull as punishment. All I am saying is that we must make an exception in Speransky's case. That is all. One exception. No more and no less."

Yakovich huffed. "I do not like it. Our program of poisoning American operatives was stopped in its tracks with Comrade Marinov's execution. What was once a shining success is now in a shambles, probably irretrievably so, all thanks to Comrade Speransky."

"Again, I am well aware of that, Slava."

"Then I am sure you understand I cannot abide Speransky getting off scot-free."

"He will not get off scot-free. I intend to make it crystal clear to Comrade Speransky that he will get one chance at redemption, and one chance only. He will be offered a single assignment in which to restore his position within the organization. If he fails at that assignment, I will not stand in the way of your administering the severest punishment available."

Yakovich sat back in his chair. He sighed and stroked his beard, lost in thought. "You really like Piotr Speranksy that much?"

"Oh no," Ilyich answered immediately. "I cannot stand Speransky. He is arrogant and cruel, and worse, he is difficult to work with. He displays a near total disregard for the chain of command and is nearly impossible to control. In fact, I will go one step farther and say I rather fear the man. He exhibits signs of instability, and the less time I must spend in Piotr Speransky's vicinity, the happier I am."

"Then, why…?"

"It is simple, Slava. And I already told you why I would go out of my way for Speransky. He is exactly that good at what he does. His value to the KGB makes putting up with his…quirks… worthwhile."

Yakovich shook his head. "I am still not convinced."

Ilyich sat silently, smoking his cigar and allowing the truth of the situation to sink into Yakovich's sometimes obstinate skull: *It doesn't matter if you are convinced, Slava, because I do not need your permission to execute my plan. This meeting is informational only.*

Finally Yakovich grunted. "What is this assignment you are proposing? What could possibly be difficult enough—and valuable enough to the KGB—to make up for Speransky's failure this past week, a failure that occurred practically right under our noses?"

Ilyich smiled. He blew a smoke ring toward the ceiling. "Let us play a little guessing game, Slava."

Yakovich blinked in surprise. "A guessing game? I have known you a long time, Fedya, and I have never known you to be a man who enjoyed games."

"Very true."

"Then…"

"Humor me."

"Fine. I will play your guessing game."

Ilyich's smile widened. "Alright, then. Say you were a covert assassin, and you had been kidnapped, tortured and humiliated by an American CIA agent, and a female agent at that, practically in the shadow of your own home. What do you suppose would be the one thing you would want more than anything else in the world?"

Yakovich answered instantly. "Vengeance, of course."

"Of course," Ilyich said, and fell silent.

Yakovich's eyes widened. "You are not suggesting…"

"Oh yes I am, Slava. Piotr Speransky will find and execute his tormentor, or he will face the fate you seem to so vehemently desire for him."

"But how on earth will he find her? She could not possibly still be in Moscow. Undoubtedly the CIA will never allow her near Russia or anywhere else in the Soviet Union, ever again. She is almost certainly sitting behind a desk at Langley in the United States. She will likely never return to the field after an operation as brazen as the one she performed here in Moscow, because the CIA knows how badly we would like to get our hands on her."

"None of that is our problem, is it?"

"But…it is an impossible assignment!"

"Again, not our problem. And if your assessment is correct, you may put two bullets into Speransky's head yourself when he fails, if that is your wish. But I am telling you, Speransky will be highly motivated. And he will either succeed and thereby justify my faith in him, or he will fail and become just another operative never to be heard from again."

Yakovich stared at his superior. "That is either the craziest or the most brilliant plan I have ever heard. But either way, it is simply impossible."

"Again," Ilyich said. "It is not—"

"I know, I know. It is not our problem."

The smile never left Fedya Ilyich's face.

1

May 12, 1988
11:35 p.m.
U.S. Embassy
Paris, France

Clayton Leavell bent over his desk, peering at a briefing document prepared by an anonymous U.S. State Department analyst somewhere in the bowels of the Harry S. Truman Building in Washington, D.C.

The information contained within the document was dry and uninteresting, even to a career diplomat like Clayton: a summary of amendments to the intelligence-sharing protocols between the governments of the United States and France. The changes were being proposed by the lame-duck Reagan administration in advance of this November's upcoming presidential election. The current Republican administration was tightening the rules in the event a Democrat were to win the election and thus occupy the White House at this time next year.

Clayton had seen it all before, every eight years like clockwork. A sitting president was rarely defeated at the end of his first term—although Jimmy Carter had managed to make himself the exception that proved the rule less than ten years ago—but following his second term, when the chances of the rival political party taking the reins of power were much greater, the flurry of changes to diplomatic protocols began.

Whether the party in power was Republican or Democrat made little difference; both approached the potential loss of influence in exactly the same way: by making it as difficult as possible for their opponent to change policy direction after assuming control.

Should a Republican win the 1988 presidential election rather than a Democrat, Clayton knew he would find himself sitting at this very desk in early 1989, poring over a summary briefing reversing many of the very changes he was being instructed to implement now.

He sipped his cognac and sighed. So much of the political process was a game; a chess match designed not so much to advance the interests of the United States as to stymie the opposing political party. And for an ambassador, the whole point of diplomacy was to gain as much intelligence as possible from the host nation while simultaneously giving up as *little* as possible to them.

It was nothing more than a massive shell game. Even when dealing with France, which along with Great Britain had been among the United States' most trusted allies for more than a century, Clayton found himself more often than not attempting to trick the French government, dealing in subterfuge and misdirection rather than cooperation.

It was the nature of diplomacy, and he knew the government of France was playing the game in exactly the same way when it came to dealing with him.

Most of the time Clayton relished the challenge.

Sometimes, though—and this was one of those times—it was simply exhausting. Clayton was a family man, and with Rebecca and the kids back in the states he felt unmoored. His wife and children's impromptu vacation was for the best, given the current situation: two U.S. diplomats killed in the past two weeks under circumstances that were unrelated as far as the world knew.

Clayton knew differently.

Arlene Nevin had been struck and killed by a car two weeks ago. A hit-and-run "accident" on a deserted West German road in which the vehicle that struck Arlene had never been found. Additionally, authorities could come up with no plausible explanation as to what the United States ambassador to West Germany had been doing on a lonely road fifteen kilometers outside West Berlin at three a.m. on a Wednesday night.

It was baffling, and the Reagan administration had voiced its suspicions—that the "accident" may not have been entirely accidental—almost immediately.

Then last week Eldon Wickheiser's administrative assistant had found the U.S. ambassador to Spain dead inside his own car in the early-morning hours one week to the day after Arlene Nevin's unexplained death. As with the Nevin situation, there were unanswered questions surrounding Wickheiser's fatality, not the least of which was what Wickheiser was doing sitting inside his car in the embassy garage in the middle of a weeknight.

Wickheiser's wife had told authorities she'd gone to bed around ten p.m. and that at that time her husband had been acting normally, watching television and eating a light snack. She'd taken sleeping medication and could not recall whether or not he'd ever come to bed.

Two inexplicable deaths of United States diplomats in separate European nations on successive Wednesday nights one week apart.

As a United States ambassador, Clayton Leavell was privy to information that had thus far been successfully withheld from the media and the public: the two diplomats had been murdered, and their killings were as far from unrelated as it was possible to get.

Evidence recovered at the scene of both deaths suggested strongly that the killings had been committed by the same person, or at least that the same organization had been responsible for both. What was being withheld from the public for the time being was that a note had been recovered at each scene.

Despite Clayton's status as ambassador to France and a very interested party, he'd not been advised of the notes' exact contents. What he *had* been told was that both were brief and cryptic. So cryptic, in fact, investigators had thus far been unable to fully decipher their contents.

While Clayton found that information fascinating from a theoretical point of view, the more important and terrifying fact was that until the crimes were solved, he had to be considered a target, as did every ambassador stationed in Europe. Secretary of State J. Robert Humphries had called him personally five days ago, and in a long conversation told him, in effect, to hunker down.

No trips outside the embassy except on official business, and even then, only accompanied by armed security personnel.

No public appearances of any kind except as necessary to perform official duties.

Basically, he was to make himself a prisoner inside the embassy.

Humphries' words hadn't frightened Clayton as much as had his tone. He was somber, and his concern was sincere and obvious.

Clayton had sent Rebecca and the children home by nightfall that day. All the media was told was that his wife and children were taking an extended vacation back in the states, reconnecting with Rebecca's parents. She had wanted to stay with Clayton, of course, but hadn't put up much of an argument out of a desire to protect their son and daughter.

And Clayton had been left alone.

That was almost a week ago, and the sad fact of embassy life was that once you removed the ceremonial duties from an ambassador's schedule—speeches to civic groups, question-and-answer sessions at schools, glad-handing host country politicians—most of the time there wasn't much actual work of substance to keep a man or woman occupied.

Clayton had been reduced to walking the embassy grounds at all hours of the night and day, giving himself more exercise in the past five days than he'd gotten in probably twenty years. In what he considered a fair display of gallows humor, he'd named these sessions his "Death Marches." When not occupied by one of his death marches, he forced himself to his desk for extended periods of time spent shuffling official paperwork.

All of which explained his presence here, alone in his office, as the grandfather clock in the corner announced midnight's arrival with all the rich, deep-throated grandfather-clock pomp and circumstance appropriate to the launch of a new day.

It was now Wednesday morning.

The murders of the two U.S. ambassadors had occurred on this day, one week and two weeks prior.

Clayton swallowed heavily, staring at the clock, the minute hand moving ever so slowly past the twelve. He knew he was safe—if isolated and alone—inside the embassy. The security staff was competent and professional.

Still, the compound felt cold and empty without Rebecca and the children.

And undoubtedly Nevin and Wickheiser had felt safe also, right up until the moment they weren't.

Clayton had requested additional security during his briefing by Secretary of State Humphries, but that request had been summarily denied. "We can't appear skittish to the public, Clayton, like we're allowing the actions of one or two lunatics to dictate our response."

"Sir, the public would never know. The public is unaware these killings are related."

"True," Humphries had said. "But at some point the news about those notes *will* leak out, and once it does, our every move in response to this crisis will be scrutinized by a critical press. We need to maintain a holding pattern, just for now, until our investigators can develop a lead on the perpetrators. Once that happens, we'll have a better handle on how to proceed."

Clayton understood Humphries' point. He even agreed with it on that damned theoretical level. But from a personal standpoint, as a guy with a target presumably painted on his back, a few extra men with guns patrolling the walls and gates of the embassy compound might have made him feel, if not comfortable, at least a little less uneasy.

He sighed and turned away from the clock.

And found himself staring straight down the barrel of a gun.

2

Clayton Leavell was no gun expert. He hated the damned things and in fact had never touched a real handgun, certainly not one that was loaded and ready to fire.

But he sure as hell knew what they looked like. What he'd never realized until this very moment was how goddamned *big* a pistol looked when it was being leveled between one's eyes.

Which accurately described his current situation.

He froze and tried not to make his terror obvious. The intruder's wry smile told him he'd failed.

"How did you get in here?" Clayton said. "This is the official residence of the United States Ambassador to France, and you are not welcome in my home."

The man's smile widened. "I understand. I think I will stay anyway. And to answer your question, there is always a way in, if you know where to look and are willing to impart the proper... motivation...to those who insist on attempting to stop you."

Despite his fear, Clayton cocked his head at the sound of the man's accent. After spending the better part of seven years as a semi-permanent resident of Paris, he'd become quite accustomed to the heavy French accent of those Parisians who spoke English, and this was not it.

This was not even close to it.

The man's English was passable, in a "foreigner-who-learned-the-language-but-doesn't-speak-it-regularly" kind of way, but the accent was as far from French as it was possible to get.

It sounded Russian.

Clayton raised his eyes and met the man's gaze head-on. It was difficult to do, but he decided anything would be better than staring down the barrel of that awful gun.

Then their eyes locked and he reconsidered his hypothesis. Because despite the smile on the intruder's face, the man's eyes were cold and stony and glittering with hostility.

It was becoming harder to keep his voice steady, but somehow Clayton managed it. For now. "What sort of 'motivation' did you impart on my security? How many men did you shoot?"

A wounded look crossed the intruder's face and then disappeared. "I did not shoot any of your men. How could I be expected to surprise you if bullets were flying outside your window?"

"Then I'll ask the same question a different way. How did you neutralize my security?"

"At the point of a knife." The glitter deepened in the man's eyes. At first Clayton assumed it was the expression of a madman, but now he wasn't so sure. He didn't think the intruder was insane, not exactly. Not clinically, at least. He was…highly committed.

To what, Clayton had no idea.

"How many men did you kill with your knife to gain access to my home?" He wasn't sure he wanted to know the answer to that question, but the intruder hadn't pulled the trigger yet, and Clayton figured if he could continue the dialogue, maybe he could figure a way out of this mess.

It was the longest of long shots, but it was better than dying where he sat.

"As many as I encountered," the man answered flatly. His amused smile was gone and Clayton longed desperately for its return.

The two men gazed at each other for what felt like an extended period of time, and then Clayton said, "What do you want? Why are you here?"

"What I want is to make a point. As for why I am here, well, isn't it obvious?" The intruder glanced down at his gun and then across the desk at Clayton, and at that moment Clayton realized he *really* needed to pee.

"Wh-what kind of point are you trying to make, and to whom?"

"That is of no concern to you."

"Of course it's my concern! You're holding a gun to my head and threatening my life, so—"

"Taking," the man interrupted.

"Excuse me?"

"You said I am threatening your life. I merely attempted to correct the inaccuracy of your statement. I will be *taking* your life."

"But…why? What have I ever done to you?"

"I already told you why. I am making a point. Sending a message. And to answer your second question, I am quite certain you have never done anything to me. In fact, you seem like a fine, upstanding, reasonable man. Please do not feel this is in any way personal."

"It is to me."

The smile returned. "*Da.* I suppose it would be."

"Don't do this. It's not too late to leave, and if you do no one ever has to know you were here. I give you my word I won't—"

"Please stop. Begging for your life is humiliating. It is beneath you, Mr. Ambassador, and more to the point, it is irrelevant. I told you this is not personal. I am simply doing what must be done to get the attention of people who have thus far ignored me, and so I have no choice but to finish what I set out to do. Anything you say, any begging you do, will be meaningless in that context."

Clayton realized his eyesight had become blurry because his eyes had filled with tears. This scene felt unreal, like something out of a nightmare, and yet it was as real as the big black gun being pointed in his direction. He thought about Rebecca, and about Lorena and Matt, and about how he would never see any of them again. He thanked God he had sent them away, but wished with all his heart he could hold each of them one more time.

"If it is any consolation, Mr. Ambassador, there will be no pain. It will be over quickly and you will never feel a thing."

Clayton swallowed heavily. His fingers felt numb and he wondered if he might be suffering the onset of a stroke. "It really isn't," he whispered.

"Perhaps not, but remember, things could always be worse. They could, in fact, be much worse. Be thankful you must not ingest the poison I forced your comrade, Ambassador Wickheiser to ingest."

"Poison?"

"*Da*. It was not over quickly for Comrade Wickhesier."

"Oh, God, why…"

"There is nothing to be gained by continuing to discuss topics we have already covered. What do you say we get started?"

Clayton's throat was suddenly as dry as the Sahara. He tried to answer but discovered the term "tongue-tied" had a literal application. He simply could not speak. He began shaking his head, breathing heavily as his blurry eyes began leaking down his cheeks.

"Do not move," the intruder said, apparently not realizing Clayton not only couldn't move, he could barely breathe. The intruder stepped back to the office doorway and bent down while continuing to train his gun steadily on Clayton. He'd placed a small gym bag on the floor and after rummaging around inside the bag for a moment, retrieved a roll of shiny silver duct tape.

The intruder displayed the roll to Clayton and said, "Duct tape would not be my first choice of binding for this operation, but as I mentioned, the point of this exercise is to capture the attention of the proper people, so I must do what will best accomplish that goal."

He stood and approached Clayton and Clayton instinctively shrank back in his desk chair, scrabbling his feet against the polished hardwood floor and rolling the wheeled chair backward.

The chair thudded into the wall and Clayton heard picture frames rattling above his head as the intruder shook his head sadly. "Please, Mr. Ambassador, do not continue to humiliate yourself. There is nowhere to go, and no means of escape."

Clayton was sweating and panting and all he could think of was begging for his life, and the hell with what this lunatic had said about humiliating himself. But his throat was still dry and his tongue still would not cooperate and he just COULD NOT SPEAK.

The intruder stepped behind Clayton's desk and pulled a strip of duct tape off the roll. The zip of the tape sounded obscene in the midnight stillness of the office. The man reached for Clayton's arm and Clayton yanked it away in a blind panic.

The intruder shook his head. This time there was more annoyance than sadness in the action. "Let me make something clear to you, Mr. Ambassador. I am happy to kill you painlessly. In fact, it is what I prefer. But if you insist on making this more difficult than it needs to be, I shall have no problem dragging your death out and making it as agonizing as possible for you. The time is barely midnight. We could quite easily spend the next four to five hours together, doing things you would not enjoy. Is that what you want, Mr. Ambassador?"

Clayton shook his head violently. That was most definitely not what he wanted.

"Then sit quietly, and place your hands on the arms of your chair. I will not tell you again."

Clayton forced himself to do as he was told. It was not easy. Every fiber of his being was telling him to spring to his feet and run, but of course he could not spring to his feet because he was quite literally frozen in fear, and he could not run because there was nowhere to go.

The intruder worked quickly. He secured Clayton's arms and legs to the chair and in a matter of sixty seconds was ready to continue. He dropped the tape back into his bag and then removed something that looked to Clayton like a long, narrow black tube from a roll of paper towels.

The intruder began threading the paper towel tube onto the barrel of his gun, and that was when Clayton pissed himself. He couldn't help it. One moment he was dry and the next he was sitting in his own waste.

The intruder didn't seem to notice. Or if he noticed, he didn't care.

He returned one more time to his bag and retrieved a sheet of notebook paper upon which something had already been written. Clayton couldn't tell what the words were and really couldn't care less. His life was in its final moments and unless the paper contained instructions on avoiding his fate, it was of no use to him.

The intruder approached, holding the paper and duct tape in one hand and his gun in the other. He bent in front of Clayton and shocked Clayton by shoving a portion of the paper into his mouth. He then slapped a strip of duct tape over the paper and around the back of Clayton's head.

Then he stood.

"Thank you for a pleasant evening, Mr. Ambassador. Unfortunately, all good things must come to an end, as must all lives. Again, this is nothing personal."

Clayton was shaking helplessly and hyperventilating as the intruder placed his gun barrel under Clayton's jaw and aimed it upward toward the ceiling. The barrel felt heavy and cold.

And then the world disappeared.

At least the intruder kept his promise. There was no pain.

3

Tracie Tanner lifted the piece of jewelry from the bowl and dabbed at it carefully with a cloth held in her left hand. A rope chain threaded through a gold cross, the jewelry was simple but had at one time been quite beautiful. Before she'd placed it into the bowl, however, it had been covered in its owner's dried and clotted blood.

She had soaked the cross and chain overnight in a jewelry cleaning solution, and by this morning much of the human tissue and unidentifiable gore had sloughed off. There had been a lot of it. Some of the blood had soaked off as well, but there was still plenty left, and Tracie had replaced the chain and cross in fresh solution for several hours before attacking it again.

Now she worked at it patiently, running the chain through the solution and then placing it on a bath towel atop her tiny kitchen table. The towel would have to be trashed when she was finished, as would the cloth and, in all probability, the bowl as well. She could wash everything, of course, but the thought of reusing any of it after being covered in bits of brain and bone was…unappealing, to say the least.

The whole job was unappealing, really. She couldn't think of a single thing she would less like to be doing. But the things she *wanted* to do had always been very different from the things she

19

needed to do, and this was something she felt strongly needed to be done.

So she took her time, moving link by link along the gold chain, dabbing with the cloth and working the blood off the finish, then moving forward and beginning the process again. It was close work, painstaking and mentally draining. In the beginning it was also emotional, as she was forced to relive the deadly events that had resulted in her taking possession of this beautiful cross and chain in the first place.

But as she worked, she was surprised to discover a sense of calm settling over her. It felt good to take her time and expend her energy in restoring the cross and chain to their original condition. The process made her feel close to the chain's owner, and she thought he would have appreciated her efforts, had he lived to see them.

She hadn't known him well; they weren't close in any traditional sense. They didn't even know each other's real names. But they'd been bound together by a shared commitment, two Amercian covert operatives toiling halfway around the world in hostile environments in support of democracy and freedom.

They had faced life and death situations together on more than one occasion, each relying on the other's resourcefulness and courage to complete their missions. It was the sort of thing that had a way of fostering closeness even between relative strangers, of bringing people together in a way nothing else could.

She worked for a while on the chain and then took a break, calling her father just to say hello, something she didn't think she'd done in years. After his initial concern that something was wrong, the delight he took in hearing from his little girl was so clear through the phone line that she vowed to make similar calls on a regular basis.

They chatted about everything and nothing, a situation so out of character for her that he asked on three separate occasions whether something was wrong. But nothing was wrong, at least nothing she could talk to her father about, and when they finally hung up she felt better that she had in a very long time.

Peaceful, if not exactly at peace.

After ending the call to her father she got back to work.

She finished cleaning the chain and then turned her attention to the cross. Covered in dried blood and gore, its gold finish was barely discernable, but Tracie knew after working on the rope chain that restoring the cross would take only time and effort.

She was more than happy to expend both.

An hour later she had placed both items on a fresh towel to dry, and this one she knew she would not have to throw away. The chain and cross sparkled like new, and although the chain's clasp would have to be repaired—it had been torn off its owner's neck the last time he'd worn it—Tracie knew the jewelry would hold a special place in its new owner's heart.

She gazed at her handiwork for a while and then turned her attention elsewhere. Her phone would ring soon enough, and when it did she would be able to deliver the restored jewelry to its rightful owner, whoever—and wherever—that person might be.

*　　*　　*

She didn't have to wait long.

The telephone call came during dinner: canned ravioli, which she was attempting to wash down with the remains of a quart of milk on the verge of going sour. She doubted she'd ever been happier to hear the damned phone ring, even if it ended up being a telemarketer or political survey on the other side of the conversation. Either one would be preferable to finishing the ravioli and milk.

But when she answered the call she discovered it wasn't a telemarketer, and it wasn't anyone taking a survey.

It was CIA Director Aaron Stallings, and he was characteristically gruff. "Get your ass in here first thing in the morning," he said as soon as she picked up. He didn't even bother with a "hello" first.

"I'm fine," she said. "Thanks for asking. And how are you?"

He ignored her comment. "What time can you get here tomorrow?"

"How early is too early?"

He snorted. "Christ, Tanner, have you learned nothing from working with me? There's no such thing as too early."

"Then what about tonight instead?"

"Tonight?" Stallings answered. Tracie knew he was still in his office at Langley and she pictured him looking at his watch, trying to figure the traffic and determine how long it would take to get from there to his suburban home. None of their meetings ever took place at CIA headquarters, given Tracie's status as an unofficial employee.

"Tonight works," he said after an extensive delay. "I said tomorrow morning in an attempt to minimize interference with your life, but I forgot you have no life."

"Look who's talking," Tracie shot back. "I'm not the one who's still in the office at seven o'clock on a Friday night."

"No, you're sitting alone at your kitchen table eating a frozen pizza and waiting for the movie of the week to start on TV."

She dropped the handset onto the table with a thud, hoping it sounded as annoying on the other end of the line as it did to her. She walked into her living room to shut off her tiny black and white television and then she returned to the phone. "Shows what you know. It's canned ravioli, not frozen pizza. And the movie of the week doesn't even start for another two hours."

"Fine. Then you were watching reruns of some stupid sitcom that went off the air twenty years ago."

Not for the first time she glanced around her apartment looking for a miniature camera or hidden listening device. "For your information, my television's not even on."

He snorted again. "Not since you turned it off a minute ago."

She sighed into the phone, intentionally loudly enough for him to hear. "What time do you want me there?"

"Give me an hour. That way you'll have enough time to meet with me and still make it home for the beginning of the movie."

"Don't worry about it. Tonight's is a repeat. I've already seen it."

He snorted again and hung up without another word.

4

May 13, 1988
8:00 p.m.
McLean, Virginia

"Took you long enough," Stallings said without raising his eyes from the stack of paperwork cluttering the desk of his home office. He'd been hard at work on the stack every time she'd ever been here, and it never seemed to change in size.

She made a point of lifting her wrist and staring at her watch, an effort that was lost on her boss because he still hadn't looked up. "It's eight o'clock on the nose," she said. "Exactly the time you told me to be here."

"Traffic was light tonight. I could have seen you twenty minutes ago."

She spread her hands in frustration. "How was I supposed to know—"

"Lets get started, shall we? Unlike you, I didn't get to lounge around in my pajamas all day. I'm tired and I've got a long day tomorrow and I'd like to get to bed."

Tracie rolled her eyes—another wasted effort—and sat in her usual chair, which had been placed in its usual location: directly in front of Stallings' desk. Every time she came here she felt like a grade school student who'd been sent to the principal's office without knowing why.

"I'm all ears," she said.

Finally Stallings lifted his head. He caught her gaze and held it. "Tell me what you know about the status of our European ambassadors."

"I know what I've seen on the nightly news, namely that they've had a run of pretty bad luck."

"Explain."

"They keep dying."

Stallings nodded. "Explain further."

"I don't know much more than that. One was killed a couple of weeks ago in a traffic accident—a hit-and-run, if I remember correctly—and another died shortly afterward of...I don't exactly recall. A stroke, maybe, or a heart attack?"

Now that he'd removed his attention from his paperwork, Stallings seemed unwilling to look away from Tracie's eyes. He stared her down and said, "What else?"

She held his gaze without blinking. Stallings' hostility toward her seemed even greater than usual, and that was saying something. There was a battle of wills taking place, but what it was in reference to she had no idea.

She thought about his question for a moment and then said, "Well, let's see. The ambassadors' deaths are related, and they're far more suspicious than the media reports would indicate."

Stallings' eyes narrowed as she was speaking until by the time she'd finished they were mere slits. "Why would you say that?"

"Isn't it obvious? I'm sitting in your office at eight o'clock on a Friday night discussing the deaths of two public figures, that's why. You and I are not in the habit of analyzing current events except as they apply to my employment situation, and you wouldn't have called me here unless you needed something from me. All of which means the deaths are related and suspicious and you want me to do something about it."

He stared at her a little longer and then returned his attention to the stack of papers. Eventually he muttered something under his breath and lifted a single sheet from the stack. He flipped it around so it was facing Tracie and then slid it across the desk in front of her without another word.

It was clear he wanted her to examine it, so she did.

The examination didn't take long.

The paper was a photocopy of a typewritten note. The note had been flattened out prior to being photographed, but it was badly crumpled, and some of the ink appeared smudged, as though the paper had gotten wet. Bloodstains flecked its edges like brownish-red raindrops.

The note was short and not terribly sweet. Its writer had used an ink pen and written in large block letters: SEND THE REDHEADED SPOOK OR MORE WILL DIE.

Tracie looked up at Stallings and found him watching her closely.

She looked back down at the paper and read it again. Its contents didn't change.

"What is this?" she finally said.

"You tell me."

"How the hell would I know? I suppose I must be the redheaded spook the writer is referring to?"

"Presumably," Stallings said. "After checking our records I found we've had two other operatives working in and around Europe with red hair in the past decade, but one of them was reassigned shortly after you were hired."

"That was eight years ago."

"Exactly. A lifetime ago in the intelligence business."

"What about the other?"

"The other is a man with short hair. It's reddish-brown, more of a rust color than blood red. It's not the kind of identifying characteristic anyone would use if they were referring to him in this type of note. Your hair, on the other hand…"

He stared at her skull, making clear he thought the connection was obvious, and Tracie couldn't really disagree with him. Her hair was thick and lustrous and flame-red. It was exactly the kind of identifying characteristic anyone who wasn't stone blind would use to describe her.

"Okay," she acknowledged. "Whoever wrote this is probably referring to me. I assume this was found on one of the two dead ambassadors?"

"It was found on both. Identical messages written with the same pen. Our analysts assure me they were almost certainly both produced by the same person."

"I don't know what to tell you," Tracie said. "It's obvious you're looking for something from me, but I don't have the first clue what this is all about."

"There's more," Stallings said.

"Of course there is."

"There's been a third death."

"Another ambassador."

"Yes. And this one wasn't even made to look like an accident. We take that as an indication that the perpetrator is getting frustrated. He's becoming more insistent you respond."

Tracie stared at the note in concentration. "If it wasn't made to look like an accident, what *did* it look like?"

"A staged scene."

"Staged how?"

"You tell me." The CIA director rummaged around in his stack of papers until pulling out another photocopy. This one was of a photograph.

The picture was disturbing and violent. A man Tracie did not recognize, presumably a United States ambassador, had been secured in a chair with duct tape. He'd been gagged with what looked like a piece of paper—the note, most likely—and then the paper had been secured with more duct tape.

Then the man had been shot in the head. Tracie thought the killer had likely placed his gun under the ambassador's jaw and fired upward, based on the damage done to the top of the victim's skull and the amount and location of blood and viscera she could see surrounding the scene.

The photograph closely resembled something in her memory from a few months ago, except in Tracie's memory the man ducttaped to the chair had been alive.

She closed her eyes and lowered her head to the desk.

"Tell me," Stallings said gently.

So she did.

*   *   *

A few months ago Tracie had been dispatched to Moscow on an assignment regarding a series of murders of American intelligence operatives working inside the Soviet Union. The men had been dosed with poison so difficult to identify that the murder spree was several months along before the agency even recognized it for what it was.

Her assignment had been to trace the poison back to the perpetrators and to stop those men and/or women permanently. She had done exactly that, identifying the KGB agent operating as the assassin, and then kidnapping and torturing him in an effort to learn the identity of the person in charge of the operation.

But the assassin had been tough and resilient. She eventually extracted the intel she needed and eliminated the KGB scientist responsible for manufacturing the poison, but only after agreeing to spare the Soviet agent's life in exchange for the scientist's identity.

She'd known it was a mistake to allow the man to live—he was a cold-blooded murderer of American assets and a career KGB assassin—but hadn't been able to bring herself to renege on their agreement. At the conclusion of the mission she'd left the man trapped inside a CIA safe house in Moscow, gagged and duct-taped to a chair.

It was exactly as he'd been secured during their torture sessions.

The helpless KGB assassin was the first thing that came to Tracie's mind when she saw the picture of the slain U.S. ambassador. The scenes were eerily similar, so much so that to assume those similarities were coincidental would require a greater leap than Tracie was willing to make, even to ease her conscience.

To her the killings of the ambassadors and the notes that had been left behind on their bodies, combined with the horrifically staged scene at the most recent murder, could mean only one thing: the assassin Tracie had known as Piotr Speransky had eventually escaped his bindings and was active again.

And he was seeking vengeance against her.

And he was killing innocent Americans to lure her into the open.

* * *

Aaron Stallings' office fell silent when Tracie finished speaking. She'd expected him to launch into one of his patented angry tirades of the sort that had been intimidating operatives and politicians alike for decades the moment she finished speaking, but he surprised her by keeping his mouth shut.

He had of course registered his displeasure in no uncertain terms months ago with the fact that she allowed the KGB assassin to live. During her mission debrief after executing the Soviet scientist and stopping their poisoning program he'd pointed out what she already knew: that the man would likely come back to haunt them again at some point in the future.

Tracie had agreed with him at the time, and as angry as Stallings had been, she'd been even angrier with herself. She had known this day was coming from the moment she walked out of the Moscow safe house with Piotr Speransky still breathing. She hadn't expected the blowback from that fateful decision to come this soon—or to be this severe, with three innocent victims dead—but, still, she had known it was coming.

But she'd been raised to believe in the seemingly antiquated notion that a person's word was her bond. Her father was a U.S. Army general and her mother a career state department diplomat. In the Tanner household, honor and commitment weren't just words or even worthy goals; they were the foundation upon which her entire value system had been built.

She simply could not bring herself to abandon that value system in the case of the Soviet assassin, even knowing all that was at stake.

The office was quiet for a long time before Stallings spoke. When he did his voice was calm, the words measured, but there was no disguising the fury behind them. "We discussed the possible ramifications of allowing a KGB dirtbag like Speransky to live a few months ago, did we not?"

"We did, sir."

"So we are in agreement, then, that your decision to spare the life of one murderous Soviet agent has resulted in the loss of at least three more innocent American lives?"

"Yes sir, we are."

"I think you know what you need to do."

"I need to get to Paris and fix this mess."

"That's right. I want you on the first plane out tomorrow."

"Sir, if it's all the same to you, I'd like to leave tonight. I thought this might be something critical, so I brought my go-bag with me. It's sitting on the floor just outside your office door. I'd like to go straight to the airport from here. I don't want to wait one second longer than I have to, in case Speransky decides to up the ante and start killing more frequently than once a week."

"Fine," Stallings spat. "I can arrange to free up the agency jet. But let me tell you something."

Here it comes, Tracie thought. It was about time. She deserved every insult he was about to hurl her way. She deserved worse. She was every bit as guilty for the murders of the ambassadors as if she'd executed them herself.

In a way, she supposed she had.

"We've worked together a long time," Stallings said, "and I know how you think. You're planning to waltz into Paris and offer your life up to this KGB asshole in some misguided mea culpa for your error in judgment. And as bad as that error was—and there's no getting around it, it was bad—I will not see one of my most valuable assets go down without doing everything in my power to prevent it."

"And how can you possibly prevent it? Speransky will expect me to come and he'll be waiting. That's the whole point of leaving the notes on the victims.

"Agreed," Stallings said.

"He's an experienced operative and will be able to elude detection."

"Maybe," Stallings said, "and maybe not. But I'm going to work with French authorities to sew up the area surrounding the U.S. embassy tighter than a drum. If this assassin tries to kill you, we'll—"

"You mean *when* he tries to kill me."

"Okay, fine, when he tries to kill you. We'll stop him before he can manage it."

"Or at least take him down after he succeeds."

"Or at least that, yes."

Tracie sat staring at the floor. The prospect of violent death didn't frighten her. She'd long ago come to grips with the knowledge she could be killed performing her duties as a covert intelligence operative.

But the notion that her actions—or in this case, *inaction*—had been directly responsible for the deaths of three innocent people, that was another issue entirely. That knowledge was like a weight resting on her shoulders, a weight that made it next to impossible to move. Her sense of despair sucked the energy out of her body. It made her feel lethargic, like she'd been awake for seventy-two-plus hours.

Stallings let her sit for a moment and then said, "Okay, Tanner, you need to get moving. I'll have the Gulfstream fueled and ready to depart for Orly the moment you arrive at National."

She nodded and somehow rose to her feet. Turned toward the door and then stopped and again faced the CIA director. "I assume you're going to coordinate with France's Directorate of Territorial Security regarding my arrival in Paris?"

Stallings had returned his attention to his paperwork, but now he looked up and said, "Of course. We don't have enough assets inside France to blanket the area surrounding the embassy ourselves, and in any event it would be a serious breach of protocol to do so without involving the DTS."

Tracie nodded again. "Do me a favor. When you coordinate with them, don't let them know I'll be arriving in Paris overnight. I want at least one day to myself to conduct my own surveillance without interference from the French or anyone else. Tell them I'll be there Sunday and they'll never know the difference."

Stallings stared at her. "You want to finish this thing alone."

"I doubt it will be possible," Tracie said. "Piotr Speransky is a professional spook and a good one, if obviously sociopathic. It seems unlikely I'll be able to locate him, sneak up behind him and then bury two slugs in his hat, but I'd at least like twenty-four hours to give it a shot."

"No pun intended," Stallings said.

"It was definitely intended."

He regarded her a little longer and then said, "Okay. I would want the same opportunity if I were in your shoes. Of course…"

"I know," Tracie said. "You wouldn't be in my shoes because you would have finished Speransky when you had the chance."

"If the shoe fits," Stallings said.

Tracie nodded again and sighed. She dropped her head and stared at the floor. She was exhausted and hadn't even begun what very well might turn out to be her final mission.

"Is there something else, Tanner?" The impatience in his tone was unmistakable.

"Actually, there is." She reached into her pocket and removed the gold cross and chain she'd spent so much time cleaning and attempting to restore. She displayed the jewelry to Stallings and he spread his hands in confusion. "What's this?"

"These belonged to Ryan Smith. He wore the cross around his neck, and I took it off his body just after he died, before I escaped the Soviet base in Bashkir a couple of months ago."

"You took it?"

"Yes."

"Why?"

"I just…I don't know, I wanted to bring something of his home for his family to remember him by, since I wasn't able to save him."

"What are you saying, Tanner?"

"Sir, I know you can't tell me Smith's real name or where his family is located."

"You're damned right I can't."

"I know he wasn't married, because he told me that much, so I was hoping you would take it and return it to his parents. Let them know he died with honor serving his country. Maybe it will bring them some peace."

"I can't do that, Tanner, you know that."

"But sir, he—"

"He was working as a covert intelligence operative inside an enemy nation. His missions and his whereabouts were—and still remain—classified. I can't return that jewelry to his family, and you know it. And there's something else, now that you've brought up the subject."

"What's that, sir?" Tracie's heart dropped at Stallings' refusal to accept Ryan Smith's cross. She hadn't thought it could get any lower than discovering she was responsible for Piotr Speransky's killing spree.

"Even if I could return the cross to Smith's family, what would we tell them? We had an operative within arm's reach and she was only able to walk out of that base with a piece of jewelry? That kind of acknowledgment would open the agency up to questions we could not answer, and rather than getting any sense of closure, Smith's family would be tortured even more than they already are."

Tracie stood motionless and Stallings said, "I'll take it from you if you want, but it will go into storage in my personal safe if I do. It can't be returned to Smith's family, and that's final."

She dropped the cross and chain back into her pocket. Her fingers felt as numb as her brain.

"I'll keep it then," she said, in a voice that sounded like someone else's.

5

May 14, 1988
12:40 p.m.
Paris, France

Tracie strolled along the Champs Elysee, trying to imagine how an American tourist might act and then duplicating those actions. She moved slowly, gawking at the exquisite French architecture, craning her neck and occasionally turning a full three hundred sixty degree circle before continuing to walk.

As a cover, the tourist angle suited her needs well. With less than twenty-four hours in which to flush Piotr Speransky out of hiding without being hindered by French authorities, it was critical she observe as much of the area as possible. The American embassy—where Speransky's latest victim had been murdered—was located one street to her left, on Avenue Gabriel, directly across the Allée Marcel Proust.

So the act of taking in her surroundings was real, it was just focused on determining where a KGB operative with vengeance on his mind might be staked out, rather than appreciating the statues and the history and the late spring sunshine.

Tracie had arrived at Orly in late-morning, the CIA G4 touching down just after eleven a.m. Unfortunately for her, between the nearly eight hours flight time and the six-hour difference between D.C. and Paris, she lost three precious hours out of what was available to her before tomorrow's seven a.m. meeting with French law enforcement and intelligence officials.

On the bright side, if this situation could be said to have a bright side, her depression and exhaustion had been so great last night that she'd slept soundly for a solid six hours as the agency jet rocketed over the Atlantic to Europe. She'd made this trip with the CIA flight crew multiple times now, but after greeting the pilots warmly at Washington National, there had been none of the previous flights' light-hearted conversation.

Tracie doubted she would ever feel light-hearted again.

The crew had apparently sensed her mood, and while they were as friendly and professional as ever, the two-man flight crew left her alone with her thoughts following their brief greeting on the tarmac.

The weather upon arrival in France was unseasonably warm, a fact Tracie appreciated only as it would apply to her ability to conduct surveillance. The airport was located about twelve miles from the heart of Paris, and after taking a bus to her hotel and checking in, she had begun her walking tour of the embassy area just after noon. There was no time to waste.

Staying in the immediate vicinity of the embassy—the area Piotr Speransky would be waiting to end her life—was not the smartest move, strategically. But Tracie was willing to risk it for two reasons.

One, if Speranksy had established any connections inside French or American intelligence services, the assassin would have been notified by now of Tracie's planned arrival tomorrow morning. He would not be expecting to see her today and thus his operational awareness would be down. It was only human nature.

Two, Tracie had disguised herself. Speransky referenced her flame-red hair in three separate notes at three separate murder scenes, so it was obvious hair color was the one physical trait he associated with her above all others. She had piled her hair atop her head on the Gulfstream prior to landing at Orly, and then covered it fully with a black kerchief.

Her hair color would be invisible to anyone looking for it.

She'd also chosen clothing that she hoped would make her appear older than her twenty-nine years. Between her dark slacks and floral-print blouse, combined with large sunglasses in a very traditional style, Tracie hoped to present the illusion of a middle-aged female tourist, say in her forties or even fifties.

Up close, of course, it would be much more difficult to maintain the illusion, but if Speransky happened to be scanning the area, even with binoculars, Tracie felt confident in her ability to escape detection.

At least for one day.

And one day was all she had. If she weren't able to flush out and kill Speransky today, tomorrow's plan would be the exact opposite: she would show off her hair fully in an effort to draw the KGB killer out of hiding and finish this thing. One way or the other.

Tracie continued to stroll at a leisurely pace, approaching the Place de la Concorde and its magnificent fountains. She passed the Obelisk of Luxor and then turned left, keeping the American Embassy off her left side. The temptation to focus on the embassy complex was strong, but doing so would be counterproductive to her current mission. Piotr Speransky would be camped out somewhere on the periphery of the embassy, likely atop one of the surrounding buildings, planning to shoot downward and toward the compound.

Tracie needed to devote her full attention to the embassy's surroundings if she was to have any chance of kicking the rock Speransky would be hiding under.

She crossed Avenue Gabriel and started down Rue Royale. It was narrow, not a main drag but a side street, almost an alleyway, with buildings looming virtually to the pavement on both sides.

She maintained her tourist cover but moved a little more quickly. It was highly unlikely Speransky would have chosen Rue Royale for his sniper's nest for the simple reason that it offered virtually no sight lines into the embassy complex thanks to the densely packed construction.

A left onto the Rue Saint Honoré took Tracie past the British Embassy. She continued to the Avenue de Marigny, and a left turn there took her back to Avenue Gabriel and her starting point.

The entire circuit took barely thirty minutes to complete, and that was with Tracie moving slowly, examining her surroundings for likely hidey-holes a KGB assassin might utilize if he wanted to fill a petite American operative with Russian lead.

The results were discouraging. Despite nearly nine years as an American covert operative working outside the United States,

Tracie had only been to Paris once or twice, and never in the vicinity of the American Embassy. She'd pictured something a little more open, not the congested—albeit breathtakingly beautiful—cityscape she discovered.

The number of potential hiding places Piotr Speransky could utilize was practically limitless. Even with French law enforcement and intelligence personnel blanketing the area tomorrow, catching the assassin *before* he opened fire would almost be a matter of sheer luck. They might be able to capture or kill him once the bullets started flying, but that outcome would provide little comfort to Tracie if she were bleeding out on the front steps of the embassy.

And if the odds of a team finding him were slim, the chance that Tracie could sniff him out, particularly while disguised as a middle-aged American tourist, seemed about as close to nil as it was possible to get. She figured the odds of getting struck by lightning were greater, and the weather was crystal clear and beautiful.

She continued walking while considering her options. Making a second pass would be her top choice. Perhaps another look would reveal some of the more likely hiding spots a professional assassin would choose.

But a second pass would also put Tracie at much greater risk of blowing her cover. The fact that Speransky had managed to access the American Embassy in the first place, much less execute three members of his personal security team as well as the ambassador himself, told her all she needed to know about his abilities as an operative, not to mention his dedication to his mission.

He was out here somewhere, and while he wouldn't be expecting Tracie to show up until tomorrow, he *would* be paying attention. Offering him a second glimpse of the middle-aged "tourist" might just be enough to bring the same hail of bullets Tracie was expecting tomorrow, only a day earlier and with no one to chase him down after he'd killed her.

The heavy sense of depression she'd been feeling since learning last night that her actions had been directly responsible for the deaths of three innocent Americans deepened.

She turned toward her hotel. Maybe she could regroup and come up with a new plan, one with a better chance of success.

It seemed unlikely.

6

It didn't take long for Tracie to return to her hotel. She'd chosen lodgings close to the U.S. embassy complex for one very practical reason: Paris was densely populated, particularly in touristy areas, and with less than twenty-four hours to smoke out Speransky, she hadn't wanted to waste valuable time riding a bus or taxi.

She walked briskly down the Avenue Gabriel, passing mere yards in front of the U.S. Embassy entrance. She continued to scan the area for any location a KGB assassin might select from which to murder an American CIA operative, but did so without any real conviction.

The area *wasn't* ideal, and a professional like Speransky would recognize that fact immediately. Any location along Avenue Gabriel would place the killer too close to his target area. He would want the benefit of some—but not too much—distance, and, again, in all probability he would choose an elevated location so he could fire down on his target.

After passing the embassy, Tracie crossed the narrow Rue Boissy d'Anglas and found herself at the entrance to the Hôtel de Crillon. She entered the building and crossed the opulent lobby to the stairs. The hotel had originally been constructed, along with an identical building across the Rue Royale, for use as a palace in the mid-1700s.

The Hôtel de Crillon and its sister structure, the Hôtel de la Marine, had rich histories and, in fact, the building that now served as Tracie's lodging had been the site of the first treaty-signing between France and the fledgling United States of America on February 6, 1778.

With a career military man for a father and a career diplomat for a mother, Tracie supposed it was inevitable she would have grown up an American history aficionado. Despite the blood-stained reason for her trip to France and the very real possibility her life would end tomorrow on the streets of Paris, she couldn't help but appreciate the knowledge that Ben Franklin, Silas Deane and Arthur Lee may well have sat in the very lobby she'd just crossed, negotiating the terms of the French-American treaty officially recognizing the Declaration of Independence of the United States of America.

In 1909 the Hôtel de Crillon opened its doors in the structure that had even then been around for more than a century and a half, following a nearly two year renovation. It had been lodging guests ever since. Given its opulence, its location and its historical significance, Tracie had known even before registering that the cost of a stay would be exorbitant, and she was right.

Room charges were far in excess of what Aaron Stallings would approve for reimbursement, not to mention far above what she could afford to pay based on her salary. Despite the danger and the—very occasional—glamor of her job as a covert operative, when push came to shove Tracie was still nothing more than a civil service employee of the United States government, albeit an unofficial one whose affiliation with the CIA had been terminated last year.

Tracie booked the room anyway. Over the course of her career, she'd done what virtually all spooks did: hidden money, weapons and numerous forged identification documents away in multiple locations around the United States and the areas in which she typically worked.

Her lifestyle was frugal and she worked nearly non-stop, so her opportunities to spend significant sums of money were few and far between. Over the years she had socked away an impressive amount of cash, weapons and IDs. Given the fact her survival beyond the next twenty-four hours seemed tenuous at best, she'd decided this was as good a time as any to access a small portion of that cash and use it on this mission.

She entered her room and eased the door closed behind her. She'd hoped for a room that looked out onto the American Embassyproperty, but none were available so she'd had to "settle" for a breathtaking view of the Eiffel Tower, the structure rising into the sky in the distance, proud and magnificent.

She made a cup of tea and then sat at the room's writing desk, sipping slowly and staring out the window. In retrospect, she decided that not being able to see the embassy complex was a good thing. She was already obsessing on the killings for which she bore direct responsibility, and on the man she had allowed to live who had then gone on to execute a half-dozen innocent people, including three American diplomats and three embassy security guards.

Staring morosely at the building where the third murder had occurred, and where she would likely die tomorrow, would accomplish nothing positive and might even interfere with her ability to think clearly and logically.

And it was hard enough to think clearly right now. It was one thing to accept the possibility of dying in the field on a mission—she'd come to grips with that prospect years ago—but it was another thing entirely to know that sometime after sunrise tomorrow morning she may well find herself bleeding out on the streets of Paris, the victim of a murder for which she'd been given advance notice.

And that outcome was becoming increasingly likely. She'd flown to Paris with the vaguely formed notion she would smoke out a professional assassin in a matter of hours, and she would do so with no assistance. Speransky had to be close if he was going to execute the "redheaded American spook," so she would use that knowledge to her benefit. She would ferret out his hiding place and then put two slugs in his skull, and that would be that.

But she'd been kidding herself, obviously. A *team* of operatives might have managed it, given unlimited resources and the benefit of days or weeks with which to work, but for one woman, alone and unfamiliar with the city, it was nothing more than a pipe dream, and a silly one at that.

She drank her tea and gazed at the Eiffel Tower and wracked her brain in an effort to develop an alternative to wandering the city aimlessly looking for a KGB agent she was clearly never going to find until he was ready to show himself.

The tea was delicious.

The view was spectacular.

Her life was falling apart.

7

Sleep came grudgingly for Tracie, and when it arrived it didn't stay long.

For more than two hours after crawling under the covers she tossed and turned and stared at the ceiling. Finally she dropped into a troubled slumber and then jerked awake, sweaty and shaking, after maybe twenty minutes. Calmed herself and tried again, eventually falling asleep only to have the same thing happen forty minutes later.

She slipped out of bed and wandered to the window and spent nearly half an hour gazing across the city at the Eiffel Tower. The time was after three a.m. so the city was mostly—but not entirely—deserted. Occasional groups of tourists wandered the streets, undoubtedly sacrificing rest to get the most out of their Paris experience.

After a while her eyes began to droop, so she gave sleep one more try. She wandered back to her bed and dropped off almost immediately, lasting almost a full hour before again awakening, this time shaking from the aftereffects of a nightmare, and with the strong suspicion she may have screamed herself awake.

It was four-thirty a.m.

Resigned to the fact that she would get no more sleep

tonight—which meant possibly ever—Tracie rose one last time and padded to the bathroom. She stepped out of her pajamas and into the shower, adjusting the temperature until the water was as cold as she could stand it. The chilly water allowed for clarity of thought unlike anything else she'd ever experienced.

The inability to sleep came as an unexpected and unpleasant surprise. Tracie had long since learned to recognize the sense of anticipation that accompanied the beginning of a new mission. Butterflies in her stomach, the slow build of adrenaline, the hyper-awareness resulting from extreme focus on a situation.

That was all very familiar.

But this was different.

This was something akin to terror. She wasn't afraid to die; she'd never feared losing her life in defense of her country. But she'd never considered the possibility she might be murdered while acting solely as a target, either, being gunned down by a disgruntled KGB agent extracting revenge on her for the sin of allowing him to live when she should have pulled the trigger on the murderous bastard the minute he'd surrendered the intel she needed.

Tracie eased off the cold water, gradually warming her now-shivering body. She would face the day with courage and determination, just like she faced every other day, no matter her fate. It was what her father and mother would expect of her and, more importantly, what she expected of herself.

If her fate was to die, she would do so with dignity.

She stepped out of the shower and toweled off, dressing slowly and then making another cup of tea, which she brought to her now-familiar spot at the window. The Eiffel Tower still rose in the distance, immutable. It had been standing long before Tracie's birth and would remain so long after she was gone, whether that day was today or in seventy years.

* * *

The knock came at her hotel room door at precisely seven a.m.

Tracie had been told to expect a visit from Deputy Chief of Mission Henry Gatlin, now the ranking American diplomat in France with Ambassador Clayton Leavell lying on a slab in a French morgue. Gatlin would brief her on what to expect during her upcoming tour of the embassy.

Tracie thought she already had a pretty good idea what to expect.

She hurried across the hotel room and said, "Yes?" raising her voice to be heard through the closed door. There was no reason to believe her early-morning visitor was anyone but Henry Gatlin, because there was no reason to believe anyone else knew she was even in France yet, but bitter experience had taught her to take nothing for granted, ever.

"Deputy Chief of Mission Henry Gatlin to see Ms. Fiona Quinn, ma'am." It was a man's voice, and it was muffled as the speaker in the hallway did his best not to disturb any sleeping guests.

Tracie pressed her eye to the peephole in the door and saw two men standing on the other side. The man closest the door was armed and wore the uniform of a U.S. Marine. On his uniform was a patch bearing the logo of the Marine Corps Embassy Security Group, the Marine detachment charged with providing security at American embassies, consulates and other official U.S. government installations.

Standing behind the armed marine was a tall, skeletal-looking middle-aged man dressed impeccably in a gray suit and blue tie under an unbuttoned black full-length overcoat. On his head was a fedora. He stood patiently, arms hanging in front of his body and clasped at the hands.

It had to be Gatlin. Tracie had spent many hours face-to-face with Piotr Speransky, torturing and interrogating him back in Moscow, and neither one of these men remotely resembled the Russian assassin.

She swung the door open and stood to the side, indicating the interior of the room. "Please come in, gentlemen."

"I'll wait out here, ma'am, thank you." The marine stood to the side to allow his boss to pass and then placed himself directly in front of the door, facing the hallway, without another word as the skeletal man in the suit entered.

She closed the door and the man turned and offered his hand. "It's a pleasure to meet you, Ms. Quinn."

"Likewise, Chief Gatlin," she said, shaking his hand firmly. "Although I wish the meeting was under better circumstances."

She wondered whether he was aware of how much responsibility she bore for the current unpleasant circumstances. If he knew, he was doing a good job hiding it. He seemed pleasant and professional, if somewhat somber. Tracie supposed having your boss gunned down in his own office and then taking over the top spot while the killer remained on the loose would have a sobering effect on just about anyone.

"Call me Henry," he said. He had removed his fedora upon entering her room and now stood fingering the brim nervously as he faced her.

"Please have a seat, Henry," she said. "Would you like a cup of tea?"

"Thank you, no. And I'll stand. I'm far too upset to sit, and as far as tea is concerned, I haven't been eating or sleeping since Ambassador Leavell's body was discovered. The last thing I need is caffeine."

I know a little bit about insomnia myself, Tracie thought, but said only, "I understand."

"So," Gatlin said after a deep breath. "The purpose of my visit this morning is to prepare you for your embassy tour." He continued to meet her gaze only with extreme reluctance, locking eyes for a moment only to slide them away, focusing on something over her shoulder.

It was unnerving and unexpected, particularly given the man's status as a professional diplomat. For a moment Tracie was thrown off, and then the likely explanation for the man's excessive nervousness occurred to her.

"How many people know about the note found on Ambassador Leavell's body?" she said, speaking quietly but focusing on the man's eyes, willing him to meet her gaze.

"Only a few. Me, of course, given the fact I am—was—second in command at the embassy as well as the person who found the body. French officials, the lead law enforcement investigator, and also the Marine Corps Embassy Security Group."

"So then, you are aware the note was left for me."

"I wasn't, until I entered your room and saw your hair. Then it became…"

"Self-evident,"Tracie suggested.

"Yes."

"Let me make something clear, Mr. Gatlin. I don't expect you, or anyone else for that matter, to accompany me outside the embassy complex. Once we get inside—" *if I make it that far,* she thought but did not say—"we can meet up to continue the tour."

Gatlin shuffled on his feet. If anything, he seemed more nervous now than he had been before. "I'm sorry," he said. "You must think the worst of me."

"Of course not," Tracie said. "I don't want to put anyone in danger unnecessarily, particularly you. You're critical to maintaining the integrity of our diplomatic mission, now that Ambassador Leavell is gone."

They stood staring at each other for a moment, neither speaking, and then Tracie said, "So you're here to brief me on the locations and tactics of law enforcement and intelligence personnel surrounding the embassy. What do you say we get started?"

Gatlin dithered a moment longer. The man was clearly shaken. Finally he nodded. He turned toward the writing desk next to Tracie's window and on it, unfolded a map of the embassy complex and surrounding area. The map was dotted with marks made in red pen.

Tracie listened carefully as he began speaking, although from her perspective his explanation was hardly necessary. The meaning of the red marks was clear from the moment she looked at them, and they had nothing to do with protecting Tracie. They were the places the good guys would lie in wait to capture the KGB assassin after he'd dropped Tracie with sniper fire.

8

May 15, 1988
7:50 a.m.
Hôtel de Crillon

She waited fifteen minutes after Gatlin and his escort departed before leaving her hotel room.

The U.S. deputy chief of mission to France—now, Tracie supposed, the acting U.S. ambassador to France—could not have been more clear in his desire to be as far away from the prospective murder victim as possible. That was her wish as well, so she gave him plenty of time to return to the relative security of the embassy complex before proceeding.

She wanted to feel anger or disgust at Gatlin for his cowardice but couldn't quite manage it. His boss had been gunned down execution style in his own office for the express purpose of luring Tracie here, and then he was given the unenviable task of meeting with her? With the assassin still on the loose and presumably still in Paris?

Tracie and Henry Gatlin had no connection other than the dead ambassador, so Gatlin had no personal stake in trying to protect her. And he was obviously bright enough to know his odds of survival took a dramatic turn for the worse in her presence, so his desire to get the hell away made perfect sense.

It didn't make Tracie feel any better, but it was understandable.

To make matters worse, there was no guarantee Piotr Speransky was holed up in some sniper blind waiting to gun Tracie down outside the embassy. That was the working theory, and why Aaron Stallings had felt comfortable instructing Gatlin to meet her here in her hotel room.

But Tracie felt it was just as likely Speransky was remaining mobile in order to avoid being discovered by French authorities and trapped before he could escape. And if that were the case, and he'd seen Gatlin and the guard leaving the embassy, it would be a simple matter for the professional operative to tail the two men here.

And if *that* were the case, she might never even make it as far as the embassy. She could be ambushed the moment she stepped into the hotel's hallway, or shot as she crossed the first floor lobby, or murdered anywhere between her hotel room and the embassy.

She'd mentioned her misgivings to Stallings as they spoke via secure satellite connection inside the CIA's Gulfstream after departing Washington National, but he'd disregarded them entirely. "The Marine Embassy Security Group is aware of the need for secrecy, so Chief Gatlin will leave the embassy complex through a little-used tunnel. No one watching the embassy will see him, and the detachment in charge of security at our Paris facility is among the best in the world. You'll be fine."

"Really?" she'd said. "If the embassy security group is so good, how did Speransky manage to access the complex and murder a sitting ambassador in his own office, and then escape undetected? Sounds like real quality protective work, there."

"Knock it off, Tanner," Stallings had said, his annoyance clear. "You know as well as I do that with proper planning a professional can access virtually any location. You could do it. Hell, you *have* done it, many times. So I don't want to hear your crap. Meeting Gatlin inside your room is much safer than meeting him anywhere in public, so that's the way it's going to be."

She'd bitten her tongue, having dealt with Stallings long enough to know she had a better chance of winning the lottery and getting hit by lightning on the same day than changing his mind once he'd made it up. But that didn't mean she felt good about it.

Especially now, pacing her room, checking her watch every thirty seconds, waiting for enough time to go by so she could go out and meet her fate. She'd never been particularly good at waiting, unless the prospective payoff at the end of the wait was going to be something worthwhile.

Getting shot in the street didn't seem to fit the definition.

She adjusted the Kevlar vest under her blouse, wishing she could leave it behind and knowing that wearing it would almost certainly be pointless. Speransky would anticipate body armor, so he would have taken up a position that would allow for a headshot instead. Any high-powered Soviet sniper rifle would pulverize her skull to the point where a closed-casket funeral would be necessary, lest mourners become sick to their stomachs.

She was starting to feel a little queasy herself just thinking about it. Death would be instantaneous, meaning there would be no pain, yet the thought of one or more rounds blasting her skull into gravel was causing her gorge to rise.

Think about something else, dammit, this isn't productive.

She paced the room a few more times and then muttered, "Okay Gatlin, ready or not, here I come." She figured she'd given the man plenty of time to lock himself out of harm's way, but more importantly she didn't think she could handle one more minute in this tiny space, alone with her thoughts.

She pulled on a light jacket, more to cover her vest and the shoulder holster housing her Beretta than because she thought she would need one, and walked to the hotel room door.

Paused with her hand on the knob and took a deep breath.

Opened the door and stepped into the hallway, bracing for the worst, one hand inside her unzipped jacket on the butt of her gun.

Nothing happened.

There was no bright flash of light, followed by a loss of consciousness.

No bullets ripped into her body.

No one attacked her.

The hallway was deserted. Tracie glanced in both directions and then began moving toward the stairway that opened onto the lobby. It was not the route she would normally have chosen with an assassin lying in wait, and it was almost certainly not the route Deputy Chief of Mission Gatlin had used, but her role in this little drama was solely to act as a target.

So she would take the stairs, and hope Speransky wasn't waiting for her in one of the stairwells. She kept her hand on her gun as she walked, determined to give him a little something to remember her by in the event he was bold—or careless—enough to allow himself to be seen.

Nothing.

She descended the stairs and crossed the lobby, a little surprised to still be breathing by the time she exited the hotel.

The morning was overcast but warm and humid, with low grey clouds threatening deluge at any moment. Tracie would have liked to wear a hat or at least use an umbrella, but the plan was to allow Speransky to identify her by her flame red hair, and to do so, he had to be able to *see* her flame red hair. She thought the only thing worse than dying by an assassin's bullet would be getting soaked to the bone first.

Her nerves were strung as tightly as she could ever recall as she turned toward the embassy. It would be a short walk, with the embassy complex located just across a narrow alley from the Hôtel de Crillon. Not for the first time, Tracie considered the possibility that she and her killer had spent the night within a few hundred yards of each other.

She walked slowly, balancing her desire to not get killed with the need to complete her mission. She couldn't imagine ever receiving an assignment that would be more distasteful than serving as a human bulls-eye, but it was her fault Piotr Speransky was still alive to target her—not to mention a half-dozen innocent Americans—so she would complete this mission to the best of her ability.

After crossing Rue Boissy d'Anglas, Tracie approached a group of a half-dozen or so men dressed in long black trench coats loitering just outside the embassy's front gate. Their status as investigators, law enforcement or intelligence personnel could not have been more obvious, and she knew they could only be there for one purpose: to meet with her.

To their credit, none of the men shied away as she approached. They must be aware of the situation and that bullets could begin flying at any moment, but unlike Henry Gatlin, they seemed accustomed to dealing with dangerous situations.

One of the men said something to the others, nodding in Tracie's direction, and then all heads turned toward her and watched her approach. When she was maybe eight feet away, one man, presumably in charge, stepped away from the others and extended his hand.

"Fiona Quinn?" he said in understandable if heavily French-accented English.

"That's right," she answered, and shook his hand. "You are?"

"I am Chief Inspector Jacques Guillard, and this is my team. We are here investigating the murder of Ambassador Leavell and were asked to escort you on your tour of the crime scene. I wish to assure you that we take your safety very seriously, and will do everything in our power to ensure your safety as we proceed."

His grip was strong and confident and despite her tension, Tracie immediately liked the man. He had to know he could be splattered with blood and bone and human tissue at any moment—hell, he might get taken out himself—but if he was feeling any fear, nothing in his demeanor gave it away.

She hoped he would get the same impression of her.

They pulled apart from the handshake and Tracie noted that none of the other men were introduced by name. None of them seemed as relaxed as Guillard, either. They nodded and smiled tightly, and she realized she'd already received the only greeting she was going to get.

Not that it mattered. If a sniper's bullet dropped her to the sidewalk, her companions' identities would be the least of her concerns.

"Well," Guillard said, "shall we conduct a little tour?"

I'd rather not, Tracie thought, even as she smiled and said, "Sounds good. Lead the way."

She was still alive.

For now.

She counted that as a win.

9

May 15, 1988
8:10 a.m.
Rue du Faubourg Saint Honoré, Paris

Piotr Speransky prepared to resume his vigil. He drained the last of his black tea and grimaced as he swallowed. This past week had constituted his first experience with Paris and he'd discovered the city had a lot to offer—it was bright and lively where Moscow was typically dull and grim—but he'd sampled a handful of cafes in the vicinity of the American Embassy and had yet to find one that could match the dingiest Russian roadside food cart when it came to the quality of their tea.

He shrugged into his jacket stepped onto the sidewalk, and as he did he glanced dubiously at the threatening skies. Rain was in the forecast, and from the looks of things it was going to start sooner rather than later. The prospect of getting wet didn't bother Piotr—he'd completed many missions with much longer timelines under far worse conditions than this—but a heavy downpour would reduce visibility and make it more difficult to see what he very much wanted to see.

He had suspected all along it would take a minimum of three murders to lure the redheaded American spy away from her hiding place in the United States, and he was beginning to think one more might be required. He'd kept the U.S. embassy complex under more or less constant surveillance since executing the ambassador, and given the timing of the killing had expected her to show up yesterday.

But there had been nothing.

It was always possible he'd missed her, of course. One man working alone could not even begin to cover all of the entrances to the facility. But he didn't think that was the case. French law enforcement had swarmed the embassy the morning after the murder, as had U.S. state department representatives and military officials.

The day after the murder would have been too soon for the redhead to make an appearance, though. That would be the day the CIA would have deciphered his note, located the spy, and sent her on her way. He'd left the same note on both of the previous corpses, but hadn't really expected the American idiots to put the pieces together until he'd staged the third ambassador's killing in a way he knew would have meaning for his tormentor.

Assuming his timeline was accurate, the little redheaded *cyka* should have arrived in Paris yesterday. Piotr had been up early and spent the day walking the streets surrounding the embassy: no breaks, just hour upon hour of watching and waiting, his senses on full alert.

But he'd seen nothing.

He wasn't worried about hanging around the scene of the killings because he knew he'd left no evidence behind that could be used to identify him. Piotr Speransky had been killing enemies of the Soviet state for years, and had long ago mastered the art of committing murder without compromising himself.

He'd been excited and hopeful at daybreak yesterday, but as the hours wore on and there was no sign of the American spook, he began to fear she was still either too dense to pick up on the clues he'd left specifically for her, or had deciphered them but was too afraid of him to be drawn to the scene.

No matter. He would keep watch all day today and again tomorrow. If she still hadn't shown by tomorrow at nightfall, he would chalk Paris up as a lost cause and leave for Rome. There were still plenty of United States embassies dotting the European landscape, and Piotr knew that no matter how much security the Americans added to the embassy staffs, he could circumvent it and kill at least one more ambassador, probably two.

Eventually the Americans would tire of losing their diplomats. Eventually they would send their spy to face the music.

And when that happened, Piotr would be ready.

He stalked along the Champs Élysée and then made the pair of left turns that would lead him directly past the front entrance to the American embassy. Security had been fortified, as Piotr had expected following the killings, so he was unsurprised to see several armed guards stationed at the gate as well as more patrolling the area.

But this time when he passed, he spotted a group of a half-dozen men, all dressed in suits and overcoats, all very officious-looking, all huddled together as if awaiting the arrival of someone else. An American spy, perhaps?

This was a good sign. This was a very good sign.

Piotr continued past the embassy and strolled a ways farther before turning left and crossing Avenue Gabriel. He didn't like the idea of keeping his back to the embassy for too long, but making a one-eighty and walking past the guards and the men in suits a second time so quickly could arouse suspicion. Piotr wasn't about to get arrested now, not when he was so close to finally extracting his vengeance on the American *cyka*.

Once out of sight of the embassy, Piotr removed his hat. He shrugged out of his reversible jacket and turned it inside out, then slipped it back on and zipped it up. He stuffed his hat into the front pocket and crossed the street once again. He'd changed his appearance only minimally, but it should be sufficient to prevent recognition. With very few exceptions, the average human being was shamefully unobservant.

He hurried along the sidewalk until the embassy was again in view. Then he slowed, anxious to take advantage of every last second of surveillance time. He continued to maintain the tourist fiction, being sure to look to his right, away from the embassy, nearly as much as he looked to the left. But his full attention was on the group of men in the suits, who were still loitering in front of the embassy as if awaiting someone's arrival.

His gut was telling him this was it, and he knew better than to question those instincts. He delayed his progress as long as possible, but eventually was forced to move past the loitering men and continue along the route he'd originally taken from the café. It was much too soon to turn around again; making a third trip past the embassy in less than five minutes might be pushing his luck too far.

He supposed he would have to circle the block in order to get into position on the far side of the embassy, and hope that the redhead didn't make an appearance while he was gone. He hated the prospect of losing eyes on the group of loitering men for even a short time, but given that he was working alone, he had no choice but to—

There she is.

Piotr had been scanning the sidewalk in front of the Hôtel de Crillon, more out of habit than because he really expected to see anything of interest, and as his gaze flitted past the entrance, the young woman who'd humiliated him back in Moscow stepped onto the sidewalk and turned toward the American Embassy.

He froze in his tracks on the busy sidewalk. A man jostled him from behind. The man cursed in French and stepped around Piotr, who barely noticed and didn't care. His attention was focused one hundred percent on the American agent.

And it was her.

It was definitely her.

He'd studied her endlessly while duct-taped to a chair undergoing interrogation and torture and disgrace. Her face and her hair—oh, that bright red hair—were burned so deeply into his memory he knew he would be seeing her in his nightmares for the rest of his life, even in the unlikely event the KGB kept to their word and allowed him to survive beyond the next few weeks.

His superiors had been livid when they learned he provided the intel the American agent used to locate and execute Slava Marinov in Moscow, right under their noses. They had cut him loose, revoking his KGB credentials and pulling the rug out from under the only career he'd ever had.

Then they'd thrown him in jail.

He had expected to disappear in the night, executed just as Marinov had been and buried in an unmarked grave somewhere, but that hadn't happened. Instead the same KGB bigshots who had completed his fall from grace by revoking his credentials and stuffing him into a jail cell had come to him with an unthinkable proposal: Piotr could resurrect his career and his stranding in the KGB, but only by tracking down and executing the American who'd so humiliated him and the entirety of Soviet intelligence services.

Bygones would be bygones, they had told him, but only if he could pull off the impossible.

Piotr wasn't certain he believed them. Hell, he was sure he *didn't* believe them. Nobody in the world excelled more at deception and manipulation than the KGB. He assumed that even if he could complete his assignment, he would likely still end up face down in the middle of the vast, empty Russian forest, bleeding out of a pair of 9mm holes fired into the back of his skull.

But anything would be better than pacing inside a six-by-nine meter cell awaiting execution, and the possibility of redemption was a damn sight better than the certainty of death, no matter how unlikely that redemption was.

So Piotr had accepted the bizarre proposal without hesitation.

His KGB superiors had unlocked the cell and set him free—more or less—and he had immediately begun planning the mission that would lead here, to Paris, and bring him face-to-face—again, more or less—with his hated enemy.

He shook himself back to reality, recovering his senses enough to begin moving again. He was angry he'd allowed himself to be so affected by the appearance of the person he despised more than anyone else in the world. He'd known she would turn up eventually and had thought he was prepared for the sight of her.

Obviously he had been wrong about that. Fortunately for him, though, he was well out of sight of the embassy's security person-nel, and also a sufficient distance away from the CIA *cyka* that she hadn't seen him, either.

She was the one he needed to worry about.

She was the exception to the general human trait of self-ab-sorption and inattention.

She would detect his presence if he were not adequately cautious.

He watched her walk away, her destination clearly the American Embassy. The urge to follow her and finish her now, pumping multiple slugs into her head from behind, was so strong he'd begun moving in her direction without any conscious thought.

But now he forced himself to turn away. It took an act of will stronger than any he'd ever exhibited.

But the delay in extracting his revenge would be worth the agony of the wait. He had more planned for the woman with the bright red hair than simply being murdered on a crowded Parisian street. He had much more planned for her.

She would be made to suffer as he had suffered.

To suffer *more* than he'd suffered.

By the time Piotr was finished with her, she would welcome death. She would beg for a bullet in the head, would view it as far preferable to the shambles he was going to make of her life.

Piotr Speransky had gone to a lot of trouble to lure the American *cyka* with the flame-red hair to Paris, and for a very specific purpose. He would stick with his plan, would focus on the long game. It would pay dividends in achieving his goal.

And he was now one step closer to achieving that goal.

10

May 15, 1988
6:20 p.m.
Hôtel de Crillon, Paris

Tracie was exhausted by the time she returned to her room inside the Hôtel de Crillon. She felt as though she'd stayed up all night and then run the New York City Marathon and the Boston Marathon back to back on the same day. With a vigorous ninety minute weightlifting session in-between.

The reality was that she'd done virtually nothing all day that should result in this degree of exhaustion. It was caused entirely by the stress of serving as a human target for the better part of ten full hours.

French authorities, accompanied by a team of three marines from the U.S. Embassy Security Group, had paraded her around in front of the embassy complex for roughly thirty minutes following her arrival this morning, and then had done the same thing a half-dozen more times at various intervals throughout the day.

They were clearly waiting for Piotr Speransky to show—or to gun down Tracie—and they were just as clearly frustrated and disappointed in the lack of activity.

By the time they took their final trip around the embassy, the French team of police inspectors and military personnel were treating Tracie as if perhaps she had somehow contacted Speransky and advised him not to kill her until later, when fewer police would be in the vicinity and he would thus have a sporting chance at escape. The men were curt, bordering on unfriendly, not exactly rude but close enough.

Not that Tracie wasted much time worrying about the feelings of the men whose presence was mostly to serve as witnesses to her murder. They were disappointed in the fact she continued to remain upright when everyone thought she should be dead by now, but she was more concerned with the knowledge that she should be dead by now.

The pressure was unrelenting. Even during the periods of time she was safe—relatively speaking—inside the embassy, Tracie's thoughts remained focused almost exclusively on her next escorted trip outside and what seemed like the only possible outcome.

Because while she was much happier than her escorts seemed to be about the fact she was still breathing, she was every bit as mystified as they were as to why that was the case. Probably more mystified. She certainly had more riding on the answer to that question than they did.

The embassy killings had clearly been staged to draw her to Paris. Each succeeding one had become more transparent as to the killer's purpose, culminating in the murder of Ambassador Leavell. Between the note left at all three murder scenes and the staging of Leavell's corpse, there could only be one possible interpretation of the evidence: that a madman was insisting Tracie come to Paris and face the music.

Now she'd done so and the result had been…nothing.

Maybe Speransky had already flown the coop and was even now en route to another U.S. embassy in another European country, where he would commit one more murder of an innocent diplomat and leave another of his goddamned notes. But that made no sense. He had to know it would take time to get Tracie to the scene. Hell, she'd arrived yesterday but that was only because she'd left Washington in the dead of night.

Speransky couldn't have planned for that, so he likely would not have expected her to materialize in Paris until today. Why would he leave town on the very day of her arrival?

It didn't feel right.

Nothing about this felt right.

Something was very wrong with their interpretation of Speransky's actions, she could feel it in her bones, and that feeling was separate and apart from the knowledge she was serving as a human target.

Yes, she'd been tense all day, her nerves strung piano-wire tight as she waited for the onslaught of Russian-made lead that would drive her to the ground and snuff out her life. But there was a difference between being tense and being unable to think straight.

She'd been thinking straight from the moment she sat down in front of Aaron Stallings' desk until just now when she stumbled, exhausted, into her room.

And something wasn't right. She just couldn't put her finger on what that something might be.

Late in the afternoon, Tracie had huddled with Henry Gatlin and the French authorities in an embassy conference room, trying to determine where to go from here. They agreed she would stay at least one more night in Paris and continue the little dog and pony show again tomorrow. The consensus seemed to be that perhaps Speransky hadn't expected Tracie to arrive in the city as quickly as she had, and so he'd spent today in hiding but might be in position tomorrow.

In Tracie's opinion that consensus was based on no evidence in particular; she felt it was nothing more than wishful thinking on the part of the authorities. But nobody had any alternative plan—Tracie included—so she agreed to endure the gut-wrenching process of awaiting execution again one for more day.

The prospect of serving as a bulls-eye for another ten hours was daunting, but after dealing with today's suffocating pressure, Tracie felt a little more at ease about tomorrow. Maybe it was nothing more than a result of her current exhaustion and she would awaken terrified in the morning, but she didn't think so.

Speransky had gone to an enormous amount of trouble and risk to lure Tracie to Paris. It was inconceivable to her that he would simply have stayed away today on the off chance she wouldn't arrive until tomorrow.

All she had to do was put herself in his place to reach that conclusion. She recalled the horror she'd felt while interrogating Piotr Speransky, the dawning realization that were it not for the fact they worked on opposite sides of the geopolitical fence, she and Speransky were not all that different. They both received orders they may or may not agree with, and they both then executed those orders to the best of their ability.

She had tried to tell herself at the time that while *he* was a sociopathic monster, murdering American operatives without a second thought, *she* was simply a dedicated intelligence professional, doing her best to further the cause of freedom and protect the interests of the finest country in the world.

It became a much more difficult distinction to maintain after she'd executed the elderly and defenseless Slava Marinov on a frozen sidewalk in Moscow.

But the point was, Tracie was every bit the professional operative Speransky was. And had the shoe been on the other foot, had she been ordered to lure Speransky to Paris for the express purpose of filling him full of holes, it would have been dereliction of duty on her part to stay away on the day of his likely arrival.

She shook her head and sighed. She'd ordered dinner from the hotel's restaurant after arriving in her room—it was extravagantly priced, as far out of her budget as were the lodgings themselves, but she was far too tired at this point to go searching Paris for a reasonably priced meal—and now she picked at it, eating mostly by rote and barely tasting the food while her thoughts remained focused on what the *hell* she was missing in this Piotr Speransky situation.

Because whatever it was, she was pretty sure it would come back to haunt her if she couldn't puzzle through it.

She finished eating and wheeled the cart containing the dishes and utensils into the corridor without any conscious thought. She closed and locked the door and undressed next to her bed. She needed a shower but that could wait until morning.

After stepping into her pajamas, Tracie pulled down the covers and crawled beneath them. The mattress was more than comfortable, it was like floating atop the fluffiest fair-weather cloud on a summer day, and the operative who'd slept on floors and in fields, in the backs of trucks and strapped into uncomfortable cargo planes, in unbearable heat and flesh-freezing cold, dropped off to sleep almost immediately, despite being certain she would remain awake most of the night as she had last night.

Her last conscious thought before floating away on the fluffy cloud was again, *What the hell am I missing?*

11

Piotr Speransky caught a cab and hurried straight to Orly after satisfying himself that the redheaded American spy had actually—finally—arrived in Paris. There was no telling how long she would hang around the embassy waiting for him to kill her, and he had a lot of work to do before he could finally realize that dream.

There wasn't much about freedom-loving nations like the United States and France that he respected, particularly after spending the better part of a decade working covertly inside them. The faith these countries showed in their citizens was, in Piotr's opinion, misplaced and dangerous. People were, with rare exceptions, dull and slow, witless animals who needed to be led, by force if necessary.

He'd grown up inside what people in the West called the "Iron Curtain," and knew how misunderstood his government really was. Only through strong centralized control could a society and its people begin to realize their full potential. If that meant a few—or even many—of those people had to be prodded into compliance with the central planners' wishes at the point of a weapon, well, what was the purpose of government if not to make the difficult choices necessary to benefit all of its people?

But one thing Piotr *did* appreciate about free societies was how easy they made it for people like him to do his job. Few in the West ever wanted even to *question* a stranger, much less challenge him, particularly if that stranger came bearing official-looking paperwork that had been drawn up by some of the world's most accomplished forgers inside the KGB.

Authorities at airports always made a show of examining his Russian diplomatic credentials. Sometimes they even took the extra step of telephoning…someone; Piotr had no idea who the calls went to and didn't care. He assumed the U.S. State Department maintained some sort of clearinghouse for approved members of foreign diplomatic missions, and the examiners were calling that clearinghouse.

In any event, his inquisitors inevitably returned after absences of varying lengths of time, smiling and apologizing for the delay and wishing Piotr well as they ushered him around any crowds and straight to his flight.

He'd been a little nervous this time, given his uncertain status at the KGB, but still only a little. His superiors had offered one last chance to redeem himself, and the only way he could hope to manage that redemption would be with the full support and cooperation of Soviet intelligence. They couldn't expect him to complete his assignment without utilizing his forged documents and KGB contacts, so for now at least those documents and contacts would remain viable.

After succeeding in this mission, there was still at least a fifty-fifty chance he would be escorted behind a government building and shot in the head, Piotr had no illusions about that. But for now he was breathing and working, and that was a damn sight better than the alternative, and far better than he'd expected after being thrown into a jail cell a couple of months ago.

Piotr Speransky knew as well as anyone the risks inherent in his KGB career. He had known since the day he began training as a covert operative that all it would take was one major fuckup to bring the wrath of the Soviet hierarchy down on him. That knowledge had motivated him to begin preparing a strategy that would allow him to disappear without a trace, should that major fuckup ever take place.

He had seriously considered implementing his exit strategy the moment the American spared his life after extracting the information she needed to eliminate Slava Marinov. That had been his plan during the long hours he spent rubbing and tearing his skin raw as he worked himself free of the damned duct tape the *cyka* had used to secure him during his torture sessions.

Then, after finally walking out of the CIA safe house, he'd changed his mind. Vengeance burned like nuclear fusion inside his entire being, and he would stand no chance of extracting that revenge without all the advantages offered him by his KGB status. So he'd decided to return to Lubyanka and spill his guts. He'd seen other operatives disappear without a trace following errors that were far less egregious than his, but he had also seen the occasional instance of an operative being allowed to survive.

To Piotr it was worth the risk. In the worst-case scenario he would suffer a few minutes of gut-wrenching terror and then everything would go black. But the best-case scenario, which was exactly what had occurred, would allow him to pursue the redhead and destroy not just her career, but also her life. He would ruin her and make her suffer, much more than he had suffered.

Only then would he end her.

And *then* he would decide whether to disappear. He would gauge the sincerity of his superiors' promise to allow him to resume his career, and would use his best judgment in determining his next move. He would either return to Lubyanka once the redhead was dead or he would vanish, never to be seen again by anyone inside the Soviet Union.

Either way, at least the *cyka* would be gone.

He spent the majority of his flight from Paris to Montreal lost in lurid fantasies about what he would do to the woman who had ruined him. He recognized them for the fantasies they were, but it brought him great joy to imagine her squirming and screaming under a sharp knife, or begging for mercy as he systematically fired 9mm slug after 9mm slug into her body in soft-tissue areas that would cause extreme pain but not end her life for a very long time.

Perhaps he would make some of those fantasies come true before he killed her, and perhaps he would not; it would largely depend upon the circumstances of their final meeting. But as he had already spent many days inside the United States, preparing exhaustively for his upcoming mission, he felt he could afford to waste his down time in such a frivolous manner.

He felt as prepared as he could be for what was to come.

The plane touched down in Montreal in the middle of the night, which was just fine with Piotr. The late hour meant fewer people milling about the airport, which meant fewer potential delays as he escaped Canada for his ultimate goal: the United States. More specifically, Washington, D.C.

His diplomatic cover worked as well as ever, and less than an hour after he landed, Piotr had rented a car and begun driving east out of Dorval. A southern route would have been faster and more direct to the United States, and given the time constraints he was currently operating under, he gave serious thought to taking it. He'd gone to a lot of trouble to ensure the redheaded CIA operative was out of his way for this portion of his mission, and it was important he make full use of every minute.

But ultimately he chose the more circuitous route, for the simple reason he'd used it before—many times, in fact—and he knew he would be successful entering the United States. The southern routing was more questionable, and this mission was far too important to Piotr to leave anything to chance.

Now that the airline portion of his trip was over, his diplomatic paperwork had gone straight into his bag, to be retrieved only in case of emergency. United States officialdom was a little dodgier about recognizing his forged documents, and while he knew his paperwork would eventually get him across the border, he'd cooled his heels for several hours at the crossing in the past, and he had no intention of doing so on this trip.

Today's border crossing would be of the unofficial variety.

After leaving the suburbs of Montreal behind, Piotr sat back and cruised through the Canadian countryside, moving as fast as he thought he could get away with without arousing the suspicions of law enforcement. In Eastman he turned south onto Route Missisquoi, aiming the Ford Granada now squarely at the U.S. border.

Straight through Mansonville and soon it was time to leave his rental behind. He eased off the road and onto a dirt trail that had been specifically engineered by some long-ago Soviet operative for this exact purpose. He stepped out of the car and shrugged an equipment bag over his shoulder, then locked the doors and zipped the key into a plastic bag, which he then weighted with a rock and placed in the crook of a dead tree just past the Granada's right front tire.

Then he started hiking. The advantage to using this crossing point was the thickly forested countryside, which ran uninterrupted for miles on both sides of the border. The disadvantage was also the thickly forested countryside, which posed a challenge for anyone in less than peak physical condition and also offered ample opportunity to become lost and disoriented should the operative allow his attention to wander.

Piotr would not allow his attention to wander. Neither was conditioning an issue.

He made minimal use of his flashlight, preferring to navigate by moonlight and lessen his risk of being seen. The tradeoff was slower movement and the loss of valuable time, but he simply could not afford to be apprehended crossing the border. His diplomatic paperwork would become much less reliable if he were caught sneaking into the country through the woods just outside one of the most remote crossing locations along the entire U.S.-Canadian border.

Even given his focus on the job at hand, the hike left Piotr's restless mind with plenty of time to wander. And when it wandered, it inevitably ended up in the same place: his treatment by the redheaded American agent and how that treatment had altered his life.

He felt his face flush with shame and humiliation, even now, months later and alone in the Canadian forest, as he recalled his time spent inside the CIA's Moscow safe house. The young woman's size and gender made the torture he'd had to endure so much more difficult to swallow. The fact that such a tiny American—and a woman at that!—had broken him made his blood boil every single time he relived the nightmare.

Piotr's worst day—even worse than the actual torture—had come when he was forced to describe his captor to his superiors at Lubyanka. While they never admonished him for allowing the petite woman to best him, such a rebuke hadn't really been necessary. He knew exactly what his handler and the other officials were thinking, because he'd been thinking the same thing. Every single day.

The pain and anger and humiliation fueled him. It had gotten him this far in his plan for vengeance, and it would carry him through to the end.

12

Piotr became aware of the bright glow of klieg lighting much sooner than he thought he should, and he smiled grimly to himself. One thing about dwelling incessantly upon his personal failings, it made the time pass quickly. Forty minutes had gone by since he ditched the rental car, and it barely felt like ten.

The Canadian border-crossing station's exterior lighting served as an effective beacon, and even though he remained far removed from the sight of anyone at the station who might be scanning the forest, he knew he was exactly where he needed to be. He'd made this crossing many times at night and had always been grateful for the unintentional assistance offered up by both the Canadians and the Americans: it simplified the crossing and made getting lost in the massive forest a near impossibility.

He gave the border crossing station a wide berth and then continued south. Thirty minutes of vigorous hiking brought the glow from the American station into view in the distance. As had been the case on the Canadian side, Piotr was too far away and the forest too heavily wooded for him to see any of the buildings or vehicles, but he'd seen all of it before. In typical fashion the Americans had decided to make their facility much larger and more imposing than the Canadians—and much larger than necessary,

71

probably—so the middle-of-the-night lighting would have been impossible to miss even had he been another two hundred yards deeper into the woods.

He left the American station behind and after thirty minutes, risked moving laterally through the woods to the road. The night's inky blackness would allow him to see the headlights of any oncoming vehicles in plenty of time to melt into the forest before the drivers could see him, and he would make much better time walking/jogging along the pavement of the lonely country road than he would struggling around trees and over fallen branches in the woods.

Fifteen minutes later, Piotr spotted the marker he was looking for: a large boulder jutting out from the edge of the forest, so close to the road it represented a real danger to any driver not paying close enough attention to his surroundings. He passed the boulder and then angled back into the woods and moments later came upon a tiny clearing located far enough from the road that it was likely to go undetected for years in this remote area.

He had hacked the clearing out of the dense forest himself during his previous trip into the states to prepare for this mission, and knew exactly what he would find when he started digging.

Piotr shrugged off his pack and dropped it on the ground in the middle of the empty clearing. He was confident no passing cars would be able to see the glow from his flashlight, but used the lantern only long enough to locate the spot on the edge of the clearing in which he'd buried his secret stash. Then he flicked it off and started digging, using a small foldable shovel he'd hidden away from the clearing and covered with leaves and twigs at the same time he buried his other supplies.

It took some time, and some digging, to find the metal box. Piotr had buried it deeper than he probably needed to, but he'd known at the time that when he needed it, he would *really* need it. He worked as quietly as possible while also maintaining a rapid pace, and by the time he heard/felt the spade *clank* against the top of the metal box his arms were burning from the exertion and sweat had begun running in tiny rivulets down his face and neck. It soaked his shirt and made him shiver in the coolness of the night.

He lifted the box out of the hole and fumbled in his pants pocket for the key that would open the heavy padlock sealing it. He inserted the key and flicked on his flashlight and lifted the lid, then smiled in appreciation. Everything was here, exactly as he'd left it:

A pair of Makarov 9mm semi-automatic pistols and several full magazines.

A gun cleaning kit.

A pair of razor-sharp combat knives.

Several thousand dollars in untraceable U.S. currency.

The metal box was filled with everything he would need to carry out his planned vengeance on the redheaded CIA agent. A car he could steal easily enough, but he stood no chance of completing his mission without weaponry and cash. His only concern had been that someone might stumble upon his hidden cache of supplies and remove them—even in a place as desolate as this, it was always a possibility—but it hadn't happened and now he would be unstoppable.

Piotr sat back on his haunches and breathed deeply of the forest air. He considered the risks inherent in lighting up a cigarette and decided to do it. He was far enough from the road that no one would ever see the tiny flare of light, and there was ample reason to celebrate. His plan had so far worked to perfection. The redheaded CIA bitch was well out of the way in Europe and should remain so long enough for him to complete his next step.

Soon she would be suffering every bit as much as she deserved.

He took a drag on the Belomorkanal cigarette and held in the smoke before releasing it in a slow, easy stream as he considered all it had taken for him to get this far. Piotr's KGB superiors had no clue as to the identity of the petite redheaded spy who'd become such a thorn in their side, and that made sense. The CIA treated the identity of its operatives with the utmost secrecy, particularly the identities of those operatives working covertly in and around the Soviet Union, for obvious reasons.

But that did not mean operatives' identities were never compromised. Any time more than one person was involved in keeping a secret it became possible to extract that secret.

Mistakes were made.

Documents were intercepted.

People acted stupidly and opened themselves up to blackmail.

And sometimes, learning a secret became a simple matter of locating the proper individual and taking advantage of the single trait most deeply ingrained in human DNA: greed.

For the right price, virtually anyone was corruptible. The problem was that the cost of taking advantage of that greed in most cases was far too high for the average person to pay.

But Piotr Speransky was not the average person. He had been operating as an elite Soviet covert operative for close to two decades, which meant that over the course of his career he'd had dozens of opportunities to earn cash on the side. Hundreds of opportunities. And all of that cash that was unknown to the KGB, unknown to Piotr's few friends, unknown to his family or fellow operatives.

Unknown to anyone but Piotr.

He had performed lucrative freelance assassinations of high-profile targets, had transported drugs between Soviet satellite states, had made use of KGB files on its citizens to blackmail bureaucrats and politicians. Through his illicit activities, Piotr Speransky had earned sums of money that would make some rich Americans blush, and he had saved virtually all of it, socking it away in various locations around the world that were safe but readily accessible to him.

While he hated utilizing that cash for anything besides its intended purpose—his retirement—Piotr had known he would stand no chance of learning his tormentor's identity without sacrificing a large chunk of it.

Given the importance of learning her identity, he accepted as the cost of doing business that the money must be spent. He had a plan for replacing it, if his superiors kept their word and allowed him to live.

But that was a concern for the future.

He had known exactly who to bribe. Vasily Labochev had been station chief at the KGB's Leningrad facility for decades. Labochev was legendary among operatives for two things: his love of hookers and his rumored ability to procure any information on any subject.

For the right price, of course.

Supposedly, Labochev's connections were so extensive he could wrangle a copy of the ignition key to Ronald Reagan's presidential limousine, or the banking information—including account numbers—for any sitting or ex-United States senator.

Anything.

But the price had to be right. Ordinary Josefs or Sergeis could not hope to obtain the kind of financing required even to approach Vasily Labochev, much less to purchase his cooperation.

Piotr was no ordinary Josef or Sergei. He raided a half-dozen of his hiding places, emptying them out until he decided he'd collected enough to make a favorable impression even on someone as powerful as Vasily Labochev.

Then he emptied out two more, leaving just one untouched.

Over the course of an exhausting nine days of continent hopping, Piotr wiped out eighty percent of the fortune it had taken him nearly twenty years to build.

But he didn't care. He still had his most lucrative hiding place. The one he left untouched still contained enough money with which to finance his disappearance, assuming the KGB didn't eliminate him before he could do so. And if it was going to cost him three million United States dollars to extract revenge on the redheaded *cyka* who had humiliated him and caused him to lose his career and his reputation, well, in Piotr's opinion that was money well spent.

He had collected all the money and approached Labochev.

And been summarily dismissed.

Until lining up the three gym bags on Labochev's living room floor and unzipping them with a flourish, bags filled to the brim with stacks of unmarked U.S. dollars.

Suddenly Vasily Labochev's demeanor changed, so much so that Piotr was thankful he'd approached Labochev armed to the teeth.

Ten days after that, Labochev provided Piotr with the information he required, in exchange for all those liquid assets. Piotr had no idea how Labochev had gotten the intel, and he didn't care.

He supposed it was technically possible Labochev's information was inaccurate, that the longtime KGB station chief had simply made something up to mollify Piotr and get his hands on that mountain of cash. But he didn't think so. Piotr's reputation was sufficiently well known to KGB insiders. Labochev would understand the consequences he would suffer for lying to Piotr, particularly given the amount of money involved in the transaction.

That being the case, Piotr felt as confident as he could reasonably be that he'd gotten what he paid for: the identity of his American inquisitor.

Her name was Tracie Tanner. She'd been a CIA operative until a little more than a year ago, when she'd lost her job, fired from the agency for insubordination. That was the official version.

Obviously, the official version was inaccurate. Obviously, her firing had been nothing more than a cover allowing the U.S. intelligence service to place her inside the most dangerous and risky locations across the Soviet Union.

The torture of Piotr Speransky and the ensuing assassination of Slava Marinov on the streets of Moscow would have been just such an assignment. Had it gone wrong, and Tanner been apprehended or killed, the United States government would have distanced itself from the operation, feigning innocence and claiming Tanner had gone rogue.

The trace of a smile flitted across Piotr Speransky's face, all alone and crouched in a small wooded clearing in extreme northern United States. Then it was gone as Piotr's now-familiar rage and humiliation resurfaced.

The CIA should never have made this Tracie Tanner the blackest of black ops agents, but she bore even more responsibility than the spy agency for the fate she would soon suffer. Had she only killed Piotr after torturing Marinov's name and location out of him, she would have been home free right now.

He'd never expected her to allow him to live, even after she agreed to do so.

It simply made no sense from a strategic standpoint. Piotr would never have made such a nonsensical mistake. He'd been in similar situations, many times, as the one holding the power of life or death over another, and he had always made the proper decision. It was an easy one to make.

But no matter. Tracie Tanner was the agent's name.

Tracie Tanner had made a grave error in judgment in allowing Piotr to live.

And soon Tracie Tanner would pay.

13

Piotr was surprised he didn't feel more tired. He'd slept for a while on his trans-Atlantic flight into Montreal, but air travel through multiple time zones was exhausting, and he'd now been awake for the better part of the last thirty-six hours.

Adrenaline can take the body far, he thought, *as can amphetamines.* Both were currently racing through Piotr's body, and while his eyes felt grainy and his eyelids heavy, he was awake and alert and ready to complete the next stage of his mission. He'd been awake for longer time frames and under more dangerous circumstances on other assignments, so he knew he would be fine.

It took less than two hours from the time he recovered his weapons and other supplies in the clearing in northern Vermont to steal a car. Most of that time was spent hiking along Route 243 into the little town of Jay.

Once there, he'd known he would have a wide range of vehicles to choose from, and he was right. Jay was rural and tiny, far off America's beaten path, and few if any of its residents were wealthy. The vast majority of the houses Piotr knew he would encounter were small and utilitarian, ranch and split-level style homes with gravel driveways. Garages were rare commodities in Jay.

Daylight was still many hours away, so activity was minimal, and the most challenging factor when it came to stealing his transportation was picking out the car that would best suit his needs.

He settled on a small Toyota. It was a few years old, silver, anonymous. During Piotr's time in the United States he'd seen thousands of cars exactly like it. Once he drove it out of the owner's yard and swapped license plates with another car, he knew there was almost no chance of being intercepted by the police.

He thought that was very fortunate for the police.

He didn't even need to break a window to access the car; it had been left unlocked. Piotr shook his head at the foolishness of its owner and in less than thirty seconds had hotwired it. Thirty seconds after that he'd backed out of the owner's driveway and was on his way toward his ultimate destination.

The distance from Jay, Vermont to Washingon, D.C. was almost exactly six hundred miles, and barring traffic issues—always a possibility in the United States, Piotr knew, no matter the time of the day or day of the week—the drive would take roughly nine and a half hours to complete.

He stopped twice for gas—the damned car's owner had left its tank nearly dry—and one for food and a quick twenty-minute catnap.

He encountered no traffic issues.

He was in the D.C. area shortly after noon on the seventeenth.

Things were going smoothly.

He would attempt to complete this stage of his mission tonight.

*   *   *

May 17, 1988
6:35 p.m.
Alexandria, Virginia

Once he learned the name of the redheaded American CIA operative, getting the rest of the intel he required was a fairly straighforward matter. Piotr had spend years operating in and around the United States, and it still amazed him how easy it was to acquire useful intelligence on just about anyone in this country.

To a man who had grown up inside one of the most closed societies in the history of the world, the concept of readily available information on citizens and business and...well, everything, really...was astonishing. In Russia, the average citizen had no chance of digging up any significant intel on another average citizen, even if they knew that person's name and address. To even conceive of such an occurrence was simply impossible.

For someone in Piotr's position it was a different story, of course. If a KGB operative decided he wanted to learn all there was to know about some random Muscovite, doing so would be no more complicated than walking into the records division at Lubyanka and poring over that individual's files.

But here in America, any interested party could learn nearly as much as they wanted to about anyone else's life if they were willing to put in a little time and effort. And while Piotr still found that notion foreign and repellant, it had suited his needs perfectly. He spent several weeks tailing his prey, making preparations, and nailing down the little details that would allow him to complete this portion of his mission and successfully escape the U.S afterward.

Once he'd made those preparations and nailed down those details, he had returned to Europe and begun the killing spree that would set his plan in motion.

Now, he felt as comfortable as it was possible to feel driving the back roads of Alexandria, Virginia, stalking his prey and waiting for the proper moment to strike.

And that moment would be soon.

He parked the Toyota along the side of the rural Virginia two-lane road Tracie Tanner's father drove every day on his way home from work. Jake Tanner was a highly regarded four-star general in the United States Army, a fact that had initially caused Piotr some concern but one that he'd ultimately decided was irrelevant to his plan.

As a career military man, Tanner would have learned self-defense techniques above and beyond those available to most middle-aged men. But an officer who'd risen as far in the ranks as General Tanner would have been sitting behind a desk at the

Pentagon for decades. He was likely every bit as soft and easily broken as any other American man in his early fifties.

If not, if Jake Tanner was a fit and formidable opponent, Piotr liked his chances anyway. He would possess the advantage of surprise over his opponent, and that was an advantage not to be taken lightly. Even longtime intelligence operatives could fall victim to confusion if taken by surprise, and an army general, no matter how imposing, was no operative. Even if Tanner were armed—a distinct possibility—the man would be unprepared to actually use his weapon.

Piotr would be prepared.

Piotr would be fine.

He concentrated on maintaining his focus while he awaited the appearance of Tanner's car, feeling the sense of anticipation build as time passed. Unless the target had been held up at work, he should be along any time. Piotr had discovered Jake Tanner—like many military men—was a creature of habit, highly disciplined, someone who could largely be counted on to follow the same routine day in and day out.

Piotr's main concern was that when Tanner showed, he would be stuck in the middle of a line of three or more vehicles all traveling the same isolated road at the same time. Such an occurrence would complicate matters, but not so badly he would have to abort the mission for the day as long as none of the vehicles was a police cruiser.

Killing a cop was the one thing that he knew he would have to avoid at all costs. Doing so would cause innumerable problems, not the least of which—

There he was.

Piotr had chosen this particular ambush location for its extended view of the rural road, and more than a quarter mile away, General Jake Tanner's distinctive red Monte Carlo had just rounded the corner and was motoring straight toward Piotr.

Even better, behind Tanner's car the road was deserted.

Piotr peered left and saw no one approaching from that direction.

Conditions were perfect.

It was time to strike.

14

May 18, 1988
12:35 a.m.
Hôtel de Crillon, Paris, France

"Something's wrong," Tracie said into her secure satellite phone. She didn't bother with a standard greeting; Aaron Stallings wouldn't appreciate his time being wasted with such a courtesy, anyway.

A moment of silence followed as the CIA director absorbed her words. Then he sighed. "Do you have any idea what time it is, Tanner?"

"Sure," she said. "It's a little after midnight. I couldn't sleep."

"Not there," came the exasperated reply. "Here. Do you know what time it is here?"

She smiled thinly. She never tired of getting under Stallings' skin, and given all he had done to her, she felt any aggravation he may experience thanks to her was no more than a tiny portion of the payback he deserved. "I guess that would make it six thirty-five p.m. on the seventeenth in D.C."

"Yes. Yes it is. It's six thirty-five. I've just gotten home after a very long day, Tanner. I haven't eaten yet, and more importantly, I haven't even had the chance to pour a scotch. May I ask why you felt the need to interrupt those important tasks with a call?"

"Well I couldn't call any earlier, sir, I was busy trying to figure out why I'm still alive after parading around in front of the U.S.

Embassy building for three days with a bulls-eye painted on my back, waiting to be gunned down."

"Obviously that didn't happen," Stallings said drily. "And since you admitted you're having trouble sleeping, I can only assume you're calling me to inform me you've failed to apprehend the man who's been running around executing American ambassadors."

"That's exactly right, which is why I started this conversation by saying something's wrong."

"So today went no better than the last two days? You haven't flushed the assassin out?"

"There's been no sign of him, and if he hasn't taken a shot at me by now, I think it's safe to say he isn't going to."

"Well, unless our entire theory about those murders is completely off base, they were very specifically designed to bait you and draw you to Paris."

"Agreed," Tracie said. "But clearly we were wrong about *why* he wanted me here."

"I assume you have a theory you'd like to share?"

"I do."

"Well then, enlighten me. It's not getting any earlier over here."

"It's simple. He wanted me out of the way."

"That doesn't make sense. Out of the way for what? It's not like the two of you have been bumping into each other on every street corner in Moscow."

"I don't know why," she admitted. "But I have a very bad feeling, and every day I hang around Paris accomplishing nothing, that feeling is getting worse."

"I'm not sure what else you could be doing, Tanner."

"Neither am I, sir, but I think it's time to call off this little wild goose chase. It's been a failure and a waste of time."

"You realize most thirty year old women would—"

"Twenty-nine."

"Excuse me?"

"I said I'm not thirty, I'm twenty-nine."

"Whatever, Tanner. My point, if you'd allow me to make it without interruption, is that most young women your age would love the opportunity to hang out in Paris. They wouldn't be calling their boss at dinner time begging to come home."

"First of all, I'm not 'begging to come home.' But if we're comparing me to 'most young women,' I think it's safe to say very few of them would have agreed to come to Paris in the first place if it was for the sole purpose of being shot at."

Another sigh from Stallings. "I know. And I actually agree with your assessment. If our assassin hasn't slithered out of his snake pit by now, he's not going to. At least not in Paris. But this isn't over. I can feel it. This lunatic is up to something, and it involves you."

"Agreed. I just don't think whatever comes next is going to happen here."

Stallings went silent. His silence stretched out for such a long time, Tracie began to wonder if he'd placed the satellite phone down on his desk and wandered off to pour his scotch. "Sir?"

"Okay. Here's what I'm thinking, Tanner. Pick an embassy city in Europe and get your ass on a flight to it tomorrow morning. Our man has killed three ambassadors on successive Wednesdays. We both agree he's not finished yet. Maybe we'll get lucky and you'll pick the right city and be in position to stop him when he goes for Number Four, or at the very least, take him down after he succeeds."

Tracie had been thinking the same thing, which was why she'd made the secure satellite call to Stallings in the first place. She hadn't contacted him to request a flight home, her intention had been to get permission to fly to Rome. But as usual, the CIA director hadn't given her the opportunity to make that request.

Now that Stallings had echoed her thoughts, though, the plan sounded more than a little thin. It sounded downright desperate, a grasping at straws that couldn't help but be doomed to failure.

It sounded like the *continuation* of a wild goose chase, not the solution to one.

Now it was Tracie's turn to fall silent.

Patience had never been one of Aaron Stallings' virtues, and after just a few seconds he said, "What?" The word came out testy and sharp. It was the sound of a man who'd nearly arrived at the end of his rope. It was a sound Tracie had heard many times.

"That's fine, sir, I'll be on my way first thing in the morning. I just feel like…"

"I know. Like we're dogs chasing our own tails. He's got us

playing defense, not offense, and that's never a good thing."

"Exactly."

"If you've got a better idea, I'm listening. But this is the best I can come up with, at least for the time being."

Tracie shook her head, alone in her room. "No. My idea was the same as yours. But I'll review everything I can remember about Piotr Speransky tonight. I can't sleep anyway. I'll write it all down and maybe something will shake loose."

They fell silent again. Things were spinning out of control; they could both feel it. It was an uncomfortable sensation and one with which Tracie was mostly unfamiliar. She was used to devising a plan, usually a bold plan, and then aggressively pursuing it to completion.

This was a novel experience, and she didn't much like it.

"If there's nothing else, Tanner…"

Tracie blinked. She'd almost forgotten she was still on the phone with her handler. The extreme stress of days spent walking around Paris waiting to be blown off her feet by sniper fire was catching up to her. She was exhausted. "No, sir. That's it."

"Then I suggest you get some rest. You sound as tired as I feel."

"I will, sir. Thank you."

"Goodbye, Tanner."

"Goodbye, sir."

The circuit went dead and Tracie lowered the sat phone's antenna. She placed the transceiver into its carry bag and zipped the bag closed. Then she padded to the writing desk.

She stared out at the Eiffel Tower in the distance and sighed. She had expected to feel at least marginally better after talking to Aaron Stallings. For all his faults, and he had plenty, the CIA director had been doing his job for decades and was considered by most in the intelligence community to be an expert in his field. He was a spymaster with the emphasis on *master*.

But rather than feeling better after disconnecting the sat phone, the opposite was true. She felt worse. Much worse. Stallings was as confused as she regarding Piotr Speransky's intentions, and that was a very bad sign.

The only thing she felt reasonably sure of was that Speransky's end game was not the murder of three diplomats and three embassy security guards. All those victims were simply collateral damage. He was up to something else, and it involved her, and it was more than a little disconcerting to realize she didn't have the slightest clue what that something might be.

She gazed out the window without really seeing anything. The scenery was spectacular but her mind was fifteen hundred miles away, inside a small CIA safe house in Moscow. She replayed her interrogation of Piotr Speransky over and over in her head, desperate to recall some small detail that might reveal the man's intentions.

There was nothing. All her obsessive replay revealed was how foolish she'd been to allow him to live. She'd known that decision might come back to haunt her, but had allowed her heart to over-rule her head and now she was paying for it, and the price was a half-dozen dead Americans.

So far.

After a while she shook her head and picked up the hotel's phone. She still had to reserve a ticket on a flight tomorrow morning for Rome. Flying there was the best plan she could come up with, but she couldn't escape the feeling that she was making another mistake.

A costly one.

15

Piotr had slewed his stolen car onto the side of the deserted two-lane, hoping it would appear as though he'd suffered a mechanical issue. Given the age of the vehicle and its generally beaten-down appearance, he thought the impression would be an easy sell.

He waited until he was certain General Tanner had gotten a good look at the car as he approached, and then he opened the driver's side door and walked quickly toward the middle of the road. He raised his arms and waved his hands over his head in the universal signal of a driver in need of assistance.

There was room for Tanner to pass him and keep going, but he knew the man wouldn't do so. Guys like him—suckers, in other words—couldn't resist lending a helping hand to a stranger in need. Sure enough, the Monte Carlo began slowing, and Piotr smiled in thanks as the Good Samaritan eased to a stop next to him.

Tanner leaned across the front seat and rolled down the passenger window. He nodded past Piotr and said, "Cars are more trouble than they're worth, aren't they?"

"Definitely," Piotr said.

"What's the problem?"

Piotr's smile widened. "Nothing."

Tanner blinked in confusion. "I'm sorry?"

"There is no problem with my car. It is running perfectly." Piotr's English, while passable, was clearly accented with Russian even after all the time he'd spent operating in the states, and while on missions here he had always tried to speak as little in public as he could get away with.

It didn't matter now, though. His victim was in his sights and would not be escaping.

Suspicion clouded Tanner's eyes and he shook his head. "Then…how can I help you?"

Piotr reached behind his back. He drew his Makarov and leveled it at the driver. "You can do exactly as I say, or you can die. The choice is yours."

Tanner shrank back instinctively but Piotr had expected that reaction and was ready for it. He reached through the still-open window and kept his weapon trained on his victim. "Do not try it," he said.

"Try what?"

"I know you are considering hitting the gas and attempting to escape. If you do so, you will die."

Tanner looked out the windshield and then across at Piotr. The road was still empty. "What do you want?" the general said.

"You," Piotr said simply.

"I don't understand."

"You do not need to." Far off in the distance a vehicle had rounded the corner and was approaching. Piotr had hoped to finished this business without interruption, but even though this particular road was sparsely traveled, the location was still less than thirty miles from the urban sprawl of Washington, D.C. He'd known there was every chance they would be interrupted and was prepared for just such an occurrence.

He leaned into the car and flicked his weapon in the direction of the oncoming vehicle. "If that motorist stops, you will get rid of him immediately or everybody dies."

Tanner nodded. His eyes hardened and he held Piotr's gaze for a long moment before turning his attention to the approaching car. Sure enough, it began slowing.

The car stopped in the opposite travel lane and Piotr felt

himself tensing. He tightened his grip on the Makarov and lowered it slightly to ensure it remained below the intruder's field of vision. It would still be a simple matter to fire into Jake Tanner's chest from this position and he hoped that fact remained foremost in the general's mind.

The other driver lowered his window. It was a middle-aged man. He said, "Everything alright here, fellas?"

For a moment no one spoke and Piotr thought he was going to have to end the general before he wanted to. Doing so would alter his plan for vengeance against the redheaded *cyka*, but would not eliminate it.

Finally, Jake Tanner spoke. "We're good," he said across the open windows. "Ran into an old friend and we're doing a little catching up."

"In the middle of the road?"

Tanner chuckled uneasily. "Yeah, I guess we should probably move our reunion to a bar or something, shouldn't we?"

The other driver shook his head angrily. "Jesus, could you be any more selfish? Blocking a public road to chat with an old friend? You're lucky somebody doesn't come by and shoot your self-absorbed asses."

The man rolled up his window and raised his middle finger at the two of them. He leaned forward to be sure Piotr could see it as well. Piotr smiled widely at the man, who hit the gas and roared away.

"Yes," Piotr said. "You are very lucky somebody doesn't come by and shoot you."

Tanner ignored his comment. "What now? I did as you asked."

Piotr kept his weapon trained on Tanner as he fumbled for the door handle. He yanked the door open and slid into the car. It was well past time to get out of here. There was nothing to be gained by risking another interaction with a passing motorist. The next one would likely not end as well.

"Drive," he said.

"Drive?"

"You heard me."

"Drive where?"

Piotr leaned across the seat and pressed his weapon to the side of Jake Tanner's head. "I know what you are doing. You are stalling because you think the longer you sit out here in the middle of the road, the less likely you are to die. You are mistaken. Put your foot on the accelerator and press down or I will blow your brains all over the inside of this car. Do not test me."

The car began to inch forward, picking up speed slowly. Piotr waited a moment and then removed the gun from Tanner's skull.

"Satisfied?" Tanner said tersely.

"For now."

"My question remains unchanged. Where am I supposed to be driving?"

"I will give you directions as needed," Piotr said. "For now, just continue along this route." He made a mental note to maintain the utmost situational awareness at all times until Jake Tanner was properly secured. Piotr had kidnapped countless men and women over the course of a long career, both in his official position as a KGB operative, and in his unofficial one as a killer for hire. Virtually all of his victims responded in the same way: with shock and terror that rendered them unable to defend themselves in any meaningful way.

This man was different. He was fearful—who wouldn't be afraid with the barrel of a Makarov 9mm pistol shoved into his ear?—but rather than being rendered helpless by his situation, Piotr could see a grim determination in his expression.

And that sort of reaction made him extremely dangerous. Piotr was holding the gun, and it appeared Tanner was unarmed, so that left Piotr clearly in charge. But he would take nothing for granted. It had become clear just in the five minutes they'd interacted that General Jake Tanner could be a dangerous adversary.

Piotr supposed he shouldn't be surprised, given the resourcefulness the redheaded CIA *cyka* had shown in capturing him and then extracting vital information from him. The fact that he hated her and wanted nothing more out of whatever life he had remaining than to make her suffer as much as humanly possible didn't mean he couldn't recognize—and even grudgingly appreciate—her abilities as a covert intelligence specialist. And he was now sitting a meter away from her father, from whom she had probably inherited the traits that made her such a dangerous adversary.

But Piotr hadn't come this far to be outsmarted or overpowered because he let his guard down. This man might be as resourceful as his daughter, but Piotr had dealt with plenty of dangerous men in his life, and on missions that meant far less to him personally than did this one.

They drove for a while, the silence interrupted only by Piotr's muttered, "Turn left here," or "Turn right there."

Eventually Jake Tanner broke the silence. He said, "What exactly is it you want?"

"I already told you. I want you to drive where I tell you to drive."

"And that's what I'm doing. What I'm asking is why am I driving exactly where you tell me to drive?"

"Because I have the gun and you do not."

"This wasn't a random kidnapping, was it?"

Piotr smiled despite the tension; he couldn't help himself. "Oh no," he agreed, "this was most certainly not random."

"And to what do I owe the honor of being hijacked at gunpoint and forced to drive to some mysterious destination for some unknown purpose?"

"Vengeance," Piotr said simply.

"I see," Tanner said, although it was clear he did not. "May I ask what was done to you that requires this sort of extreme vengeance?"

Piotr turned in the seat. He faced Jake Tanner and realized he'd begun lifting his Makarov and pointing it again at Tanner's head. "My life was destroyed."

Tanner glanced over at Piotr before returning his attention to the road. "What could I possibly have done to you that warrants this response? I don't even recognize you."

"It was not you who ruined my life."

"And yet it is me who is being kidnapped."

"Yes it is."

"Who was it?"

"You know who it was. You just do not want to say it."

Tanner shook his head. "I'm quite sure I don't—"

"It was your daughter. And that is all you need to know on the subject."

"My daughter?"

"Shut up."

"How could you have learned the identity of—"

"SHUT UP OR DIE!" Piotr shouted.

The car fell silent again.

"Turn left here," Piotr said.

Before long they had arrived.

16

May 17, 1988
7:10 p.m.
Somewhere near Alexandria, Virginia

The minute the asshole stuck a gun in his face, Jake Tanner knew he'd made a mistake with his split-second decision to stop for the stranded motorist. The road was a remote country two-lane, but there had still been plenty of room to drive by if he'd decided just to mind his own business and let the unlucky bastard with the broken-down car fend for himself.

But of course, he'd never been one to let people in need fend for themselves, not even strangers. The concept of service to others was a thread running through the Tanner family, and the thought of driving past the man had never even occurred to him.

Until the ungrateful prick stuck a gun in his face.

At first, Jake assumed this was a random occurrence. A man who'd committed some kind of serious crime and then experienced a breakdown as he was making his escape. A criminal who had panicked and flagged down the first poor sap to drive by, resorting to Plan B: an armed carjacking.

But that assumption had begun to fade almost immediately, replaced by a cold dread that told him he'd been targeted specifically. His kidnapper was far too calm and calculated to be a criminal whose car had died at an inopportune moment. And it took a little time to place the man's accent because it was so unexpected. And having a gun thrust into his face wasn't helping him think clearly, either.

Then it came to him, and when it did his blood ran cold.

The accent was Russian. And his immediate thought was, *This has something to do with Tracie.*

Not a day had gone by since his only child told him she'd hired on with the Central Intelligence Agency as a covert operative that he didn't worry about what she might be doing and where she might be doing it. She was able to share almost nothing about her career with him—as a U.S. Army general, he well understood the concepts of classified information and top secret clearances—but given the fact the United States had only one major geopolitical rival in the world, it didn't take much imagination to assume her work regularly brought her in contact with representatives of the Soviet Union.

Representatives like the man sitting a couple of feet away in the front passenger seat of his car, calmly holding a gun on him and tossing out directions like an old hand at public kidnappings.

But even if his assumption was correct, what the hell was a Russian operative doing in rural Virginia kidnapping a four-star general in his own car?

And where were they going?

And most importantly, what was going to happen when they got there?

Jake didn't know the answer to any of those questions and he doubted very much he wanted to find out. But he was going to, because after maybe thirty minutes of driving, following left and right turns dictated by the kidnapper that seemed random but were not, they finally turned into a long gravel driveway that was choked with weeds and strewn with potholes.

At the far end of the driveway stood the remains of what at one time had been a single family home but was now nothing more than an abandoned wreck, a shell of a building that even from a distance and approaching nightfall Jake could see had not been occupied in a very long time.

Shutters sagged, torn partially away from siding that featured faded, peeling paint. Every window Jake could see had been smashed out, and what he assumed were gang symbols had been spray-painted across virtually the entire front of the house.

The man sitting in the passenger seat with the trace of a Russian accent and the calm, threatening demeanor didn't strike Jake as a Washington gang member, so he assumed this choice of destinations had been selected for its ease of accessibility and the remoteness of its location.

Jake moved slowly up the driveway, the car practically at idle, not anxious to hurry things along. Whatever was going to happen here, he knew it would not be healthy for him. The longer he could delay the man's endgame, the greater his chances of figuring a way out, either by making a play for the Russian's gun or making a break for freedom under the cover of darkness.

For his part, the Russian seemed perfectly happy to allow Jake to move as slowly as he wanted. He'd been tense and nervous back at the ambush point, but now that they'd escaped, he seemed relaxed, almost jovial, a man without a care in the world.

They reached the end of the long driveway and Jake eased to a stop. It was either that or drive into the side of the house, an option he actually considered doing for the briefest of moments. It seemed increasingly obvious the man's intentions were deadly, and if Jake were doomed to die, he certainly wouldn't be opposed to taking his captor along with him. Dropping a house onto the asshole's head would be no more than he deserved.

But he pulled to a stop instead. All things being equal, he preferred attempting escape over dying in his own car next to the man with the gun.

He left the engine running and said, "Okay. What now?"

"Now we go inside."

"How about you go inside and do what you need to do, and I'll wait for you out here? I'll keep the car warm for you."

The Russian had been holding his weapon in his lap but now he raised it and trained it on Jake. He held it close to his body, being careful to give himself enough time to squeeze off at least one shot should Jake make a play for it. "Let me warn you. Do not mistake my good humor for weakness, General Tanner. I will not hesitate to put you down like a rabid dog."

"Fair enough," Jake said. He worked hard to keep his voice steady, determined not to give this asshole the satisfaction of sensing fear in his captive. "But now it's my turn. Do not mistake *my* good humor for weakness, either. The first chance I get, I'm going to take that gun away from you and shove it up your ass. Then I'm going to snap your neck and leave you inside this wreck of a house, which is a better fate than you deserve."

The Russian gazed at Jake, his expression flat. Jake knew immediately he'd made a mistake in speaking to the man the way he had, but he just couldn't stop himself. Passivity and victimhood were every bit as foreign to him as the Soviet system of government, and every bit as repugnant.

"Perhaps I should protect myself then, and just shoot you where you sit."

"Maybe you should," Jake said, meeting the Russian's gaze with a steely one of his own and refusing to look away until his kidnapper had.

For a moment nothing happened and then the Russian said, "Having met you, General, I now understand your daughter much more clearly."

"My daughter is a better operative than you'll ever be, and a better person, not that the bar is set too high on that one. If you think you'll ever get the drop on her, you're kidding yourself."

The Russian ignored his comment and said, "You will roll down your window, and then open the door and step out of the car. Once you are outside you will stand perfectly still until I tell you to move. If you get the bright idea to slam the door and run, I will shoot you before you make it three feet in any direction."

Jake did as he was told. He couldn't see any reasonable alternative. This man was a professional. If there had been any doubt up until now, his instructions eliminated it. By forcing Jake to roll down the window before stepping out of the car, the Russian minimized the possibility of a gunshot being deflected by the glass and giving Jake a few precious seconds to escape.

He stepped out of the car and then stood next to it as his captor slid across the bench seat and stopped behind the wheel. "Now step back six feet," the man said, and Jake did as instructed.

Then the man climbed out of the car and indicated the house with his gun. "Get moving," he said.

So Jake did.

It wasn't like he had much choice.

He crossed the front yard and climbed the crumbling concrete front steps, stopping in front of the closed front door.

"Do not be shy," the Russian said. "Please, walk right in."

Jake turned the knob and pushed on the door and it swung open with a creak that belonged in a horror movie, a Grade B drive-in feature where a chainsaw-wielding maniac terrorized a slew of teens. He stepped inside and considered trying to slam the door on the Russian, trapping him outside, but the man was too quick, slipping a foot into the doorway to block just such an attempt.

Besides, even if he managed to trap himself inside the wreck of a house and leave his captor standing outside, what then? He couldn't exactly outwait the Russian, and the other man was holding a deadly weapon while Jake was unarmed.

He took three steps inside and the man behind him said, "That is far enough," so he stopped. From behind, the Russian produced a flashlight that illuminated the interior of what at one time must have been a living room. The hardwood floors were filthy and water-stained from years of rain and snow blowing through the shattered windows and leaking through the porous roof.

And the room was empty, save for a single wooden chair placed squarely in the center. The chair was heavy, hewn out of what looked like white oak, with a sturdy back and blocky arms and legs that would be perfectly suited to securing, say, a two hundred pound kidnapping victim.

A few feet away from the chair a canvas bag lay on its side. It was a good-sized bag that had been zipped shut but appeared filled with…again, Jake didn't know but doubted he wanted to find out.

Again, he was going to.

"Take a seat, General Tanner."

He turned to face the Russian. "You first."

The man lifted his gun and trained it right between Jake's eyes. It seemed unlikely he would shoot yet, because he had gone to a lot of trouble to get Jake here and if all he wanted to do was blow Jake's head off he could have done that way back at the ambush site. Still, it was all he could do not to flinch at the sight of that black barrel pointing directly into his face.

"I insist," the Russian said. All traces of his previous good humor had vanished. His voice was cold and his face was hard and Jake knew that whatever his plan was for an endgame, it had already begun.

17

"I will not tell you again," the Russian said.

Jake nodded tiredly. He walked to the center of the room and turned to face his kidnapper, who had trailed him as he moved and now stood just out of arm's reach, his weapon still aimed at Jake.

"Tell me why you're doing this," he said, standing in front of the chair. "I want to know what it has to do with my daughter." He'd been careful not to mention Tracie's name on the off chance the KGB man was bluffing and didn't know for certain who she was. That seemed a remote possibility, but he wasn't taking the slightest chance of putting his own child in even more danger than she clearly already was.

"Sit down and I will tell you."

"If I sit, I won't ever be getting up again, will I?"

The Russian's eyes narrowed. "We can do this the easy way or we can do it the hard way. It does not matter to me. In fact, I would almost prefer you resist."

The sick feeling Jake had gotten in the pit of his stomach the moment the crazy Russian bastard pulled a gun on him had never gone away, but now it solidified into a solid mass roughly the size of a basketball. The man's refusal to respond to his question served as all the answer he needed, and the thought that he would never again see the wife and daughter he cherished more than life itself struck him like a sledgehammer to the face.

He swallowed heavily and dropped into the wooden chair. Now he wished he'd taken a shot at escape as he exited the car. A bullet in the back would likely be far preferable to what this man had in store for him.

The Russian stepped to his canvas bag and unzipped it, careful to keep his weapon trained squarely on Jake as he did so. He lifted out a roll of silver duct tape and held it up for Jake's inspection. "Does this have any meaning for you?" he said.

Jake shook his head, mystified. "No. Should it?"

The Russian shrugged. "It seems to mean a lot to Tracie. I was just curious if she had inherited her affinity for duct tape from her father." He smiled. "They say you can fix anything with it, and I have to admit, I have found that to be mostly true."

Jake stiffened. "How do you know her name? Is she all right? Where is she?"

The Russian smiled coldly. He tore off two long strips of tape and slapped them over Jake's wrists, moving more quickly than Jake would have predicted. The man was big and bulky but moved with the fluidity of an elite athlete. He added another strip to each arm, taking the time to pat them down firmly until their adhesive bonded securely with the wood on the underside of the chair's arm.

Then he spoke. "Do me a favor," he said. "Please try to remove your arms from the chair."

"I'm not doing anything until you tell me where my daughter is."

The Russian laughed. With Jake secured, some of the affability he'd shown earlier seemed to have returned. "It is a little late to be making demands," he said. "But do as I ask and I'll tell you whatever you wish to know."

Jake's concern for his own fate had vanished at the sound of Tracie's name. He tugged hard at the tape, making the good-faith effort at escape his captor obviously wanted to see.

He got nowhere. His arms would not budge.

The Russian nodded. "Very good." He bent and began repeating the taping procedure on Jake's ankles, taking his time and doing it right. "Your precious little girl is fine. For now. As we speak she is searching for me in Paris."

"Paris?"

"*Da*. She thinks I am there."

"Why would she…" Jake's voice died away as he made the

connection. "The dead ambassadors I heard about on the news. That was you?"

"You are fairly intelligent. For an American."

Jake shook his head, certain he must be missing something. "You murdered three American diplomats just to lure my daughter to Paris? Why in God's name would you do that?"

"Do not forget about the three security guards I also put down. I worked hard to gain access to the embassy compound, the least you can do is give me credit for a job well done."

Jake felt his eyes widen in horror. "You're…"

The Russian smiled. "Brilliant?"

"I was going to say insane."

The man shrugged, utterly unaffected by Jakes' words.

Jake tried again. "Why? Why would you kill all those people?"

"To be certain your little girl was out of the way so I could do…this…without having to be concerned about the possibility of interruption."

"But you haven't harmed her."

"Oh, no. I have not harmed her. Not yet. I want her to suffer as much as humanly possible before I kill her. And what better way to hurt a young woman than to torture and kill her daddy?"

Jake heard the reference to torture but it barely registered. All he could think about was Tracie's welfare. "I'm going to ask you again: how do you know her name? The CIA would never divulge that information."

This time the Russian actually laughed. It was a hearty guffaw, the sound of a man who thoroughly enjoyed the joke he'd just heard. "One can always access the information one needs as long as one knows where to look and whom to bribe."

"What did she ever do to deserve all this?"

The Russian's voice turned hard and cold again. "She destroyed my life. Took away my career and my dignity. She humiliated me. And she will pay for doing so."

"You're afraid of her." The realization came to Jake out of nowhere, and he was instantly certain he was right. Even in the midst of fear for his own welfare, he was filled with pride for his only child.

The Russian scoffed. "Hardly."

"She's going to kill you, you know."

Without warning the man snapped. He'd been holding the gun in his right hand and now he swung it at Jake's head, pivoting his wrist at the last moment and clubbing him with its butt. Jake felt a gash open and blood begin to flow, warm and wet.

Then the lights went out.

When he awoke, it was to an intense pain, the likes of which he had never before experienced.

He wished he could drop back into unconsciousness.

He did not.

18

May 18, 1988
6:00 a.m.
Hôtel de Crillon, Paris

Someone was shooting at Tracie. The darkness was impenetrable, making it impossible to tell from which direction the shots were coming, but the steady *thump-thump-thump* of semi-automatic weapons fire was impossible to mistake.

And she had no idea where she was.

She thrashed in the dark, reaching for her weapon to return fire, but the back of her hand struck something heavy and metallic, and she flashed awake just as the antique alarm clock supplied by the Hôtel de Crillon dropped to the floor with a teeth-rattling crash. It smashed into dozens of pieces.

She was instantly wide-awake.

Thump-thump-thump.

The Hôtel de Crillon.

She was in Paris thanks to her failed mission to flush out Piotr Speransky, but would be leaving for Rome in…she looked for the clock before remembering she'd just smashed it. Then she checked her watch. It was six a.m. Paris time.

Thump-thump-thump.

Someone was pounding on her door, likely awakening the guests inside every room along this section of corridor. And who-ever was doing the pounding was insistent. He or she continued to rap on the door with the steady insistence of a metronome.

Tracie threw her covers to the side and slipped out of bed, shrugging on a robe and grabbing her weapon, which was on the bedside table exactly where she'd left it. If her hand had thrashed a few inches to the left, she would have knocked *it* to the floor and not the clock.

She hurried to the door and pressed her eye to the peephole. She half expected to see Piotr Speransky on the other side, armed and angry and bent on vengeance, although why he would ignore her for three days while she paraded around in front of the American Embassy like an idiot, only to confront her inside a hotel filled with potential witnesses she couldn't imagine.

But it wasn't Piotr Speransky.

It was the young Marine Corps Embassy Security Group guard who had accompanied Deputy Chief of Mission Henry Gatlin to her room yesterday. He had entered the room briefly and then stood sentry in the hallway during her meeting with Gatlin.

Now he was just on the other side of the door, banging incessantly, showing no interest in giving up and going away.

Tracie slipped her gun hand behind her back and reached for the doorknob. There was no reason to believe the young man was anything other than what he appeared to be—an American soldier carrying out an order to the best of his abilities—but there was no reason to take unnecessary chances, either.

She eased the door open an inch or two, bracing it with her bare foot in the event the man attempted to bull his way inside. It wouldn't prevent him from entering, but should give her time to remove her gun hand from behind her back and make him regret his decision.

"What is it?" she said quietly. There was no reason to ask if he had any idea what time it was, or if he knew he might be waking up other guests. He was here because Gatlin, or someone else at the embassy, had sent him.

"I have a message from Director Stallings, ma'am."

Tracie blinked. "Excuse me?"

"Chief Gatlin asked me to pass along a message from Director Stallings. He said it was of the utmost importance, and that I was not to return to the embassy until I had relayed it."

Tracie stepped back and opened the door fully. "Please, come in." she said. She had turned off and stored her secure satellite phone after speaking with Stallings last night, so he would have been unable to reach her directly. If he'd found it necessary to use Gatlin as a go-between, whatever message was about to be passed should probably not be passed in a public hallway.

The soldier stepped inside and eased the door closed behind him. If he felt awkward in the presence of a beautiful, half-dressed young woman he didn't show it. He looked her straight in the eyes and started speaking. "Director Stallings has instructed me to drive you to the airport immediately. The agency jet is waiting, and he wants you on it as soon as possible."

Tracie blinked in surprise. "That doesn't make sense," she said. "I talked to Stallings last night and he told me to buy a ticket for this morning on a commercial flight to Rome. Why would he tell me that and then send the Gulfstream for me? For that matter, why would he fly me on the company plane, anyway?"

The soldier shook his head. It was an abbreviated little movement and he never took his eyes off hers. "I can't answer that, ma'am. I'm just following orders. I do know the call came just a few hours ago, and Chief Gatlin conveyed to me that this was a matter of the utmost importance."

A few hours ago? There was a six-hour time difference between D.C. and Paris, so a few hours ago for Stallings would have been shortly after they spoke via secure satellite phone. Tracie's mind was whirring as she tried to consider the possibilities. What the hell had changed in the short time since she had talked to Stallings herself?

One thing was certain. If this Marine had been tasked with taking her to the airport, he wasn't about to stop until he accomplished his mission. The only way she could change his mind would be by force, and without additional information she couldn't justify disabling an American soldier who was just trying to do his job.

"I'll need a few minutes to get dressed and get my things together," she said.

"I understand, ma'am. I'll be in the hallway when you're ready." He opened the door and stepped through it, and she waited until he had closed it completely before moving toward her dresser.

* * *

She had exaggerated the time she would need to prepare. A career in covert ops had taught her to be ready to move anywhere, at any time, at a moment's notice.

But she wanted a few minutes to think, to consider what this new development might mean. Why would Stallings have changed the plan so dramatically, and so soon after speaking with Tracie?

She threw on jeans and a sweatshirt and tossed the rest of her things into her go bag, acting almost completely by rote. Her mind was elsewhere.

The obvious next step would be to haul out her secure satellite phone and call Stallings herself before ever leaving her hotel room. Let the embassy security guard cool his heels in the hallway while verifying the information he'd passed along.

But having the director of the Central Intelligence Agency as a handler complicated matters immensely. Mission briefings and debriefings were conducted not at Langley in a meeting room filled with analysts and agency experts, but rather they took place after hours, inside Stallings' own home. With very rare exceptions, their meetings consisted of just two people: Tracie and Stallings.

The arrangement afforded the CIA director the plausible deniability he required should things go sideways on a mission, but the opposite was the case for Tracie: even more so than other covert ops specialists, she was often truly on her own. It was a high-wire act that that worked for her, because she'd always been a loner, had always preferred working solo to having to worry about one or more partners.

But it also meant that the backup and support typically available to covert specialists working in a more traditional role was not always there for her. Six a.m. in Paris translated to noon in Washington, meaning Aaron Stallings was in the middle of his workday. He might be eating lunch, or he might be glad-handing U.S. senators in an effort to secure funding for a secret project, or meeting with senior advisors, or performing any one of dozens of other responsibilities of which Tracie was unaware.

Regardless, it wasn't like Tracie could just ring him up on an unsecured outside line. They spoke only one of two ways: face to face or via secure satellite telephone communication. Stallings wouldn't have his sat phone with him in the middle of the day inside Langley, so he would remain effectively unreachable for the next several hours.

Tracie finished packing her bag. She secured her shoulder holster and strapped her backup weapon to her ankle. One advantage of flying in the CIA jet was that Tracie didn't have to bother disassembling her guns and traveling unarmed. She always felt naked when doing so, uncomfortable to the point of worry until she could once again feel the soothing presence of the Beretta strapped firmly against her ribs.

She stood and took one last look around the room. She was ready to go. The more she considered this new development, the more it occurred to her that she didn't really want to verify anything with Stallings. Because if he actually *had* relayed instructions through the embassy for her take the agency jet to Rome, she would find out why immediately upon landing, or perhaps even once she boarded the Gulfstream at Orly. The most likely explanation would be that the CIA director had somehow gotten a line on Speransky, that the killer was even now stalking another diplomat, and it was essential she waste no time getting to her destination.

That was if Aaron Stallings actually had contacted the embassy in the middle of the night to change their agreed-upon plan. If he hadn't, then there was only one other rational explanation for this morning's events—the Soviets had co-opted the young man standing guard outside her door, and the "change in plans" was nothing more than a ruse designed to lure her away from the embassy.

And straight to Speransky.

But if that were the case, what the Soviets didn't realize was that was exactly what Tracie wanted. The man had executed at least six innocent Americans—hell, maybe more by now, she had no way of knowing—since that fateful moment in the shabby little CIA safe house in Moscow when she'd decided to spare Speransky's life, and she had every intention of rectifying her costly error in judgment.

There was nothing she could do to erase the blood of those

innocents from her hands; it stained them now and would stain them until the day she died. But she sure as hell could make sure he never harmed anyone else, and she would accomplish that goal or die trying.

So if this was a trap, and Speransky was waiting for her in the hallway, or in the car waiting outside the hotel, or along the route to the airport, or any other goddamned place, she would be ready.

And she would take him down.

19

By the time they'd gotten halfway to Orly, Tracie decided the early-morning knock on her door had not been a trap. The Marine Embassy Security Group guard was exactly what he appeared to be: a young soldier carrying out an order.

The realization did not cause Tracie to let her guard down, of course. She'd been wrong before and nearly gotten killed because of it. She would continue to remain alert for any sign of Speransky or any other KGB attack dog right up until the moment the CIA jet lifted into the air, but she knew in her heart the extra vigilance would be unnecessary.

The ride across the streets of Paris was uneventful. Traffic was light and in the early morning hours the city seemed peaceful, a slumbering giant, a beautiful throwback to a simpler age. During her relatively infrequent down time, Tracie tended to stay close to home—her career required enough travel as it was—but she decided this city might be worth a return trip if she were ever able to take a vacation.

She smiled to herself, imagining sharing a room at the Hôtel de Crillon with Marshall, then snapped back to the present, becoming instantly alert when the young soldier behind the wheel bypassed Orly's main entrance. She snaked her hand under her jacket and rested it on the butt of her weapon while showing no outward sign of concern.

A moment later she removed her hand, satisfied nothing was amiss. The CIA had apparently struck an agreement with France's

ALLAN LEVERONE

intelligence services to utilize their airports much in the same way they utilized Washington National, and the soldier was searching for a little-used secondary entrance to the airport that would allow them to bypass the busy main terminal area.

It was a time-consuming maneuver, given the size of Paris' main international airport, and more than a little irritating. Tracie was anxious to leave France behind and get to Speransky's location, wherever that might be. Eventually the driver hooked a sharp left onto a virtually invisible access road. The car passed through a screen of shrubs camouflaging a chain link fence with a security gate that had already been opened. A series of three large hangars stood off by themselves in the distance, far removed from the bustle of Orly's runways, and Tracie could see the agency Gulfstream parked in front of the hangar closest to them.

The car skirted the tarmac, paralleling the chain link fence, and then turned left and eased to a stop next to the plane. Its engines were running, and even at idle power the high-pitched whine of the twin turbines sounded deafening from up close.

The soldier stepped out from behind the wheel, clearly intending to open Tracie's door for her like some kind of military chauffeur, but she beat him to the punch. She leapt out of the car almost before it had stopped moving. She met the driver halfway to the plane and thanked him for the ride even as she felt marginally guilty for having doubted his motives.

Just another day in a career where trusting people can get you killed faster than just about anything else, she thought.

The Gulfstream's access door stood open, its drop-down stairs extended and a pilot standing next to it. She'd ridden in the jet multiple times by now, including just a few days ago on the flight from Washington to Paris, and every trip had featured the same two-man crew. But this was a different pilot, and for a moment Tracie's suspicions skyrocketed, just as they had with the ESG marine who'd appeared at her hotel room door.

But then she forced herself to relax. Of course the agency would employ more than one flight crew. Federal aviation regulations enforced strict rest requirements for pilots, and Tracie had no way of knowing where this plane had been since dropping her off at Orly to begin her mission. Undoubtedly the usual crew was

112

enjoying a day off, or was at home in the states with their families, or whatever.

There was a difference between vigilance and paranoia, and Tracie realized she was coming disturbingly close to crossing it. Between having to parade around in public waiting to be shot and knowing that the man she'd spared in Moscow was traveling around Europe executing innocent civilians, her nerves had been working on overdrive the last few days.

She was as safe here as she would be anywhere. If Speransky and/or the KGB had managed to hijack the CIA's own private jet and was using it as bait to lure one wayward spook, Tracie realized she may as well give up her career, because the battle between the United States and the Soviet Union was over and had been lost.

The man in the captain's uniform watched her cross in front of the car and then stepped forward. He extended his hand and smiled. "We're ready to go as soon as you are, Ms. Quinn. Climb aboard and make yourself comfortable, and we'll be in the air shortly."

"Thank you," she said, returning both the smile and the handshake. "What's the flight time to Rome?"

The pilot's eyes were hidden behind the clichéd aviation sunglasses preferred by fliers everywhere, but Tracie got the impression he blinked in surprise. "Rome? Why would you think we're going to Rome?"

"Well, that was the destination I'd been assigned last night by Direct…uh, by my handler."

"I don't know anything about that, ma'am, but apparently things have changed. My first officer and I are under strict orders to get you stateside as soon as possible."

"Stateside?"

"Yes, ma'am. D.C. And we really need to get in the air immediately, so if you don't mind…"

"Of course." Tracie hurried up the steps and into the plane, her bag slung over her shoulder. If she'd been confused by the situation before, she truly had no idea what to make of it now. Asking questions of the flight crew would be pointless, because they wouldn't have been told anything, and even if they had, they would be as miserly with information would any other CIA employee.

She had no choice but to wait.

And wonder.

She strapped herself into a seat, barely noticing the plane's plush interior.

The feeling that had been lingering over the past few days, the one that said things were careening badly out of control, hadn't gone away. It had been lurking in the back of her mind and now it was intensifying.

Something was wrong.

Something was very wrong.

And she had no idea what it might be.

20

May 18, 1988
10:10 a.m.
Washington National Airport

Tracie didn't think she'd ever been so anxious for a transatlantic flight to come to an end. She'd made the journey countless times, having spent the vast majority of her career working in and around Russia and the various Soviet satellites.

It was inevitably long and boring, but this trip was different. She felt like a caged animal. She alternated between pacing inside the Gulfstream's passenger cabin and sitting with her eyes glued to the window, staring down at the endless expanse of ocean far below. From an altitude of thirty-nine thousand feet, the water passed so slowly beneath the airplane it almost felt like they were standing still, suspended in midair like some sadistic magician's trick and not rocketing along at more than five hundred miles per hour.

She could only keep still for so long in one of the leather captain's chairs before her restlessness got the better of her and she once again found herself wearing a pathway in the carpeting.

Back and forth.

Back and forth.

Typically on these flights, she occupied her time in one of two ways: sleeping or studying intel related to her latest assignment. In this instance, however, she could do neither. She had been awake most of last night but was still too keyed up to sleep. And since she had no clue why she was being flown home, there was obviously no mission briefing to study.

The time passed with excruciating slowness, but it did pass, and eventually Tracie felt the jet begin its long, slow descent for landing. The drop in altitude was a gradual one, and she might well have missed it had she not been so attuned to every aspect of the flight and so anxious to get on the ground. She couldn't even see the eastern coastline of the United States yet in the hazy distance, but he moment the descent began, Tracie buckled in for landing, willing the airport to come into view.

It took longer than she would have liked for that to happen. The final phase of flight was interminable, but at long last the G4 touched down at Washington National and began taxiing toward the secluded corner of the airfield reserved for cargo flights, quarantined aircraft, and the Central Intelligence Agency.

As they approached, Tracie could see a Chevy Suburban parked in front of the agency's hangar. It looked brand new, a 1988 model, with an all-black paint job, blackwall tires and smoked-black windows. Despite her tension, Tracie had to smile. The vehicle screamed "CIA," and she thought if the agency had bought it in an effort to maintain anonymity they had failed mightily, even in a town filled with similar vehicles carrying diplomats and heads of state.

The G4 was still taxiing when she popped out of her seat and approached the exit door. One of the pilots, she thought it was the first officer but wasn't sure, turned and barked at her to remain buckled in until the engines had been shut down, but she ignored him and after a moment he shrugged and turned back toward the front.

Finally the men opened the door and lowered the stairs. Tracie's custom was to thank the crew for their hospitality, and she did so today, shaking both men's hands. But her heart wasn't really in it. She shrugged her bag over her shoulder, refusing the chauffeur's offer of assistance, and climbed into the back seat.

Seconds later they were on their way. The moment the young marine embassy security guard had told her back in Paris that Aaron Stallings was sending the agency jet for her, she had known a car would be awaiting her arrival. The car would bring her straight to a briefing with him, and she wanted nothing more.

Traffic was heavy, and if Tracie had felt trapped inside the relatively roomy Gulfstream jet, she felt like she'd been straight-jacketed inside the Chevy truck. She gazed out the window and tried to formulate a line of questioning for her handler.

After a while she gave up. Without even a shred of knowledge about what had changed in the Piotr Speransky situation, it was impossible to come up with any questions that might be relevant. She sat back in her seat and closed her eyes and waited for the drive to be over.

* * *

Aaron Stallings met her at the car door.

She was so surprised to see the CIA director standing in front of her when she climbed out of the Suburban that she froze in her tracks.

This was completely out of character for the man she'd come to know as cold, calculating and brusque. In all the briefings he'd conducted with her at his home—every single one—he had never once stepped foot outside his office. Typically he ignored her even after she entered, forcing her to stand awkwardly in front of his desk while he pretended to examine paperwork, or sign documents, or do whatever the hell the director of the world's foremost intelligence agency did to occupy his time.

But today he was standing not just outside his office but outside the house, in his driveway, waiting for Tracie.

The little voice that had been yammering inside her head, telling her something was very wrong, intensified. *This can't be good.*

She recovered her composure and thanked the driver, who had circled the car to assist her. She shook his hand, never taking her eyes off Stallings. He rarely smiled and never joked with her, but today he looked somehow different.

Somber and uncomfortable.

Something's very wrong.

The driver returned behind the wheel of the Suburban and started the car. He accelerated slowly away along the circular drive. The vehicle disappeared into the trees and Tracie was alone with her boss.

She still hadn't moved.

Neither had he.

He offered her a smile and said, "Come on in, Tracie," as he turned toward his front door.

She felt as though she'd been hit in the stomach with a sledge-hammer. "What did you say?"

"I said come in."

"No, after that." A black dread descended on her, a desolation that made her previous unfocused concern feel like a walk in the park on a sunny spring day. "You called me Tracie."

"Well, that is your name."

She shook her head. "No. That's not right."

"You're name's not Tracie?"

"Of course it is, but you don't use it. You never call me Tracie. It's always 'Tanner' this, and 'Tanner' that. I don't think you've ever called me by my first name. I wasn't sure you even knew what it was, or cared. So what the hell is going on?"

They'd been walking slowly toward the house as they talked, and now Stallings stopped and waited for Tracie to come next to him. He took her hand and put his arm around her shoulders as he led her up the steps.

"Lets go inside and talk," he said, and she knew it was bad. Really bad.

*   *   *

"Have a seat," Stallings said as he closed the door to his home office behind them. He had removed his arm from Tracie's shoulders as they walked through his front door, but the sensation of dread she felt hadn't lessened. If anything, it seemed to be increasing, building toward some kind of titanic explosion.

She moved toward his desk and froze in confusion for the

second time in a matter of minutes. Every time she'd been inside this office she had been forced to sit in a metal folding chair placed directly in front of Stallings' massive desk, like a fourth grader who'd been sent to the principal's office.

There was a chair in front of the desk, all right, but it wasn't the rickety metal one she expected to see. It was large and comfortable-looking, plush and leather-covered, the sort of chair she imagined a bank president might sit in as he smoked a cigar and denied mortgage applications. It was so big she wasn't even sure how he'd managed to squeeze it in through the office door.

She looked from the chair to Stallings and then back. "That's for me?" she said.

"You don't see anybody else here, do you?" A little of the old Stallings sarcasm resurfaced with the comment, and rather than making Tracie angry or annoyed, she felt a little comforted by that fact. The world hadn't completely gone off its axis.

Not yet, at least.

"I think I'll stand for now, if it's all the same to you."

He didn't answer. Instead he moved behind his desk and stood gazing at her.

"What's going on?" she said quietly. "Why did you change our plan in the middle of the night? And why...all this?" She gestured at the chair, confused. "I assumed you had gotten a line on Speransky, but if that was the case, why pull me all the way back to the states? And now, with you acting so strangely, I'm starting to think this isn't about Piotr Speransky at all."

Stallings sighed deeply. "It's about Speransky," he said after a long silence. "But it's also about...something else."

"What else is it about? Stop beating around the bush and just tell me," Tracie said.

"It's also about your father," Stallings said.

Tracie went numb. Her arms and legs, her fingers and toes and lips, all numb.

Her hair went numb.

She couldn't breathe.

In one overwhelming rush of insight she knew the truth, but somehow she still managed to mumble, "What about my father?"

"He's dead, Tracie. I'm sorry."

21

She felt her legs give way but somehow managed to avoid smashing her face on Stallings' desk as she toppled to the floor.

He rushed to help her but she raised one hand and said, "I'm okay," even though she knew she wasn't. Her ears were ringing and she felt herself begin to hyperventilate so she concentrated on controlling her breathing as she struggled to push herself up into the chair.

It was important to her that she do it herself, and to his credit the CIA director seemed to understand as much. He stood next to her, arms half raised as if to catch her should she fall again, but he never touched her and after a struggle that was much more difficult than it should have been, she found herself slumped in the leather chair, suddenly grateful for the padding.

She squeezed her eyes shut, determined not to cry in front of her boss, although why the hell that mattered at this point she had no earthly idea. With her eyes still closed she said, "What did Speransky do to him?"

"It doesn't matter. Not to you."

"Of course it matters." She opened her eyes and fixed Stallings with a glare. She hadn't begun sobbing yet, although how long she might manage to continue that magic trick she had no idea. "It matters more than ever."

"What I mean is this is over, at least for you. I give you my word the agency will find him and deal with him, but you're too close to this now. It's too personal. You're off this assignment."

"Too personal? It's always been personal, boss. From the moment Ryan Smith and I kidnapped him off that snowy road in Russia it's been personal to him. And now it's personal to me. So I need to know what was done to my father. I need to know everything. I need to."

"Listen to me," Stallings said. "That's not how it works. You just found out your father is gone and you're going to need time to deal with that. Time to grieve. I know how close you were to him and I will not allow you to put yourself in harm's way while you're not thinking clearly."

"At least tell me what happened to him."

"You don't want to know the details, Tracie, trust me."

"I don't want to know the details? I *have* to know the details. I have to know everything. Most importantly, how do you know it was Speransky?"

"Tracie...please just let it g—"

"I can't just let it go, sir. Don't you see? I can't. I feel numb and empty and it's going to take a long goddamned time to come to grips with the knowledge that my father—the man I grew up idolizing, the person I've tried to model my life after—has been ripped away from me and my mother and everyone else who loved him. It would be hard enough to deal with if he died in a car accident, or suffered a heart attack, or even was killed in a mugging, for Christ's sake. But if Piotr Speransky is responsible, I have to know everything, because I will not let it stand. So no, I won't let it go. I can't let it go. Tell me. Please."

Stallings continued to stand next to her chair. He looked her up and down and then stared at the floor. He shoved his hands into his pockets. Even lost in her grief and bewilderment, Tracie thought he looked more human than she'd ever seen him.

Finally he wandered back behind his desk and sat, thrumming his fingers on the surface.

"Please," she repeated, and he nodded tiredly.

"I guess I understand the need to know," he said softly, and then sighed. "Alexandria police got an anonymous tip by telephone last night alerting them to a murder. The tipster identified the victim by name."

"The victim being my father."

"Yes. The person calling in the tip was male, and he spoke with a slight but detectable Russian accent."

"That doesn't mean it was Speransky," Tracie said, although she knew it was, because she knew what was coming next.

"No it doesn't," Stallings agreed. "But the details of the crime scene make the connection unmistakable."

She closed her eyes again. This was her fault. This was all her fault. "He'd been duct-taped to a sturdy wooden chair and tortured, before being shot in the head, exactly like the last of the three ambassadors."

"Yes."

"The similarities were intentional. He wanted me to know."

"Yes."

"Speransky murdered those three diplomats for one reason: to draw me to Europe, so he could be sure I was out of the way while he tortured and murdered my father."

"Yes."

"I need to see the crime scene photos, and don't tell me you don't have them. I know you can get them, which means I know you have them."

"Yes, I have them. But you don't want to see them, Tracie."

"No, I don't want to see them. But I need to, and you're going to show them to me. You owe me that much." She thought he would get defensive like he always did, that he would rant and rave about not owing her a goddamned thing, that he would tell her to understand her place in the pecking order, that he would say all the things she had heard dozens of times from him whenever he felt she was questioning his authority.

He didn't say any of them. He locked eyes with her, testing her, gauging her resolve.

She held his gaze, steely-eyed and determined, all trace of her tears gone, at least for the time being. She would grieve for her murdered father, of course she would, but she would lock the grief and pain away until she could at least look at herself in the mirror and tell the person staring back that she'd settled the score.

Or she would die trying. It was really that simple.

They measured each other for a long time. Tracie didn't care. She would stare at her boss for as long as it took to get what she needed.

Finally he nodded.

Then he shook his head.

Then he reached into a drawer and pulled out a yellow file folder and tossed it across the desk. It spun once and landed directly in front of Tracie, the photos spilling out onto the polished walnut surface like the desecration they were.

She clamped her mouth closed and ground her teeth and steeled herself for the worst. Then she began sorting through the pictures, each a visual stab in her heart that was every bit as real as if Piotr Speransky had snuck into the office and was even now thrusting a combat knife into her back, over and over.

Her father lay slumped to the side, a portion of his skull blown off by one or more slugs from a weapon far more powerful than it needed to be to accomplish its task. That had been done for effect too, Tracie knew. What was left of his head lolled on his shoulder, gore covering his face. The amount of blood that had been spilled was sickening. It ran down his neck. It soaked his shirt. It covered virtually all of the surrounding area.

His body strained in death against the bonds keeping him in the chair, and Tracie's heart broke, over and over, as she sifted through the photos.

"He was taken to an abandoned house in a secluded area of Alexandria, on Telegraph Road," Stallings said. "A stolen car was found abandoned on the side of Route 644, which, as you know, is along your father's commute home from the Pentagon."

Tracie closed her eyes and ran her hands through her hair.

"Are you sure you want to hear this?" Stallings asked gently.

"Keep going."

He sighed. "The current working theory by law enforcement is that this was a random act, that your father stopped to help what he thought was a stranded motorist and was kidnapped, tortured and robbed, possibly in a gang-related incident. But of course we know differently."

"Do they know how long he was tortured?"

"They suspect the call was made to the police shortly after your father died, and given the fact he typically left work at the same time every evening…they think it was five hours, give or take."

"What was done to him, specifically?" Tracie asked, doing her best to ignore the drumbeat of accusations screaming inside her skull that said she was to blame, that she had killed her father, that she was the reason he lay slumped in a chair with his head blown apart.

"Chemicals were involved," Stallings said, choosing his words carefully. "As were blades. But they won't really have any more specifics until after the autopsy has been completed."

She shuffled through the photos again before slipping them neatly back into the file folder. She had seen enough. The images they contained would be burned into her memory for the rest of her life.

"I assume you've arranged protection for my mother?" she said.

"Of course. She's under round-the-clock surveillance. There's no way Speransky can get anywhere near her even if he's still in the country, which I very much doubt."

"Thank you," Tracie said. "And thank you for sending the Gulfstream to bring me home."

"The murder of a four-star general is big news. I didn't want you finding out from the television."

"I appreciate that," she said. Her hands were folded in her lap and she stared at them as if they were the most fascinating things she'd ever seen. Then she raised her eyes and met Aaron Stallings' steady gaze. "There's something else."

"I know there is."

"How the *hell* did Piotr Speransky find out who I was?"

22

They stared at each other for a long time, nobody speaking. As the silence stretched on, Tracie felt the shock and grief draining from her system, replaced by something else.

Something diamond-hard.

Something cold and furious.

Something beyond furious.

"The mole," she said.

"Yes," Stallings agreed. "There's a mole."

"No, you're not hearing me," Tracie said. "I'm not saying, 'Gee whiz, Director, there must be a mole.' I'm saying the mole *I told you about* at least a year ago is still there, leaking information, doing what moles do, and now, because you ignored me and did nothing, I've been compromised and my father is dead. That's what I'm saying."

Stallings' complexion began to change, his face coloring and his expression darkening. Nobody talked to him the way Tracie just had, and she knew he would not tolerate it, not even from an operative lost in her grief. She knew it; she just didn't care.

He started to speak, only to slam his jaw closed and stop himself.

Then he cleared his throat and said, "There are things of which you are unaware." It was obvious he was biting back his legendary temper, but Tracie didn't care about that, either.

"No," she said, interrupting her boss before he could continue. "That doesn't cut it. You don't get to sit behind your desk and dismiss me with the excuse that I don't have clearance to know everything, or that you know the identity of the mole but have been allowing him to continue to operate because you're gaining valuable intel from him. That's not acceptable. I've been outed to a Soviet assassin and now the best man I've ever known is dead. And he wasn't just killed. He was tortured for hours and *then* killed. And there's no justification for that. None."

Stallings had shown no reaction while she spoke, other than the steady coloring of his face. By the time she finished, it was just shy of purple, the shade of an overcast sky before a vicious thunderstorm.

He sat for a moment and then said, "Are you finished? Have you gotten it all out of your system?"

"For the time being."

"Good. Because now it's my turn to talk."

Tracie stared at him without speaking.

"Last year you accused me of sitting on the intel you extracted from Winston Andrews regarding other leaks inside the agency, and now you're doing it again. I know you're devastated by the loss of your father, so I understand you lashing out. I certainly understand your anger and frustration. I feel it, too.

"And if you truly believe I was dismissing your concerns back then or I'm dismissing them now, I'm very sorry but there's nothing I can do about that. Because the fact of the matter is that I can't and won't run everything I'm doing as head of this agency past a field-level operative. The system doesn't work that way, and it *shouldn't* work that way.

"All I can tell you is that it is, by nature, extremely difficult to flush out a mole, particularly inside an organization filled with people trained better than anyone else in the world in the skills of deception and stealth. But I have been working steadily on identifying the leaker, and I've been making progress.

"I am heartily sorry I wasn't able to do so in time to prevent what happened to your father, and that's the truth. Whether you choose to accept that explanation is up to you. Frankly, it's more than you're entitled to as an employee, and I wouldn't be offering any elucidation at all were it not for the horrible murder last night of General Tanner.

"But I *will not tolerate* you coming into my office and accusing me of intentionally allowing a mole to operate for the past year, undermining the security of this nation and resulting in the deaths of some of its citizens, because I felt I was getting something out of it, professionally or personally. That's where I draw the line. *That's* what is unacceptable."

Tracie was at a loss. She had no idea how to respond. She'd expected a full-on barrage of invective from the CIA director, an unleashing of insults that would allow her to respond in kind and maybe, just maybe, release some of the awful tension and grief and fury swirling inside her. Subconsciously, she suspected that was why she had attacked him so heatedly in the first place.

But instead, his response was measured and fair, probably more so than she deserved. And he was right. Her job had been to deliver the information about a possible leak inside the agency to her superiors, and that was what she had done. What happened to that information after she passed it along, how it was processed and what became of it, was far above her pay grade. That would have been the case even if her father was still alive and had never been kidnapped.

She had lowered her head and was again staring down at her hands fidgeting in her lap, seemingly of their own accord. She steeled herself and raised her eyes and met those of her handler and held them steadily.

"You're absolutely right," she said. "That was unfair of me and I apologize. We've had our disagreements over the course of working together, and I've felt unfairly treated at times. A lot of the time, in fact. But never once in my nine years working inside this agency have I ever seen you act with anything less than the safety and security of this country as your foremost consideration."

"Apology accepted," he said quietly. "You've been blindsided and I would have been shocked had you *not* reacted strongly."

"That's still no excuse, but thank you. And I suppose it goes without saying, but I'm going after Speransky. I'll be leaving right after the funeral."

"I can't let you do that," Stallings said firmly. "I meant what I said before. I give you my word we'll handle this, but you're not to get involved."

"Then I quit."

"Excuse me?"

"You heard me. If I can't do this as an operative, I'll do it on my own." She stood and faced the CIA director, still seated behind his desk. His jaw hung open and he stared at her, nonplussed. In other circumstances she would have derived great pleasure from the sight, but right now she just felt numb.

"Thank you for everything," she said. She extended her hand and he shook it reflexively. "It's been an honor serving this country and a privilege working with you."

She turned toward the door and walked out, closing it softly behind her.

23

May 19, 1988
2:30 a.m.
Leningrad, Russia, USSR

Vasily Labochev arranged his daily briefing papers into a neat stack and slid them to the side of his desk. By now they were eighteen hours old and he'd been over them four times already, but what else was there to do in the middle of the night when the hooker he'd paid good money for was sleeping alone in his bed?

He sipped from a large tumbler of vodka and stroked his beard. Sometimes the cost of amassing wealth was high.

Vasily had been in charge of the KGB's Leningrad station for well over thirty years. His rise through the ranks of the Soviet Union's legendary spy agency had been meteoric, thanks in large part to the success he'd had developing sources of information inside the United States' Central Intelligence Agency in the years following World War II, and continuing to this day.

A young intelligence operative at the time the Red Army surrounded Berlin, Vasily had struck up something like a friendship with an American operative also developing intel in the area. The American's name was Winston Andrews, and despite the fact that with the end of the war, the United States and the USSR turned from reluctant allies to hated enemies, the two men remained in contact.

Although their personalities were about as different as it was possible to get—Vasily was oversized and ebullient, a heavy drinker and inveterate womanizer while Andrews was slim and serious—through many hours spent drinking and talking, Vasily began to realize the serious-minded Andrews shared his interest in profiting personally as well as professionally from his work.

And a career in covert intelligence offered a unique opportunity to do so.

A feeling-out process began, one that was lengthy and incremental, taking place over the course of several years as each man gauged the other's dedication to his country and willingness to sacrifice ideals—or at least bend them a little, and sometimes a lot—in favor of personal gain.

The early, tentative exchanges of intelligence were successful. Both men received high praise from their handlers for collecting intel on the enemy, while successfully concealing the fact they were selling intelligence of equal or greater value to the very same enemy. It was a decades-long high-wire act; with a treason charge certain to follow for either man should the illicit arrangement ever be exposed.

But Vasily's arrangement never came to light inside the KGB, and for the longest time, neither did the CIA tumble to Winston Andrews' activity. By the nineteen-fifties, each spy was rocketing up the ranks inside his agency. Vasily became the youngest station chief in KGB history when placed in charge of Leningrad in 1957, and he'd remained in his position ever since.

The key to his success, and the factor that allowed him to act both as a traitor to his country and a valuable collector of intelligence at the same time, was the fact that Vasily never overstepped. He only utilized his CIA contacts for information once of twice a year on an official basis, making the flow of information slow and occasional rather than rapid, which would have drawn far too much attention from the wrong people and resulted in his—and his American comrade—getting caught.

And then shot; at least in his case.

Shortly after assuming his duties in Leningrad, Vasily expanded his operation to include contract work: utilizing his American contacts to gain intelligence not for the benefit of the Soviet government, but for private entities willing to meet Vasily's extremely steep asking price.

In this manner, he was able over the years to amass exorbitant wealth through the sale of intelligence to mercenaries and other interested parties, while charging an extremely steep fee, thus assuring he did not run the risk of going to the well too often and seeing the entire operation blow up in his face.

From the early nineteen-sixties until last year—a span of more than a quarter-century—the mutually beneficial arrangement between Vasily and Winston Andrews ran with the smoothness of a finely crafted Swiss watch.

And then, last year, abruptly and without warning, Andrews disappeared.

Details were sketchy and hard to come by, even for a KGB station chief, and it took Vasily a long time to learn Winston Andrews' fate. He was still uncertain of all that had happened. But apparently someone inside the CIA finally uncovered Andrews' status as a KGB collaborator and the man had taken his own life to avoid suffering the humiliating consequences of his treachery.

This should have marked the end of Vasily's long run as a collector of intelligence for the KGB—not to mention his lucrative private business—but Vasily was nothing if not resourceful. He had long ago envisioned a scenario whereby Andrews was outed or killed, and he had planned for the future accordingly.

He had developed a second conduit of intelligence inside Langley.

An even more valuable one.

As soon as Vasily learned of Andrews' disappearance he withdrew from all activity with his secondary source, like a turtle retreating inside its shell. He kept a low profile for months, concerned that prior to his suicide, his old comrade Winston Andrews might have revealed the identity of his collaborator to someone inside the CIA.

A revelation that would most likely get Vasily killed.

When nearly a year went by and that dire consequence never materialized, Vasily cautiously renewed acquaintances with his second contact, his big fish. The contact's name was Roger Thornton, one of just three deputy CIA directors. Like Vasily and Winston Andrews, Thornton had begun his career as an operative, rising through agency ranks over the years until eventually ascending to a position just one rung below that of Director Aaron Stallings himself.

Unlike Andrews, Thornton had become more reluctant to share intel the higher he climbed on his organizational ladder, but that fact was irrelevant to Vasily. He had Thornton by the balls, because he'd recorded multiple conversations with the man in which information was exchanged that was damaging to the United States of America.

Vasily had only needed to mention this fact to Thornton once to make his point: he would cooperate fully with Vasily when asked, or the KGB station chief would leak some of his hours of incriminating conversations with Thornton to the American press, and Thornton would be finished. His career would be destroyed and he would face life in prison—perhaps even execution—for treason.

Despite having been nearly a year since they last spoke, Vasily found it unnecessary to remind Thornton of the consequences for not complying with a request when they renewed acquaintances in January. They made a bit of small talk and then got down to business

Thornton reacted angrily to Vasily's request. "The name of a covert operative? That's going too far, Vasily. I can't possibly provide you with that information. It's…it's just…impossible."

"It *is* possible, my friend," Vasily had answered, speaking calmly and quietly. "In fact, not only is it possible, it is exactly what you are going to do."

Thornton had gone quiet for a long time, and Vasily let the silence drag on, knowing the CIA deputy director was considering his options, knowing also that he had none.

At last Thornton had said, "Hypothetically speaking, if I were to provide you with a name, what operative would we be referring to?"

"We are referring to the young woman who tortured our man inside a CIA safe house over the winter and then assassinated one of Russia's preeminent scientists on the streets of Moscow."

Thornton had hemmed and hawed and sputtered and complained, but in the end he had promised to "see what I can do."

He came through much more quickly than I would have expected, too, Vasily thought with a smile. Within days, Thornton had gotten back to Vasily with not just the name of the operative, but with a fair amount of associated biographical information as well.

Shortly afterward, Vasily's net worth had increased dramatically. It was the single biggest score of his illicit career trading in information. Because he had held Piotr Speransky up for a small fortune in exchange for that name.

As KGB station chief, Vasily was well aware of Speransky's humiliation last winter at the hands of a CIA operative in Moscow. When he combined that knowledge with a familiarity of just how unstable and prideful Speransky was, Vasily concluded—correctly, as it turned out—that Speransky would be willing to pay a king's ransom to learn the name of the woman he needed to kill in order to regain his reputation and save his career.

But that gain in net worth was a double-edged sword. It also placed Vasily squarely in Piotr Speransky's crosshairs. Vasily knew that if Speransky survived his mission and was successful in eliminating the American, his next move would be to return to Leningrad to recover the fortune in cash he'd been required to pay Vasily.

And that scenario could not be permitted to occur.

Speransky was cold-blooded and remorseless. He would execute Vasily and take every last American dime of his money back, along with whatever else of value he could get his hands on. He would never stop until Vasily was lying dead in a pool of his own blood.

The notion that *he* could find himself the target of a man like Piotr Speransky was terrifying. But he wasn't dead yet, and he wasn't out of ideas yet, either. Vasily Labochev hadn't risen to a top post inside the Soviet Union's premier intelligence service without being able to deal effectively with risky contingencies.

He had a plan, and if successful, his plan would preserve his life, not to mention his fortune. This was why he was sitting behind his desk at two-thirty in the morning and not cavorting in his bed with one of the many prostitutes he single-handedly kept in business.

Because two-thirty a.m. on May nineteenth in Leningrad was six-thirty p.m. on May eighteenth in Washington, D.C. and he very much needed to speak to someone in Washington.

Someone very specific.

He took a long sip from his tumbler of vodka and smiled into the telephone handset. "Hello, Comrade Thornton, and how are you this fine evening?"

24

A long silence followed Vasily's greeting.

It was exactly what he had expected.

When Thornton responded, it was with obvious reluctance. "Uh...what do you...I mean, I didn't expect to hear from you again for a very long time."

"What do you mean? It has been several months. The last time we spoke was, what? Late January? Early February?"

"Something like that, yes. I was hoping for longer."

"Understandable, given the lengthy delay between our previous communications. But I so enjoy speaking with you, I decided to... what do you Americans say...chat you up again."

"Nobody I know says that."

"Nevertheless, I do enjoy our conversations."

"You want something else from me. You always want something else."

"So cynical, my friend. You do not believe I might simply wish to pass the time with you?"

Thornton had been speaking quietly, but now he lowered his voice further. When he spoke, though, it was with barely contained fury. "I most certainly do *not* believe that. And this is not the time to be talking. The murder of General Tanner is all over the news here. We shouldn't speak for a very long time. We certainly shouldn't be speaking right now."

"And yet we are. And we will, as often and for as long as I wish."

"What do you want, goddammit?"

"As pleasing as it always is to chat with you, I *am* calling for a specific purpose."

"That's a shock."

"I need a favor."

Thornton chuckled bitterly. "And the surprises keep coming."

Vasily couldn't help smiling. "Obviously you have made the connection between the intelligence you provided me last January and the breaking news in your country."

"Made the connection? Of course I made the connection! How stupid do you think I am?"

"I do not think you are stupid at all, my friend, which is why I know you will do exactly as you are told."

"For the last time, what do you want?"

"I need you to make a piece of intelligence available to your operational assets."

Another long silence followed, as Thornton tried to decipher what he'd just heard. Then he said, "You want to pass information along to *our* operatives? As in, the CIA?"

"See?" Vasily said. "I told you I did not think you were stupid."

"Why would you want to provide intel to our side? To set up our operatives so you can murder more innocent Americans? No. I will not be a party to any more killing of my countrymen, Vasily. I don't care what you threaten me with, I won't do it."

"Slow down, my friend. I am afraid you misinterpret the nature of this call. I am not interested in passing along false intelligence. I am not interested in setting up American operatives to be killed. Quite the opposite, in fact."

"Then why would you voluntarily provide intel to the CIA that would be damaging to your side?"

"Because I believe this information would *not* be damaging to my side."

"I don't follow."

"This is one of those very rare instances where one event can be beneficial to both sides."

"Keep going."

"You see, the man who committed the murder of which you spoke a moment ago, the killer of General Tanner, has—"

"It's not 'the man,'" Thornton interrupted. "It's your agent. A KGB operative. Just to be clear."

"*Da,*" Vasily agreed. "The KGB agent. This man has gone... how do you say...off the rails. He has taken the intelligence you so graciously provided and run with it in a direction entirely unanticipated—and unapproved—by his KGB handlers. We have thus reached the determination that this man is no longer capable of following orders and confining himself to strict mission protocols."

"And? I'm supposed to care about this because?"

"We have decided it is necessary to end him."

"Then why don't you get off the phone with me and just do it? That seems to be the sort of thing you people are exceedingly good at."

Vasily laughed. "Why, thank you, my friend, I'll take that as a compliment." He sipped his vodka before continuing. "We understand the execution of General Tanner has caused untold headaches for your agency, and would like to offer up our man as some small measure of...fence-mending, as you Americans would say."

"Nobody I know says that, either."

"Still."

"Let me get this straight," Thornton said incredulously. "You blackmail me into giving you the name of the agency operative who executed Slava Marinov, and then claim to be surprised when one of your men murders our operative's father in a clear case of revenge? That's the biggest pile of steaming bullshit I've ever heard, and I've spent my entire adult life working with some of the most deceitful people in the world."

"That may be so," Vasily said calmly, "but, still, it is the truth. I give you my word as a gentleman and fellow career intelligence professional that the information I am going to pass along is not meant to entrap any of your people, or even to put them in any danger whatsoever, beyond the risk they will take completing the assassination of our man."

"I don't believe you," Thornton said simply.

Another sip of vodka. It was smooth and slightly spicy and made Vasily's belly feel as though a small, cozy campfire was burning inside it. He'd anticipated Thornton's response; the conversation really couldn't have gone any other way. What Vasily was proposing was antithetical to the philosophy not just of the

KGB, but of America's CIA as well. There was no greater sin for any intelligence professional than to reveal the identity of another operative to the enemy, and after Vasily had forced Thornton to do just that the last time they spoke, he was now offering to do the same thing? Expecting nothing in return?

It made no rational sense. So Vasily understood Thornton's reaction.

He also didn't care about it. Thornton wasn't the person whose opinion mattered. When he had forced Thornton to reveal the identity of Marinov's killer, he hadn't just passed that intel along to Piotr Sperasky. He'd also done a little research into the CIA covert operative known as Tracie Tanner.

What he'd learned was that Tanner, in addition to being petite and beautiful, was one of the most deadly and resourceful agents in the Central Intelligence Agency's arsenal. She must be, because she no longer had any official ties to the agency, and yet Vasily knew for a fact she had accomplished multiple missions inside the Soviet Union, including, of course, the infamous—and brazen—assassination of Slava Marinov mere blocks from the Kremlin.

Based on what he'd uncovered in his research, Vasily would have bet his life that this Tracie Tanner person would never rest until she hunted down and eliminated the man who murdered her father. In fact, he *was* betting his life on it, because he knew that if Speransky survived, he, Vasily, was the next target on Speransky's list.

And since the upper echelon of KGB management had decided to offer reinstatement to the assassin, Vasily couldn't very well countermand their orders and use another Soviet assassin to take out Speransky. His choice was stark and terrifying: offer Speransky up to the CIA or wait to be murdered by the most deadly and unstable man in the KGB's arsenal.

The decision was a simple one.

But in order for the American operative known as Tracie Tanner to do Vasily the great favor of saving his life by eliminating his murderer, she would need to know where to find the man.

Vasily had that base covered as well: it would be right here in Leningrad. Speransky had emptied out almost all the hidden caches of funds he'd stashed away over the course of his career, but there was one he had left untouched.

The one he kept in Leningrad.

Vasily knew it hadn't been touched because he'd known about Speransky's Leningrad safe house for years. Nothing that went on inside his city escaped Vasily's attention, and he had been aware of Speransky's cache almost from the day the assassin established it. One thing Vasily *didn't* know was how much money had been stuffed inside the small, square concrete-block building located inside a dying industrial park on the outskirts of the city, but he knew it was a lot.

Vasily had paid a small fortune to a low-level KGB operative to tail Speransky around Eurasia from the moment Vasily advised him of Tracie Tanner's identity until the moment the assassin had departed for the United States, and at no time had the man come within shouting distance of his Leningrad safe house.

There could be only one reason Speransky would have left this particular cache untouched: he planned to return to Leningrad and transfer the money he would reacquire after killing Vasily—along with much of the remainder of Vasily's personal fortune—to his hidden storage area right here in the city.

This meant Vasily's time was running out.

Quickly.

"Are…are you still there?" Thornton's voice was half fearful and half hopeful that Vasily had suddenly dropped dead, and Vasily realized he had gone silent for at least half a minute as he mentally reviewed his plan. He shook his head in disgust at himself; it was a measure of how badly Speransky had shaken him that he'd allowed such a show of weakness when dealing with his American mole.

"Of course I am still here," he answered gruffly. "But our connection is bad, and I missed your last comment. What did you say?"

"I said I don't believe for one second you are offering General Tanner's killer to us as some kind of olive branch between our two agencies. That's patently absurd." Thornton's voice was stronger and more forceful than it had been at any time during their conversation and Vasily mentally cursed himself for allowing the man to believe he may have gained the upper hand.

Or any hand.

No matter. He would put the American in his place right now. "I do not care," he said curtly.

"Excuse me?"

"I said I do not care what you believe or do not believe. I am not soliciting your opinion, nor am I asking your permission for anything. You are merely to act as a messenger, nothing more. You will pass the intelligence to your superiors, exactly as I give it to you. If you do not, you will find your name splashed across every newspaper in your country as the most despicable traitor in American history. Am I making myself clear, Comrade Thornton?"

"I hate you."

"I know that. Am I making myself clear?"

Now Thornton's end of the line fell silent as the American considered his possible responses. Vasily didn't push him. There was only one conclusion Thornton could reach, and Vasily was content to let him take as much time as he needed to reach it.

"Yes." The word came through the staticky earpiece loud and clear, and it was obvious it had been uttered through clenched teeth.

Vasily smiled. "Good," he said. "Here is what you will tell your superiors."

"There's only one."

"I am sorry?"

"I have only one superior, and it is the CIA director himself."

Vasily sipped his vodka and allowed himself another smile, a self-satisfied one. "I am well aware of that, my friend. Now, pay attention. It is important this information gets relayed exactly as it is issued. There can be no mistakes."

"Jesus Christ almighty, just get on with it. I know how to do my job."

"I hope so," Vasily replied. "For your sake."

He proceeded to spell out the details that would allow him to survive the mess he'd gotten himself into. Hopefully.

When Vasily finished speaking, Thornton seemed stunned. The entire conversation had clearly thrown him for a loop, and that was just fine with Vasily. A man unmoored and lost was much more likely to do as he was told than a man confident in his standing.

The conversation drew to a close just as Vasily emptied his tumbler of vodka. He felt warm and fuzzy and optimistic.

It was now well past three a.m. in Leningrad, but despite the time, he walked to his bar and refilled the glass. It seemed there was every reason to celebrate.

25

May 19, 1988
10:00 a.m.
Arlington, Virginia

The morning of the funeral dawned overcast and drizzly. The weather was a perfect match for Tracie's mood, which she doubted could get any bleaker after first being responsible for the murders of six innocent Americans overseas, and now her own father here in the D.C. area.

Jake Tanner had seen combat in two separate wars—three if you counted the undeclared "police action" in Korea thirty-plus years ago—and come through it all with no more serious injury than a sprained ankle, only to be shot to death just miles from his home.

After being tortured for hours.

Tracie knew she would suffer from the unrelenting horror of her accountability every day for the rest of her life, starting with today. She liked to think she was tough; hell, she *knew* she was tough. But she dreaded attending her father's funeral, had no idea how in God's name she was ever going to get through it.

She loved and cherished her mother, but was a daddy's girl through and through. She's been her father's daughter as long as she could remember. Some of her earliest memories were of hiking with her dad through the Virginia woods, of learning to disassemble and clean a pistol and then reassemble it, of going to the shooting range on Sunday mornings after church and then following that up with a five-mile run.

When she was six years old.

She knew she would have to be strong for her mother but wondered how to accomplish that feat when just thinking about her dad's fate was enough to make her break out in a cold sweat and begin shaking, as though she might pass out at any moment.

And what the hell was she supposed to wear to a state funeral? She rarely spent more than a few days in D.C. at a time, and even though it was where she kept her apartment, she had never been one to stockpile clothing. She owned only a handful of dresses, none of which was appropriate for today's somber occasion.

She hated shopping with a passion, but sucked it up and did it anyway yesterday, settling on a black knee-length dress with an understated black lace collar and new shoes that were as uncomfortable as they were expensive. Tracie knew she would never wear either item again after today, not because they weren't pretty but because they would forever be stained with the memory of why she'd bought them in the first place.

She arose far too early, having slept far too little, showering and dressing in a matter of minutes and then tending to her mother, who seemed utterly adrift. Tracie could tell she'd been crying but said nothing. If her mother wanted to talk, she would do so when she was ready.

But, really, why would she even consider discussing her husband's murder with the person who had set the whole thing in motion?

They ate a tasteless breakfast and the minute Tracie placed the dishes into the dishwasher she couldn't have said what the hell the meal had been, and she'd cooked it. Then they sat in the living room of her parents' home—her mother's home, she corrected herself—and stared at the TV news mostly in silence until it was time to leave for the service.

Tracie didn't think her heart could break any further.

She was wrong about that.

*　*　*

Having grown up the only child of a decorated U.S. Army general and highly regarded state department official, Tracie Tanner was thoroughly familiar with the pomp and circumstance with which official Washington approached everything. But nothing in her upbringing had prepared her for the spectacle that was her father's funeral service.

The burial of a four-star general, particularly given the circumstances of Jake Tanner's death, was more than just an occasion. It was An Occasion, and as such, made the time pass even more slowly from Tracie's perspective than it otherwise would have. And that was saying something.

From the service conducted inside Washington's National Cathedral, packed with mourners and covered by television news crews, to the transportation of the casket to Arlington National Cemetery by marine color guard and horse-drawn carriage, the day was a study in misery for Tracie.

She sat in the front pew fiddling with her imitation-pearl necklace, wishing she were even now hunting down Piotr Speransky.

She tried to pay attention to the words of the minister but could not.

She tried counting how many times she broke down and wept but lost track somewhere around ten.

Finally, a couple of hours or a thousand years after the funeral service had begun, she found herself standing with her mother and the rest of her extended family in front of the gaping hole in the ground that would serve as her father's eternal resting place.

The weather hadn't improved over the course of the morning. If anything the drizzle had intensified and turned into a light but steady rain. Umbrellas sprouted above the mourners like black mushrooms, but although Tracie had brought one she refused to open it. The rain soaked into her overcoat and her dress and flattened her hair to her skull.

She was miserable.

It was what she wanted. She *should* be miserable. She deserved nothing better.

People whispered and chatted under their breath and the occasional titter made its way to Tracie's ears. Instead of being upset that someone would find anything funny about her father's burial, she was glad to hear the suppressed laughter. Despite his lifelong service to his country and lofty position in the military, Jake Tanner had never been one to stand on ceremony. If forced to come up with a one-word description of him, the word "somber" would never have occurred to her.

Had he been alive, and commemorating the life and death of a fellow soldier instead of lying inside a box waiting to be lowered into the ground, he might well have been the one cracking a joke under his breath. Not to denigrate the dead man or to show disrespect, but to remind everyone around him that life was for the living, that mourning must be a temporary condition, and that even in the midst of extreme sorrow it is possible—even necessary—to see the potential for happiness.

Tracie had begun to shiver from the effect of the steady rain when the carriage drawn by a team of white horses rounded a corner and approached the burial site. It came to a stop and a contingent of soldiers, wearing their dress uniforms and intensely white gloves and hats, lifted General Jake Tanner's casket from the carriage and transported it to the gravesite. They moved slowly, rain dripping from their hats and their uniform coats.

They paid the weather no more mind than did Tracie.

They placed the casket onto the bier. A minister read a passage from a bible and Tracie hoped the book didn't hold any particular meaning to the man, because rain was splattering off its pages as he held it open. She was aware of her mother sniffling softly beside her, supported on one side by Tracie's uncle and on the other by her aunt.

The twenty-one-gun salute had just begun when Tracie began shaking again, exactly as she'd been doing on and off since last night, only much more intensely. A thin buzzing noise began in her ears. It started off barely noticeable, like the sound of a faraway train whistle, but it grew louder, quickly, and she didn't even have time to register surprise that she was about to faint when the darkness closed in and she was gone.

* * *

She was only out for a moment.

When she opened her eyes she knew exactly where she was, and exactly what had happened, and assumed that she must be lying flat on her back, staring into the leaden overcast as raindrops pelted her face and horrified spectators muttered to each other about how she'd not only killed her father but had ruined his funeral for good measure.

But she wasn't flat on her back.

She hadn't fallen at all.

She was still nearly upright.

She was being supported by a pair of heavily muscled arms encased in a wet black overcoat, with the cuffs of a navy blue suit peeking out the ends. Two large, dark-skinned hands held her securely around the waist, and she raised her eyes, blinking against the steadily falling rain, to see the concerned gaze of Marshall Fulton staring down at her.

Marshall Fulton, the agency analyst who had risked his life and his career to help her successfully track down and rescue Secretary of State J. Robert Humphries last year after he'd been kidnapped by a team of Iraqi intelligence operatives.

Marshall Fulton, the man from Louisiana Bayou country whom Tracie had been sort-of-but-not-exactly, on-and-off romantically involved with for months. The man with a seemingly infinite supply of patience, who understood her reluctance to commit to anyone after the tragic fate that had befallen her last love, Shane Rowley.

Marshall Fulton, the man with the deepest, softest brown eyes she'd ever seen.

Those eyes now bored into her own as his arms pulled her into his body, protecting her and sheltering her in an expression of tenderness unlike anything she'd ever experienced.

"I've got you," he whispered, and she realized he'd been standing directly behind her, which was why she hadn't seen him. She had briefly wondered earlier where he was but had been so lost in her grief and guilt she hadn't expended much energy worrying about it.

But she had no doubt Marshall had positioned himself close to her intentionally. During one of their many heart-to-heart chats since their relationship deepened, she had shared with him how close she was to her father, how much she felt she owed him in terms of moral compass and work ethic, how much she admired him, not just as a father but as a human being. She was certain Marshall had stood directly behind her because he wanted to be prepared should she become overwhelmed by grief during the burial ceremony.

And she had done exactly that.

He moved so quickly as she started to fall that no one in the crowd, save the half-dozen or so people in their immediate vicinity, even knew she'd fainted. Almost no one realized anything was amiss.

"Thank you," she mouthed, and pushed herself up to her full height, once again supporting herself on her own two feet. She would be eternally grateful to Marshall for his quick reflexes, and the action he'd taken that had prevented a somber ceremony from turning into a circus sideshow.

But Tracie Tanner's default setting was one of independence and self-reliance, and she was determined to finish out this awful day as she'd started it—strong and dignified. Marshall recognized what she wanted and offered one last, lingering hug. Then he released his grip and stepped back, once again just another onlooker here to pay his respects to the life and death of General Jake Tanner.

The rifles continued firing as the rain continued to fall, twenty-one lonely reminders of a life given in service not just to a nation, but to an ideal.

When the last piercing shot echoed away into the rain and the mist, Tracie felt her attention begin to turn to the cause that had already begun to consume her: finding her father's murderer.

She would not rest until she had tracked down Piotr Speransky.

And once she located him, she would end him.

Or she would die trying.

26

May 20, 1988
8:30 a.m.
Washington, D.C.

"Hello?"

"Hello, Tanner. It's Director Stallings."

"I know who it is."

"Yes, well. It was a beautiful service yesterday, aside from the weather, of course."

"Of course. Yes. Beautiful."

"I spoke with your mother for a few minutes at the grave site. I passed along my condolences, along with those of everyone at the agency. She's a lovely lady."

"Yes, she's a lovely widow. She's also in danger. Speransky executed my father, my mother might very well be next."

"I highly doubt that. After a crime as high profile as the murder of your father, the greatest probability is that Piotr Speransky fled the country immediately. The murder was intended to get our attention and he would know we would devote every possible resource to tracking him down. He has either already left the states or is making his escape as we speak."

"So now we're discussing probabilities? I agree with your assessment, but what if we're wrong? What if Speransky doesn't care about being caught? What if he's so focused on making me suffer that he's still hiding under some rock in D.C. waiting to take a crack at my mother? Or what if he's working with one or more other KGB operatives, and those men or women are even now preparing to murder her?"

"I understand your concerns, and—"

"Maybe weighing probabilities is good enough for you, but it's not good enough for me. I just lost my dad, I have no intention of risking my mom as well."

"I understand you're upset, Tanner, but please let me finish."

"Fine. Go ahead."

"I mentioned my assessment of the situational probabilities because I wanted to set your mind at ease, if possible, regarding your mother's safety. But of course I'm not willing to put her life at risk while the Speransky situation remains unresolved. I put in a personal request the D.C. Police Chief Marvin Harris to place your mother's home under surveillance and provide round-the-clock security for her while your father's murder remains under investigation."

"But the investigators think it was a gang thing, a random carjacking and murder."

"Exactly, and that's why it took my personal intervention to convince Chief Harris. He was reluctant and would only agree to a few days of protection, but he did commit at least to that much."

"A few days won't be enough."

"I know it won't, and that's why I wanted to tell you I've committed agency resources to protecting your mother as well. It's a commitment we can't really afford in terms of manpower, but I'm doing it anyway because I don't want you to be worrying about your mother's safety."

"I...I don't know what to say, Director Stallings. It means a lot to me that you would do something like that."

"You don't need to say anything. I had great respect for your father, as I do for your mother. While diplomats and intelligence operatives rarely occupy the same turf or have the same priorities, I've crossed paths with your mother numerous times over the years and always found her to be of the highest integrity. A true professional and, as I said, a lovely woman."

"You've met my mother before yesterday?"

"More than once, yes, typically at official government functions."

"I find that…hard to picture."

"Part of my job description is to maintain a working relationship with state department officials. In any event, as I mentioned earlier I spoke briefly with your mother at the burial service. If she's anywhere near as perceptive as you, and I have every reason to believe she is, I felt she may well suspect there is more to the murder of General Tanner than the authorities realize. That being the case, I wanted to assure her we would spare no expense keeping her safe, and for as long as necessary."

"Again, I don't know what to say, other than thank you."

"You're very welcome. When we spoke, I told her also how proud I am to be working with you and what a fine job you do serving your country. I told her both she and your father would have been extremely proud if I could share all you'd done to help keep this nation safe and secure."

"Aside from the part where my actions resulted directly in my father's death."

"Everyone makes decisions in the heat of the moment that they would change if they could, Tanner. Everyone has regrets."

"I know. But most people's regrets don't include being responsible for the murder of their own father."

The telephone line lapsed into silence. It stretched out, an invisible wall separating two people who rarely saw eye-to-eye on anything.

Finally Tracie spoke. "If there's nothing else, I have a lot to—"

"We need to talk, Tanner."

"Isn't that what we're doing now, more or less?"

"I mean in person. We need to meet."

"Why would we do that? I no longer work for the agency, remember?"

"You didn't officially work for the agency before this, either. You haven't been a company employee for over a year now."

"You know what I mean. My only goal now and moving forward is to find and end Piotr Speransky. You won't allow me to do that, so I quit. Even if you're calling because you want me back on the team, unless your next assignment to me is to assassinate Speransky, I'm not interested. He's not going to face a judge. He's not going to see the inside of a jail cell. The last thing he will ever see is the business end of my Beretta right before I blow his fucking head off. So I can't imagine what we have to discuss in person."

"I disagree. I think there's plenty to discuss."

"Have you backed off your position that I'm not allowed to go after Speransky? Because that's the *only* way we have anything to talk about."

"We can't have this conversation over an unsecured phone line, Tanner. But to answer your question, yes, I still feel we need to talk. Can you come here tomorrow?"

"I can be there this afternoon. I can be there whenever you want. I can be there in thirty minutes."

"Good. See you in thirty."

The line clicked dead and Tracie pulled the handset away from her ear. She stared at it for a moment, replaying the strange conversation in her mind, convinced she must have misunderstood.

But she hadn't. She'd been very clear with Stallings, clearer than was prudent on, as her boss had stated, an unsecured telephone line. Aaron Stallings was a lot of things, but he was not stupid.

And he still wanted to meet with her.

Which meant she would have the backing of the agency in her mission to avenge her father's death. Not only that, but the director of the entire CIA had cleared time at the beginning of a workday to return to his home just to meet with his most unofficial black ops asset.

He had never done that before, and he'd assigned Tracie to some extremely time-critical missions in the past.

Something had happened over the past few days that changed everything from Stallings' perspective. And that something had to be big for him to call Tracie at home and invite her back to work, never mind offer to meet with her at literally a moment's notice.

She realized she was still seated at her kitchen table staring at her telephone like a damned fool. She replaced the handset into the cradle, thankful Stallings couldn't see her through the telephone line. If he could, he would probably change his mind—again—and fire her.

Again.

It was close to a thirty-minute drive to Stallings' home from her apartment; more if the traffic was heavy, which it almost always was. She needed to go. Now.

She didn't have to waste time getting ready to go out because was already dressed, so she stood and grabbed her car keys from the hook on her kitchen wall. Then she marched through the tiny living room to the front door, slamming it behind her and trotting across the parking lot to her car.

She didn't care if she had to drive on sidewalks or over the tops of any vehicles in between her apartment and Stallings' home, she was going to make it to Georgetown in less than half an hour.

She was highly motivated.

27

May 20, 1988
9:00 a.m.
McLean, Virginia

As usual, the door to Aaron Stallings' home office was closed as Tracie padded along the second floor corridor. As usual, she paused in front of it and offered a quiet rap of the knuckles against the stained oak.

Then, not as usual, she turned the knob and entered without waiting for a response. She had neither the time nor the inclination for politeness or the observance of niceties.

She had taken less than two steps across the room, Stallings seated behind his massive desk as always, when he lifted his head from his ever-present mountain of paperwork and said, "Please take a seat, Tanner."

He spoke quietly and matter-of-factly, and the complete about-face from his usual modus operandi was unsettling. Aaron Stallings was legendary inside the CIA, and in fact throughout official Washington, as a master of gamesmanship.

He played political parties against each other to achieve agency goals, dangling veteran politicians on strings like it was their first day in D.C.

He intimidated men and women alike, agency employees and civilians, with his acerbic wit and his ability to grasp all nuances of a situation faster than anyone else in the room.

He was loud and bombastic.

His current calm, quiet tone was the last thing Tracie had expected, particularly after entering the office without waiting for an invite. Normally he would force her to stand in front of his desk unacknowledged upon her arrival while he completed whatever task he was working on, sometimes stretching the process out over what felt like several minutes.

The entire charade was meant to reinforce their relative positions in the hierarchy, to demonstrate who was in charge and who was not. Tracie had understood his methods from their very meeting and had never allowed them to intimidate her.

She had expected something along those lines this morning and to say she was surprised by the abrupt change in Stallings' manner would be an understatement. She tried not to let him see he'd thrown her off her game, though, and sat as instructed.

Stallings spoke immediately. "Thank you for coming on such short notice."

"Like I said on the phone, my only priority is finding and finishing Piotr Speransky. I'm here because something has obviously changed between the last time I sat in this office and this morning. If that change won't aid in my mission, I'll be out of here so fast it will make your head spin. Sir."

"Don't beat around the bush, Tanner," he said drily. "Tell me what you really think."

"I just don't want to waste your time. And in that vein, why am I here?"

"I told you a couple of days ago you would not be permitted to go after Speransky. I've changed my mind on that subject."

Even though that was exactly what she'd expected to hear, a jolt of adrenaline blasted through Tracie's body at Stallings' words. She had serious doubts she would be able to locate Speransky without the assistance of the world's preeminent intelligence agency, but had been committed to trying. If the CIA director was telling the truth now, though, it might mean the difference between success and failure.

She maintained her composure, not wanting to let her boss see the emotions playing out inside her. "Why?" she said.

"Because I put myself in your shoes," he said simply.

"I don't understand."

"As I told your mother yesterday at the funeral service, you've completed some critical assignments in service to this country, usually operating alone or with only minimal backup and always in harm's way. You've proven yourself to be tough and resourceful, as well as extremely reliable. You've earned the opportunity to track down your father's killer."

"You understand I won't be bringing Speransky to justice, at least not of the official variety. The only justice he's going to receive is the kind administered with a gun."

Stallings stared at her for a moment, his face an unreadable mask. Then he said, "And *you* understand I cannot officially endorse or even respond to your words."

"Of course I do," Tracie said.

"Then I believe nothing more needs to be said on the subject."

"No sir, it doesn't."

"Good."

"Thank you, sir."

"You don't need to thank me, and I still feel I may be making a mistake. You're too close to this situation. I never do anything like this. I shouldn't allow it. But I'm going to allow it."

They held each other's gaze for a moment and then Tracie said, "With that out of the way, why, specifically, am I here? You wouldn't come home from work in the middle of the morning just to tell me I'm back on the team. You could have done that tonight, after spending a full day at Langley. Something's happening. What is it?"

Stallings nodded. "I have a line on Speransky. In fact, I have more than just a lead. I know exactly where he can be found."

A second lightning bolt ripped through Tracie. "How is that possible, so soon after he killed my father?"

Stallings regarded Tracie appraisingly. He looked away for a moment and then back into her eyes. For the first time since they'd begun working together, Tracie sensed a certain…reluctance to speak on his part. It wasn't fear, not exactly. Tracie doubted the CIA director was capable of fear. But there was a definite hesitation in his manner that was utterly uncharacteristic of the Aaron Stallings she had come to know.

Stallings cleared his throat and said, "I'm sure you recall the discussion we had a couple of days ago regarding your claim following Winston Andrews' suicide, where he told you there was one or more people high in the CIA's chain of command who were collaborating with the Soviets?"

"I didn't *claim* that was what he told me," she said, speaking slowly. "*That was what he told me* just before killing himself. I made that as clear as I possibly could to you, and you—"

"We've already had this discussion," Stallings interrupted.

"I know, so why are you bringing it back u—"

"I've identified the traitor."

Time stopped as Tracie processed the director's words. She realized her jaw was hanging open and she slammed it closed. "Excuse me?" she finally managed.

"You assumed at the time that I would ignore Andrews' charge, and you accused me of doing exactly that just days ago. But I take the security of this agency—and this country—seriously. Of course I was going to pursue the possibility Winston was telling the truth."

"What does this have to do with Piotr Speransky?" A cold fury was building inside Tracie as she asked the question.

"We were able to learn Speransky's short-term future plans from a wiretap we placed on the agency traitor's telephone."

"I see." Tracie swallowed heavily, the fury mushrooming in her gut, exploding with nuclear speed. "So you've been tapping a Soviet collaborator's phone while plans were being discussed to murder my father, and you didn't feel the need to, oh, I don't know, *take action to stop the murderer?*"

She had risen to her feet as she was speaking without even realizing she was doing so. Her voice rose from a near-whisper to a shout, shaking and cracking, and she leaned over Stallings' desk, her fists planted on it as she screamed into his fleshy face.

She breathed deeply and continued, Stallings gazing impassively up at her. "You say you care about the security of the agency and the country, and that's wonderful. You should care about that. But you're so concerned about the agency that you'll allow an innocent man to be slaughtered without lifting a finger to help him? That's monstrous!"

"Are you finished?" Stallings said quietly. "Because if you're done disparaging my character—again—it's my turn to speak, and I'll thank you to listen quietly and without interruption, as I've done to you."

Tracie realized her entire body was shaking from anger and regret. She blew out a breath and dropped slowly into her chair.

Then she nodded. "Talk to me. Please."

"The very day last year that you told me about Andrews' charge, I began investigating it."

"But you told me the matter was closed. You made it seem like Andrews' death was the end of the traitorous activity."

"Of course I did. As I may have mentioned once or twice, no operative, not even you, is—or should be—privy to all that's happening behind the scenes at an agency devoted to intelligence gathering and national security. To involve you or update you on my progress would have made no sense and, in fact, would have complicated matters immensely."

Tracie nodded. Stallings' words made sense and she was immediately angry with herself that she hadn't considered that possibility on her own.

"I understand," she said. "But the larger issue remains unchanged. How could you allow my father to be victimized if you were tapping the traitor's phone?"

"We agreed it was my turn to speak, did we not?"

"Yes, we did. Sorry."

"It takes a long time to identify a traitor with any degree of certainty. You might think it would be simple, given the relatively small number of people inside the CIA who held positions above Winston's. But the opposite is actually true. I couldn't involve any high-ranking agency members in my investigation for fear that I might unwittingly involve the traitor himself. And obviously, a man committing treason against this country is going to be extremely careful to cover his tracks, particularly given his standing within the agency."

Stallings breathed deeply and continued. "It took almost a full year to identify the security leak. I narrowed the traitor down to the three most likely possibilities—my three deputy directors— and then fed false intelligence to each, information that would seem valuable enough to pass along to the Soviets, and that would eventually show up on our analysts' desks after being intercepted. However, it also had to be essentially harmless."

"So none of our secrets would be at risk or our assets exposed," Tracie said, now beginning to grasp the enormity of the problem Stallings had faced.

"Exactly," the CIA director said. "And if I've learned anything from working so closely with you over the last year-plus, it's that you would want anyone engaged in treason against this country's welfare to suffer the full weight of legal consequences for his actions."

"You're damn right I would," Tracie said softly. The fog of fury that had dropped over her was lifting, replaced by a dawning understanding. She thought she knew what was coming next but waited for her boss to spell it out.

"That being the case," Stallings continued, "while it would have been a simple matter to tap the traitor's phone internally, anything we uncovered using such a wiretap would have proven inadmissible in a legal proceeding. So I had to involve the FBI and wait for them to convince a federal judge to approve the wiretap. This was another step that took much longer than you might expect."

"And the approval came through just recently."

"The day of your father's murder," Stallings said gently. "I'm sorry."

Tracie covered her face with her hands, almost unable to believe the awful, ironic timing. Had the wiretap been approved earlier, it might have given Stallings or the FBI time to prevent Speransky from executing her father.

The news was horrific, but even through the dull, throbbing pain Tracie realized something needed to be said. She removed her hands from her face and looked her boss straight in the eyes.

"I owe you an apology," she said. "I was so far out of line in accusing you of somehow being complicit in my father's murder that I wouldn't blame you if you never spoke to me again."

He waved his hands like a man shooing away a pesky mosquito. "Water under the bridge," he said simply. "I've been there, so I understand."

"Thank you."

"I'm telling you all of this because the information gained from the wiretap not only identified a traitor who will never take another breath of air as a free man, but also served up Piotr Speransky on a silver platter. I assume you're interested in this information?"

"You assume correctly."

Stallings opened a drawer in his desk. He reached down and lifted out a reel-to-reel tape player and placed it squarely in the middle of the desk. A tape had already been loaded into the machine, and when he pushed a button the tape began to turn.

28

"I don't believe for one second you are offering General Tanner's killer to us as some kind of olive branch between our two agencies. That's patently absurd." The voice on the tape was male and clearly American. Based on the words coming out of his mouth, he was a CIA employee. Tracie was certain she'd never heard his voice before, though, and had no idea who was speaking.

"I do not care," a second man said. This voice clearly belonged to someone to whom English was a second language. Tracie was unsurprised to hear a Russian accent but couldn't place the voice. She didn't think the speaker was someone she'd ever met.

The tape continued to turn. "Excuse me?"

"I said I do not care what you believe or do not believe. I am not soliciting your opinion, nor am I asking your permission for anything. You are merely to act as a messenger, nothing more. You will pass along the intelligence to your superiors, exactly as I give it to you. If you do not, you will find your name splashed across every newspaper in your country as the worst traitor in American history. Am I making myself clear, Comrade Thornton?"

"I hate you."

"I know. Am I making myself clear?"

Tracie had lowered her head as she concentrated on deciphering every nuance of the taped conversation. Her eyes had narrowed to slits and her forehead furrowed. But now her head shot up in alarm and she discovered Stallings was staring at her steadily.

"Stop the tape," she said, but he was already reaching for the button. She sat for a moment, frozen, almost but not quite unable to comprehend what she had just heard.

"Thornton?" she whispered, and Stallings nodded.

"*Roger* Thornton?" she repeated. "CIA Deputy Director Roger Thornton? Is that the Comrade Thornton this KGB officer is talking to?"

The pain of betrayal was clear in Stallings' eyes as he answered. "The one and only. I've known Roger for nearly forty years. I would have trusted him with my life. I did, in fact, numerous times, although all of those times were decades ago, and clearly the man on that tape is not the man I thought I knew."

Tracie shook her head slowly. *One of the CIA's three deputy directors is a traitor.* The words felt foreign to her even as they rattled around inside her head. "Now I understand how difficult it must have been to identify the leaker. Who would ever have imagined the number two man in the entire agency was a Soviet collaborator?"

"Unfortunately, not me," Stallings said. "Had I tumbled to it a little sooner, your father might still be alive."

Tracie thought she now understood how Alice felt after she'd fallen down the rabbit hole into Wonderland. *The CIA's deputy director.* She'd been shocked last year when Winston Andrews admitted at least one highly placed agency member was collaborating with the Soviet Union against the interests of the United States, but now she realized he'd undersold the extent of the betrayal.

The deputy director of the CIA.

Stallings sighed deeply. "Are you ready to continue?" He was clearly troubled; Tracie had never seen him this shaken.

She nodded and he punched the button on the tape player and the discussion of murder and treachery resumed.

"I hate you."

"I know. Am I making myself clear?"

The line fell silent for a moment, and then, "Yes."

"Good," the Russian voice said. "Here is what you will tell your superiors."

"There's only one."

"I am sorry?"

"I have only one superior, and it is the CIA director himself."

"I am well aware of that, my friend. Now, pay attention. It is important this information gets relayed exactly as it is given. There can be no mistakes."

"Jesus Christ almighty, just get on with it. I know how to do my job."

"I hope so," the Russian said. "For your sake. Here is what you must pass along. Comrade Speransky maintains a small safe house in Leningrad. He has doubtless gone underground in your country, while he waits for the opportunity to complete his mission by eliminating Agent Tanner. Once he has done so, he will leave the United States and return to Leningrad."

"How do you know that?" Thornton asked.

"Excuse me?"

"I said, how do you know Speransky will run to Leningrad? If he's anything like most CIA operatives, he will have established multiple safe houses all over Russia and probably all of Eurasia, independent of the KGB and unknown to you."

"I am sure he has."

"Then how do you know he will choose Leningrad?"

"That is none of your business, my American comrade."

"It *is* my business."

"Is that so?"

"Yes. I'm not passing any intel on to my people unless I know it's accurate and is being provided to me for the stated purpose of eliminating your man."

The tape fell silent again. Tracie watched the clear plastic reels spinning on the machine, the tiny brown magnetic strip churning between them through the heads as the KGB caller considered Thornton's words.

"Fair enough," the Russian finally said. "I know he will come to Leningrad because it is the only one of Comrade Speransky's personal safe houses that still contains any cash or other items of value. My intelligence does not come cheaply. Comrade Speransky was forced to liquidate his other remaining assets in order to pay for the information he required to even the score with your Agent Tanner."

"You extorted him."

"My business dealings are none of your concern, Comrade Thornton. You asked how I knew Speransky would be found in Leningrad after murdering Tracie Tanner, and I have told you. That is all you need to know."

"I know this: if we're certain Speransky is going after Tanner, we can save the trouble and risk of placing a team inside Russia. We can simply wait for him to make a move on Tanner here in the states and take him down when he does."

"I would not recommend that, my friend."

"Really? And why is that?"

"Piotr Speransky is the finest assassin in the KGB arsenal. His status as such is the sole reason he is not rotting in a shallow grave outside Moscow after causing Slava Marinov's death. If you try to trap him using Tanner as bait you will never succeed. He is better than anyone you have. He will kill Tanner and slip through your fingers and you will never see him again.

"Your only chance is to wait until his guard is down and execute him then. Once Tanner is dead and Speransky has returned to the Soviet Union, he will assume he has completed his mission successfully and will not be expecting reprisal, at least not immediately. That is when your team will have its greatest—indeed, its only—chance of success."

Again the tape fell silent and again Tracie found herself questioning reality. Could she really be listening to a high-ranking KGB officer discussing her murder and the murder of her father with the man who occupied the number two rung on the CIA's organizational chart?

It was outlandish, beyond belief, and yet the evidence was there, spooling through the little tape machine on Stallings' desk. The evidence was there, in the paleness on Stallings' normally ruddy face, in his obvious shock at the betrayal of one of his most trusted associates.

The evidence was all there.

Finally the voices on the tape resumed and when they did Tracie was thankful. They enabled her to again concentrate on the operational aspects of the discussion, and not on her stunned disbelief that a man in Thornton's position could turn against his country and the people fighting to keep it safe.

"Fine," Thornton said. "Whatever you say. What is the address of Speransky's unofficial safe house in Leningrad?"

"The structure is located inside Druzhba Industrial Park on the outskirts of Leningrad. It is a small concrete block storage building roughly two hundred meters inside the park on the left-hand side. Commit that location to memory, please."

"I'll remember, don't worry," Thornton said.

"I need you to remember *everything* we have spoken about today. Do you understand all I am asking you to pass along to your CIA contacts?" the Russian-accented voice said.

"I understand," came Thornton's cool reply. "I'm not an idiot."

"Do not answer so flippantly, Comrade Thornton. It is critical this intelligence be relayed promptly, and it is equally critical your operatives do not delay traveling to Leningrad. Speransky will move quickly once Tanner is dead. He will return here, he will clean out his safe house, and he will be gone, and once he has dosappeared you will never find him."

"I still don't understand why your people don't just eliminate Speransky if it's that important to you." A tone of doubt and suspicion ran through Thornton's words, as if he could not believe the Soviets were truly interested in giving up their own man.

When the Russian answered, his voice was sharp. Insistent. "You do not need to understand, Comrade Thornton. There are forces at work that you *cannot* understand. All you need to do is relay the information I have given you, exactly as it has been provided. If you do not, you will find yourself a media star in your home country, and not in a good way. Are we clear on this?"

"I hate you."

"I know. Good day, Comrade Thornton."

28

Stallings pressed the button to stop the tape machine and then picked it up and slipped it back into his desk drawer. He removed a set of keys from his pocket and locked the drawer.

Tracie watched him work and when he'd finished, she said, "I've been in the field for almost ten years. I've listened to wiretapped phone calls dozens of times, both of the legal and illegal variety, and that is without question the strangest conversation I've ever heard. I'm glad you ferreted out the mole, although I'm sorry it turned out to be someone you trusted so implicitly. But are you buying any of what the Russians are selling here?"

"Yes," Stallings said simply.

"It smells like a trap to me. Why in the hell would the KGB assign Speransky to travel all the way to the United States to kill my father and me, and then offer him up to us for assassination? That's not how they do business. If they want Speransky dead, they'll haul him behind a KGB station house and put two slugs in the back of his head and dump him in a shallow grave. Then they'll wipe their hands clean and move on. They've done exactly that dozens of times, probably hundreds."

"You're absolutely right."

"Then why the hell do you believe any of it? What the hell is the KGB really up to?"

"The KGB's not up to anything."

"I don't follow. It's obvious from the telephone conversation that the Russian is a high-ranking KGB member. He would have to be to co-opt someone like Roger Thornton."

"I know who the Russian is, and you're right. He's the KGB's Leningrad station chief, a man named Vasily Labochev, who has been in his position at the KGB nearly as long as I've been in mine here. But the murder of your father is not a KGB operation, Tanner, and never has been. Sure, I believe the KGB would put a bounty on your head after you took out Slava Marinov, but to assassinate a man as high profile as your father, and in such a messy, public manner? The Soviets stand to gain nothing from that. Killing him was a freelance operation on Speransky's part. Trust me on this."

"But that just brings me back to my original question. Why would the Leningrad station chief employ a CIA mole to get us to do what the KGB could do themselves, with much less fuss?"

"Think about it, Tanner. You've spent enough time in Russia and other Soviet states to know how their system operates. What is the time-honored communist business tradition?"

"To profit on the side from official business relationsh…" Tracie's voice trailed away as she connected the dots.

She raised her eyes to meet Stallings'. "Piotr Speransky is not the only one freelancing on this operation, is he? The KGB station chief is doing exactly the same thing. That explains all the talk about money, and how Speransky had to spend so much of his own to get the intel Labochev provided."

Despite the seriousness of the conversation, the corners of Aaron Stallings' mouth curled up in a wry smile. "This is why I put up with all your bullshit, Tanner. Your ability to intuit things is among the finest I've ever seen, and I've watched a lot of operatives come though Langley."

Normally Tracie would have been taken aback by Stallings' words. He was not a man accustomed to offering compliments, especially to her. Acerbic criticism was more his style.

Today, though, she was so focused on the Speransky situation she barely noticed his praise. "So Labochev offers to sell Speransky the intel he needs, which is the identity of the CIA operative who tortured and humiliated him in Moscow."

"You."

"Yes, me. Labochev squeezes his mole. He gets the information Speransky needs and passes it along to the assassin. Speransky comes to the United States and kills my father and is lying in wait to finish the job by executing me."

"Exactly."

"But the operation hasn't been completed yet. I'm still breathing. Why is Labochev suddenly reversing course and offering up Speransky to the CIA?"

"I asked myself the same thing, and there's only one answer that makes any sense."

"Labochev squeezed Speransky for so much cash that he's afraid Speransky is going to come back and kill him to retrieve all his money once I'm dead."

"Bingo. And Labochev is using the CIA to get to Speransky because—"

"Because the KGB wants Speransky alive," Tracie interrupted. "Labochev is the only one who wants him dead, so he has no other choice than to use the CIA to do his dirty work."

"Exactly. Typically, a KGB operative who'd made the kind of error Speransky made in allowing you to capture and interrogate him would be summarily executed. But because Speransky is so good at what he does, the KGB was willing to overlook his indiscretion in order to continue utilizing him to assassinate their enemies."

Tracie sat back in her seat, staring at the rear wall of the office over Stallings' shoulder, seeing but not seeing any of the framed photographs of the CIA director with various presidents, senators and congressmen as she considered the implications of what she'd learned.

"So if this isn't a trap, if the intel about Speransky's safe house in Leningrad is accurate, I actually have a chance at avenging my father's death," she said wonderingly. She refocused her attention on her boss, drilling her eyes into Stallings'. "Assuming you meant what you said about allowing me to complete the mission, of course."

"I meant it," he said. "I wouldn't have called you here if I didn't."

"I swore I would devote the rest of my life to taking out Speransky if that was what it took," she said. "But, honestly, I wasn't sure I would ever be able to dig him up once he slithered under a rock somewhere. And now it looks like he's fallen right into my lap."

Stallings nodded.

"It will make my final CIA mission my most rewarding."

"Your final mission? Why would it be your final mission? I refuse to accept the resignation you offered the last time you were here, by the way. I fully expect to refuse it in the future."

Tracie shrugged. "I have to choice but to resign. My cover is blown. The Soviets know my identity. I'll never be able to work covertly again."

Stallings smiled. "I know you've had a lot to absorb, between your father's murder, the funeral service and now this tape recording." He nodded toward his closed desk drawer. "But there's one more dot you haven't connected yet."

She shook her head. "What am I missing?"

"The Soviets *don't* know your identity. Only Labochev does, and we can be certain he hasn't shared that with anyone else inside the KGB, because if he does that, he has to explain why he robbed Speransky blind to give him the intel he needed to complete an official mission. There is no way Labochev has told anyone in any official capacity about you. None."

"Unless KGB leadership knows Labochev is getting rich selling intelligence."

"No way."

"How can you be so sure?"

"Because if that were the case, they would want in. In fact, I'll take it a step farther and say they would *demand* to be cut in. Labochev must keep his operation a secret from everyone in the KGB or he'll find himself on the outs. He'll end up with nothing. His bosses will extort everything from him that he extorted from Speransky, and presumably from others before him."

Tracie nodded slowly. "Wow," she said. It was all she could manage.

"Yes," Stallings agreed. "Wow."

"And this Vasily Labochev lives in the same city where I'll be renewing acquaintances with Piotr Speransky."

"Yes he does."

"And if he dies, so does the information about my identity."

"Yes it does."

"And if Labochev dies, my mother will be able to live the rest of her life without looking over her shoulder."

"Yes she will."

"And I'll be able to continue my career without worrying my cover's been blown, assuming I survive when I go up against Speransky."

"Yes you will."

Discussing the murder of her father when he'd only been dead a few days was like rubbing heavy-grade sandpaper over a fresh wound, but Tracie was discovering that if she concentrated on the details of the mission she was about to undertake, and not on how badly it hurt to suddenly have such a massive hole in her life, she could think clearly and—she hoped—plan properly. She would have to be able to do both to stand any chance of taking down Piotr Speransky, even with the advantage of surprise on her side.

This wouldn't be like any other assignment; it was far too personal for that to be the case. But the mere act of listening to the wiretapped tape recording and discussing the ramifications of the intel it contained with her handler had an almost soothing effect.

Here was a mission to be undertaken. It was concrete and specific, similar in many ways to dozens of other assignments she had completed over the years.

This was familiar ground.

This was the work to which she had devoted her entire adult life.

This was doable. And if she failed, she would die knowing she had at least done all she could to avenge her father's murder.

She chuckled softly. "Ironic, isn't it?"

"What?"

"The Druzhba Industrial Park is where I'll finally come face-to-face with Speransky again."

"So?"

"'Druzhba.' It's Russian for 'friendship.'"

29

May 22, 1988
12:30 p.m.
Gaithersburg, Maryland

Piotr Speransky was tired of sitting around doing nothing.

He was a man of action, a predator, a lion among sheep. To hang around a shabby little safe house day after day, deep inside the country he despised, when the target of his hatred was practically within arms reach more than tried his patience; it stretched his patience to the limit.

But the *cyka* named Tracie Tanner had not suffered enough through the death of her father.

Not yet.

Not even close.

In a perfect world, he would allow her to dangle on the end of the string of misery he had constructed, guilt-ridden and suffering, not just day after day but week after week. And then, far down the line, when she finally began to feel like herself, when the memory of her father's torture and murder began to fade, only then would Piotr take her.

And torture her.

And eventually, when he'd tired of making her suffer in fresh and original ways, kill her.

But this was not a perfect world, far from it. In a perfect world, he would never have fallen victim to the petite woman less than half his body weight. He never would have been interrogated by her, and made to suffer humiliation at her tiny hands.

He certainly would never have cracked under that interrogation.

But he had, thus proving beyond a shadow of a doubt the *im*perfection of this world. And while the fantasy of causing Tracie Tanner months of suffering before torturing and murdering her was enough to sustain him during the long days spent huddled inside the empty wreck of a home he was using as a safe house, his craving for vengeance demanded he *move*.

The end result would be the same, even if the timeline of Tanner's suffering were shortened. Piotr would ensure the young woman's physical pain more than compensated for the emotional trauma she would avoid by being taken so quickly after learning the fate of her father.

He might even use her sexually before killing her. Rape wasn't typically a part of his torture routine—and he had quite firmly established a routine after torturing so many dozens of victims throughout his long career—but in Tanner's case he thought he might make an exception. Most of his past victims had been men, and none of the few women he'd worked over had even been close to a match for Tanner where beauty was concerned.

But that remained to be seen. It was entirely possible the fantasy of using her in that way would be far superior to the reality, and Piotr wanted nothing to spoil that delicious fantasy.

He would play it by ear. Either way, he would ensure she suffered plenty before finishing her. By the time she took her last miserable breath, she would have been begging to die for hours.

For days.

He packed his few belongings and prepared to exit the empty shell that had at one time—years ago, by the looks of the structure—been a small, secluded single-family house. A retirement home for an elderly couple, maybe, or some rich landlord's rental property.

Whatever. The place had served Piotr's needs and that was all he cared about. It was located deep in the woods outside Gaithersburg, Maryland, far from the similar empty wreck inside which he'd tortured General Tanner before killing him. One thing he'd learned from his operations inside the United States was that there were plenty of places available to use as hideouts, even for days or weeks, thanks to the disposable culture so prevalent in the decadent West.

Even houses often fell victim to that culture.

Piotr shrugged his pack over his shoulder and took one last look at the implements of torture he had stored inside the home during his previous visit to the country. Then he nodded, satisfied they would be sufficient to cause all the suffering he wished on the woman he hated more than anyone else in the world.

This was where she would scream and beg and plead for her life.

This was where her blood would be shed.

This was where she would perish, but only after he had wrung every last ounce of misery from her small body.

He enjoyed his fantasy a few seconds longer and then crossed the room and pushed through the creaky front door. It hung drunkenly off the frame, so locking it behind him was a pipe dream, but that wouldn't matter. Nobody had been inside this structure in decades, and if someone happened to be here when he returned with his prospective victim, say a homeless man in search of shelter or teenagers looking for a place to drink and party, Piotr would simply kill them before getting down to work.

It wouldn't even slow him down.

He tossed his pack into his stolen car and started the engine. Then he turned around in the weed-strewn front yard and headed down the long gravel driveway.

*　*　*

Piotr wasn't concerned with Tanner's whereabouts. She would either be home when he broke into her apartment or she would not. Life would be easier if she were there upon his arrival, obviously, but if that were not the case he would be happy to await her return.

He would certainly be more comfortable killing time inside her apartment than he'd been over the past few days. He'd familiarized himself with the location of her home, although he had never been inside it. But no matter how rudimentary its furnishings—and as a woman who spent most of her time working in foreign countries, Piotr doubted Tanner would have wasted much time or effort decorating her apartment—it would have to be in better condition than the abandoned house in which he'd spent the last few days.

The abandoned house inside which she would soon die.

He pulled into the parking lot next to her apartment building and automatically scanned the cars in the lot for hers. It was the middle of a workday, so there weren't many to examine. This was a working-class building and most people could not afford to spend their time during the week holed up inside their apartments watching soap operas.

Tracie Tanner's car was not here.

Piotr was disappointed but not particularly surprised. At least if he had to spend the rest of the day awaiting his victim's return, he could make good use of his time and maybe find something decent to eat inside her refrigerator. He'd had more than enough of his recent diet of American fast food.

He backed the car into a slot next to the parking lot's exit. It meant a slightly longer walk, meaning he would be exposed for a few extra seconds after kidnapping the *cyka*, but that minor negative was more than offset by the advantage of being able to hit the street and disappear once he forced Tanner inside the vehicle.

He unzipped his pack and removed his lock picking tools, stored inside a smart-looking leather case. His Makarov was secured inside his shoulder holster and covered by a light windbreaker, and between the gun and the tools it would be all he would need to kidnap Tracie Tanner, CIA operative or no.

After sliding out of the front seat, Piotr closed and locked the doors, double-checking to be certain he got them all. The car was old and dented, certainly not one any thief with a modicum of self-respect would be interested in stealing, but his pack was stored under the front seat and he absolutely could not risk *that* disappearing.

Then he strode across the lot and directly to Tanner's front door. He had long ago learned that moving confidently, like a man with a purpose, eliminated most of the risk of appearing suspicious to onlookers.

Not that there seemed to be any around.

He unzipped his carrying case and removed his lock picking tools the moment he arrived at the door. Standing flush against the front of the building meant no one inside any of the apartments could see what he was doing if they happened to look out a window, but there was no way to conceal his actions from anyone who might drive into the parking lot.

He glanced back at the lot and saw no activity.

Not a single vehicle had come or gone since his arrival.

Piotr turned back to the door and set to work.

It took even less than the sixty seconds he'd allotted to the task; Tanner's lock was cheap and easily breached. In maybe half a minute, he'd stepped into his victim's apartment and closed the door behind him.

Smiling, Piotr crossed the living room, moving quietly. He was certain Tanner was not here, but there was never a reason to take unnecessary chances. He stayed close to the wall until reaching a short hallway off his right side. The apartment was small, even by Washington standards, and it was obvious Tanner's bedroom and bathroom were located off the hallway.

He drew his weapon and eased his head through the open bedroom door. The bed was neatly made and the room was empty. The bathroom was right behind the bedroom, and Piotr cleared that as well.

That left only the kitchen. Piotr reversed course down the hallway and entered the kitchen, which was as tiny as the rest of the apartment, and just as empty.

He shrugged. Oh well, he hadn't really expected his victim to be home in the middle of the day.

He turned to open the refrigerator door and froze. A piece of paper had been torn out of a notebook and was lying in the middle of Tanner's small kitchen table. Something written on the paper had caught the attention of his subconscious even as he turned toward the refrigerator.

It was his name.

His heart thudded inside his chest as he spun on his heel and returned to the table.

His name was on a note inside the CIA operative's empty home.

This could not possibly be good.

He realized his mouth had become dry and his throat scratchy, and he ignored that realization as he read the note the *cyka* had left for him:

Hello Piotr, it read.

It was cowardly of you to kidnap and murder an unsuspecting man just to get at me. But I would expect no less from you, given that you are, in fact, a coward.

I spared you once when I shouldn't have, but by killing my father you have sealed your fate. As you read this, I am on my way to loot your safe house in Leningrad and take from you everything of value you have left.

Yes, I know about your safe house.

Yes, I know what is inside it.

Yes, I am going to rob you and leave you with nothing.

This is the fate you deserve, to be penniless and adrift.

After I have removed and safely stored your liquid assets, only then will I end you. You will never see me coming. You will never feel the shot that kills you.

I almost feel sorry for you.

But not quite.

You've brought your fate on yourself.

Tracie.

A heavy veil of panic and confusion fell over Piotr.

How could the *cyka* know of his safe house? How could she know of the cash he'd salted away? How was this even possible?

He stumbled away from the table and toward the front door. Everything had changed in an instant, and although he'd only just begun to consider the ramifications of the note Tanner had left for him, one thing he knew without a shadow of a doubt was that waiting to ambush his CIA tormentor had been a fool's errand.

Labochev had sold him out to the Americans. It was the only logical way Tanner could have learned of his last remaining Soviet safe house. For that, the CIA station chief would pay. Piotr's original plan had been simply to shoot Labochev in the head and take back was what rightfully his upon his return to Leningrad, but now he vowed he would torture the fat, old, double-dealing *mudak* for nearly as long as he intended to torture Tracie Tanner herself.

Right now, though, it was critical he get moving. He should *already* have been moving, because there was literally no time to spare. He had no way of knowing how long the note had been sitting inside this empty apartment waiting for him, and thus it was impossible to know how extensive Tanner's head start was.

His mind was whirring, calculating possibilities and potential responses to this betrayal. He must get to his safe house to stop the American before she removed what was left of the fortune it had taken him decades to amass. But it was clear he could never beat her there, not with her lead time of a day or more.

He would need help.

The man who prided himself on always getting the job done alone would need help. The very notion of asking anyone for anything was anathema to Piotr. But he must force himself to do it, because to cling stubbornly to his pride at a time like this would represent the worst kind of hubris.

But the logistics of acquiring that help would be problematic. He was in the middle of a country he had worked his entire adult life to undermine, a country he hated with every fiber of his being.

More importantly, it was a country that would like nothing better than to get its claws into him and execute him for espionage, so it was not like he could simply drive to any corner telephone booth and ring up the person he desperately needed to talk to.

So before he could escape the United States and return to Russia to deal with Tanner, who had now made a fool of him for a second time, he would have to take a detour. He must drive to the Russian embassy and speak with the KGB's Washington station chief. It was a man named Dmitri Smyrnovich, and his official title was Special Assistant to the American Ambassador.

But Dmitri Smyrnovich was no one's assistant. His real purpose in Washington was to coordinate the Soviets' anti-American propaganda machine from inside the capitol of the very nation he was working to destroy. Piotr had met Dmitri once or twice over the years and taken an instant dislike to the man. Smyrnovich struck Piotr as arrogant, with a superiority complex he'd done nothing in the real world of espionage to earn.

That was beside the point. Personal feelings were irrelevant. Dmitri would have access to secure KGB telephone lines between

Washington and Moscow, lines Piotr could use to make the call he so desperately needed to make.

Today's developments were bad; Piotr was not so foolish as to try to convince himself otherwise. But while he had lost a key battle, he would still win the war.

He would unfortunately have to expend more of his precious fortune to pay the man he was going to call—favors were never free—but the end result would permit him to assassinate Vasily Labochev and recover the rest of his cash. He would similarly recover his standing inside the KGB. And most importantly, he would still get the satisfaction he craved: torturing and eventually killing the little *cyka* Tracie Tanner.

At least there was now no mystery as to where she would be found.

Piotr crumpled up the note and jammed it into his pocket. He was shaking with rage. The redheaded bitch would pay.

Oh, yes she would.

30

May 22, 1988
12:40 p.m.
Gulf of Finland
Finland/Russian border

The boat ride across the Gulf of Finland felt endless to Tracie.

It was a trip she'd made numerous times, wedged into an ancient fishing vessel piloted by a bearded Russian whose name she did not know. His age was open to debate also: he may have been thirty-five, sixty-five, or anything in between.

But he'd been accepting CIA cash to ferry passengers across the Baltic Sea from Finland to Western Russia and vice-versa—no questions asked—for as long as Tracie had been working in the region, probably a lot longer.

The ride was never a comfortable one. The water was invariably choppy, with gulf swells rising above and beyond what Tracie felt comfortable with in such a small boat. But beggars couldn't afford to be choosers, as the saying went, and with limited access into and out of Russia, Tracie had no choice but to suck it up and deal with a queasy stomach.

The unnamed Russian captain—Tracie thought of him as "Gorton," for his salt-and-pepper bearded resemblance to the fisherman in the seafood commercials she'd seen on television—had met her at the Helsinki airport, ushering her into a car almost

185

the moment the CIA's Gulfstream jet stopped taxiing. Where he'd gotten the car and what he intended to do with it when they set sail for Russia, Tracie had no idea and didn't much care.

They drove wordlessly south after leaving the airport, skirting Helsinki proper and then turning east along the Finnish coast. Within minutes of departing the city the countryside turned steadily more rugged and desolate. With its endless inlets and hidden coves, the Gulf of Finland offered hundreds if not thousands of potential mooring spots for someone looking to conceal a small boat for a few hours.

After passing Kotka, a small Finnish coastal city, Gorton exited the main road onto a bumpy trail that was nearly impossible to see, even while driving on it. Still without speaking—Tracie didn't think the man had ever said more than a few words to her at one time—the captain drove on as the trail became ever more difficult to navigate. Fifteen minutes later, Gorton pulled to the side, although Tracie couldn't have said why he would bother. It didn't seem likely another vehicle would come this way for months.

As they climbed out of the car, Tracie could see the boat in the distance, bobbing inside a small sheltered cove. It was the same craft she'd ridden on every time she made this trip, but always with a new paint job and a different name emblazoned on the side, all courtesy of Central Intelligence Agency dollars.

Tracie watched their transportation as it scraped against the large boulder to which it had been carelessly secured. She thought about asking how long the massive rock may have been eating through the boat's hull, and how much damage the vessel could take before springing a leak in the middle of the crossing, but didn't waste her time.

It wasn't like Gorton would have answered, and it wasn't like she had any alternatives, even if he'd said the damned thing was about to plummet to the bottom of the ocean at any moment.

They clambered aboard and the captain fired up the engine. Within three minutes of climbing out of the car, the little boat was headed out into open water and the Russian coast, roughly thirty miles southeast across the gulf.

The plan was to set Tracie ashore along the mostly uninhabited area north of the tiny town of Vistino in extreme western Russia, hard by the Estonia border. That portion of the crossing would be simple. She knew so because she'd done it before. That location was even more remote than the area in Finland they'd just left behind.

But the Soviets weren't stupid. They were every bit as aware as Tracie of their security vulnerability along the Baltic coastline. They combatted that weakness by heavily patrolling the southern Gulf of Finland using armed Zhuk class Russian Naval patrol boats. They further bolstered those patrols with an amalgam of retrofitted craft, some of them not unlike the boat Gorton was piloting right now.

It made for a tense ninety-minute expedition across the open sea. More than once Tracie had found herself taking refuge from patrols beneath the false bottom that had been built into Gorton's boat as the captain calmly explained his business on the gulf to young Red Fleet commanders: he was a humble fisherman merely trying to support his wife and family the only way he knew how.

It had always worked. Gorton was sent on his way while the defenders of the Soviet coast moved on.

But the boat's false bottom hadn't been constructed for comfort, and Tracie hoped it wouldn't become necessary to crawl into it today. When not ferrying CIA passengers the boat actually did serve as a fishing vessel, and Tracie knew from the almost unbearable stench beneath the floorboards that the narrow crawl space did not go unused by Gorton when it came to storing his catch.

The sky was overcast and darkening in advance of a storm, the seas even choppier than usual, and Tracie sighed. She still had to hike a fair distance before she would have any reasonable opportunity to steal a car, and the thought of doing so while being assaulted by a cold rain was not a pleasant one.

The time dragged, the crossing interminable, and while she was grateful they hadn't encountered any Soviet patrols—yet—Tracie found herself worrying whether she would have sufficient opportunity to prepare for Speransky's arrival in Leningrad. There was a lot to do and he wouldn't be sneaking into Russia at ten miles per hour aboard an ancient, stinking fishing boat, and Tracie could feel the time slipping away.

She took solace in the knowledge that as time-consuming

as it was for her to get *into* Russia, it should be equally so for Speransky to get *out* of the United States. And while she had no way of knowing how far behind her the KGB assassin was, she assumed she would have at least twenty-four hours to herself once she finally entered Leningrad. Hopefully that would be enough.

Sea spray soaked Tracie's hair and her clothing, and it occurred to her that no matter the weather, she was probably going to be waterlogged by the time she could take shelter in a stolen car. She tried to sit lower in the boat and silently cursed Piotr Speransky for roughly the thousandth time.

At last the Russian shoreline came into view, still without Gorton's little boat encountering any patrols. It felt like a minor miracle. Ten minutes later, Gorton had maneuvered as close to the rocky beach as he dared. After shaking his hand, a solemn ritual she repeated every time they successfully completed a crossing, Tracie leapt over the side, splashing up to her knees and wading to the shore.

The beach was deserted, as she had known it would be. Vistino was located more than five miles from here and it was miniscule, with a population of well under a thousand. Had Tracie seen anyone while sweeping the area with her binoculars during their approach, she would have waved off the landing and instructed Gorton to find another drop-off location.

She had taken maybe a dozen steps toward the narrow road running along the beach when she turned around. Gorton was already at least fifty feet out into the Baltic, headed for wherever he kept his boat moored. She wondered how much money he'd just made, and whether his boat would receive another new name and paint job, even though they hadn't encountered any Soviets during the trip.

Then she put Gorton and his boat out of her mind. The rain had thus far held off, although the sky continued to darken. Tracie slipped her backpack over her shoulder and began hiking. With any luck she could acquire a car sooner rather than later.

And if that were the case, she would be in Leningrad by tonight.

31

May 22, 1988
11:50 p.m.
Leningrad, Russia, USSR

Vasily Labochev's arm was trapped under a sleeping hooker. Nikita, she called herself, or Natasha. In his drunken haze, he couldn't quite remember which. Or maybe it was something else.

It didn't matter for a number of reasons, one of which was that he was certain the girl's real name was neither Nikita nor Natasha. Call girls were a lot like covert intelligence operatives, he thought with an intoxicated grin: they never wanted you to know their true identities.

Vasily's personal life included many rendezvous with girls just like Nikita/Natasha. At least twice a month for as long as he could remember, Vasily had shared his bed with prostitutes. It was a habit he took great pains to conceal from his KGB superiors, because it was exactly the sort of thing they would worry might prompt extortion by an enterprising Russian criminal type, or much worse, by the American CIA should they become aware of it.

This latest call girl, Nikita or Natasha, had practically set up shop inside Vasily's palatial home. She'd spent every night here over the past week, and Vasily expected she would continue to sleep in his bed until this nasty business with Piotr Speransky was over. He was paying her handsomely, and he knew she would be more than happy to continue earning triple or even quadruple her normal nightly pay until the income stream dried up.

And he needed her. He hadn't been sleeping well since beginning his unofficial business transaction with Speransky. It was a natural by-product, he thought, of committing extortion against one of the most lethal assassins in his country's long and storied history of lethal assassins.

At least with Nikita/Natasha here, Vasily could drink himself numb and then tire his body to the point of exhaustion through bedroom gymnastics, at which his current paid partner was exceptional. He would then fall into a troubled slumber. He would still awaken multiple times overnight, sometimes to pee and others to fret.

Often both.

But at least he was able to manage a few hours rest each night.

He felt his arm going numb and tried to slip it out from under Nikita/Natasha without waking her. He didn't care about the quality of her rest; she was a contract employee, nothing more, and normally he would have poked her in the ribs or shoved her off his arm, and the hell with her if she didn't like it. But if he woke her, she would think he was ready for another round, and he was too prideful to turn her down if she awakened and expected sex.

The problem was all he wanted right now was to get out from under her damned body so he could roll over and get back to sleep.

He worked his arm out slowly and carefully and had almost freed it when he heard a loud THUMP from downstairs. Every once in a while his cats would knock a candlestick off a table while roughhousing; it was a sound he'd heard more than once in the middle of the night.

This was something else entirely.

It was heavier than a candlestick, and muffled, and less metallic.

It was more like a dead or unconscious body hitting the floor; another sound he'd heard plenty of times over the course of his KGB career.

One thought flashed through his alcohol-addled and sleep-deprived brain: *It is Speransky.*

Speransky is here.

He finished his revenge job in the United States and he got here before those amateurs at the CIA could eliminate him, and now he has come to kill me and take back his money.

Vasily bolted upright in bed, yanking the rest of his arm out from under Nikita or Natasha or whatever the hell her name was, waking her but now not caring. He slipped out of bed and lifted the edge of the mattress, removing a Makarov 9mm semi-auto pistol. He knew the magazine was full but he ejected it anyway to be sure, then slammed it back home.

The hooker blinked rapidly and yawned. "What is happening, baby?" She was halfway through a languid stretch when she caught sight of the weapon and yelped. "What-what-what is—"

"Shut up," Vasily growled, accomplishing nothing. She continued to stutter nonsensically.

He lifted the weapon and pointed it squarely at Nikita/Natasha and said, "Shut your damn mouth right now," and she shut her damn mouth.

He flicked the gun in the direction of the door and said, "Get out of bed and come to me."

The hooker had lifted the bedcovers in a pathetic—and point-less—attempt to shield herself from Vasily's gun, and now she lay half-upright in bed, whimpering.

"Now," he whispered fiercely. "Do it or I'll shoot you where you lie."

She gave him a wounded look, like she actually thought she was the lady of the house and the big, strong man should be protecting her from whatever threat they were facing, not menacing her with a loaded gun.

Vasily was shaking badly and losing patience. Speransky was coming, he would be here any moment, and if the assassin entered the bedroom now, he could simply shoot Vasily in the back.

But Vasily could not turn and face the door just yet. He needed the hooker if he was to have any chance of escaping Speransky's wrath.

"Now," he whispered one more time, and the word seemed to shake Nikita/Natasha out of the terror that had frozen her to the bed. She was still clearly afraid, but seemed to recognize she had no reasonable alternative than to obey. She pushed the covers down and reluctantly began crawling toward Vasily.

"Please, do not shoot me," she begged. "I will just leave, you do not even need to pay me for tonight. Consider it a freebie, a gift to remember me by. I will simply leave and we can forget this ever—"

She sucked in a breath in surprise and renewed fear as Vasily grabbed her by the hair and yanked her the rest of the way out of his bed. She crumpled to the floor at his feet and he reached under her armpits and lifted her to a standing position, placing her directly in front of him.

"Now," he said, speaking softly into her ear, "we are going to walk into the hallway. You are to stand in front of me at all times. If you scream, I will shoot you in the back. If you try to run, I will shoot you in the back. If you do anything other than exactly what I tell you to do, I will shoot you in the back. Do you understand?"

"Why are you doing this?" she said, sobbing and sniffling.

"Do you understand?" he whispered.

"Yes. Yes, I-I understand."

"Good. Do not forget, or you will never feel the bullet that kills you."

Nikita or Natasha moaned miserably.

"Now," Vasily said, making the plan up as he went along. "Open the bedroom door and move slowly into the hallway."

32

Tracie cursed inwardly as the third member of Vasily Labochev's three-man personal security team hit the floor.

She'd been dragging his unconscious body across the kitchen with the intention of placing him next to the other two men she'd disabled, when she lost her grip and the heavy security guard thunked onto the ceramic tile. The back of his skull bounced noticeably and she decided he would probably be the last of the three to regain consciousness.

She hauled him the rest of the way and shoved him up against the other two men. All had been secured by duct-tape around the ankles and wrists, with their arms behind their backs and gags taped into their mouths. They would be exceedingly uncomfortable when they regained consciousness, but they would all survive.

Tracie had known Labochev would employ private security. She'd come to the home prepared to kill them, but it hadn't been necessary. Less than an hour of surveillance had been enough to convince her the men were not KGB professionals, or professionals of any kind. They were nothing more than local thugs that Labochev must have recruited on the side.

Hunting them down and disabling them had been a simple matter, one that had taken less than thirty minutes to do, and all without firing a single shot.

She shoved the final security guard against the other two, then turned and hurried through the kitchen. She crossed the large dining room and beautifully furnished living room, moving carefully but swiftly to the stairway located at the rear of the room. The third security guard had been more than willing to give up the location of Labochev's bedroom when presented with the alternative: a gunshot to the back of the skull.

Interrogating a prisoner was all about providing the proper motivation.

She crept up the stairs, weapon held chest-high in both hands. The plan had been to approach Labochev while the man was sleeping, and Tracie still hoped to do so. But the third security guard had hit the floor hard when she dropped him, and it was entirely possible the noise had been sufficient to awaken the KGB man, even all the way up on the second floor.

The security team had left lamps burning in each of the downstairs rooms, so there was enough ambient light in the stairway that Tracie was able to avoid using her flashlight. The stairway itself was constructed of highly polished redwood with a sweeping ninety-degree turn in the middle and what appeared to be an ornate, hand-carved banister. It looked like something out an old American South slave owner's mansion. "Gone With the Wind," Soviet style.

She reached the top of the stairway and flattened against the edge of the hallway wall. Then she peeked around the corner, leading with her gun.

And cursed inwardly.

She *had* awakened Labochev when she dropped the unconscious security guard. The KGB station chief stood at the far end of the hallway outside his open bedroom door. He was using a terrified woman as a human shield. The woman was dressed only in a sheer nightgown, gun held to her head.

"Do not move another..." Labochev commanded, his voice fading away as he stared the length of the hallway in obvious surprise.

"It...it is you," he said a moment later, shock competing with wonder in his tone. "But you should be..." His voice trailed away again. Even in the dim light of the hallway, Vasily Labochev looked as though he'd seen a ghost.

"Dead?" Tracie offered helpfully, and Labochev nodded.

"Sorry to disappoint you. The assassin *you* sent is going to have to be a little better if he wants to pull off that particular trick."

The human shield was sobbing and moaning and shaking visibly. Labochev had one hand wrapped around her hair, holding it in his meaty fist, and in the other he held his gun flush against her skull.

"Please," the girl said in Russian. "Please..."

"Shut up," Labochev barked in her ear. To Tracie he said, "I do not know what you are talking about. I sent no assassin to kill you. I do not even know who you are."

Tracie laughed. "Drop the innocent act. The entire last conversation you had with Roger Thornton was captured on tape, and I've listened to it multiple times. You know exactly who I am, and exactly why I'm here."

"I do not," Labochev insisted, but his already pale complexion seemed to have whitened further.

"Oh, you do," Tracie said. "And furthermore, my father is dead because of you."

"I had nothing to do with—"

"Spare me," she interrupted bitterly. "Maybe you didn't pull the trigger, but you didn't have to. If it weren't for you, Piotr Speransky would never have known who my father was or where to find him. So as far as I'm concerned, you are every bit as guilty as Speransky, and thus every bit as deserving of the fate I'm here to deliver."

Labochev had begun shaking his head, as if he wanted to continue arguing but knew doing so would be pointless. "How did you get in here?" he asked. "I have armed security patrolling my property."

Tracie smiled. "I know what you're doing. I've been in your situation, and when I was, I did exactly the same thing."

"I do not know what you are talking about."

"Bullshit. You know you're screwed, so you're trying to keep me talking while you attempt to figure a way out of the mess you've found yourself in."

Labochev started to speak but Tracie cut him off. "But that's fine. I'll humor you. Have you ever heard the expression, 'you get what you pay for?' Is there an equivalent cliché in Russia?"

"I do not—"

"I know," Tracie said. "You don't know what I'm talking about. I was able to get past your 'armed security' because you cheaped out when it came to protecting yourself. Instead of hiring professionals who know what they're doing, you went for three idiots who are big and scary-looking but don't know the first thing about defending property."

Labochev had no answer for that.

Tracie continued. "Want to know a secret, Vasily?"

"I do not think so."

"Probably not," Tracie agreed. "But since you're paying the Three Stooges down there, I feel it's only fair to inform you of this: two of your men were fast asleep in the living room. All I had to do was disable the first guy outside and then I was in."

Labochev swallowed heavily and Tracie said, "But don't feel too badly about it. I would have gotten past your guys anyway, even if they were professionals. It might have taken me a little longer and I maybe would have broken a sweat, but the end result would have been the same: me taking you out."

"You are not going to take me out. We are at a standoff. I have an entire staff of employees coming to this house first thing in the morning. Once that happens, you will have no chance at escape. Therefore, you will have no choice but to flee before their arrival. I do not mind waiting."

"Hmmm," Tracie said, pretending to consider Labochev's words. "That's only true if you assume I have any objection whatsoever to shooting your little girlfriend to get her out of the way, and *then* taking you down. What in the world would make you think that's the case?"

Labochev smiled wickedly. He continued to train his weapon on the young woman's head. "What would make me think that? I know a little bit about you, Miss Tracie Tanner of the American CIA. I did my research on you when I was acquiring the intel to pass along to Comrade Speransky. You are wired a little differently than the typical assassin. You possess...what is the word...oh yes. Ethics. You have a code of ethics. It does not serve you well, Miss Tracie Tanner of the American CIA. I am certain you will not shoot this young lady, because you possess that code of ethics."

"Well, imagine that," Tracie said sarcastically. "You've gone from knowing nothing about me, not even who I am, to being an expert on my entire life and career in a matter of seconds. That's about as close to a miracle as I think I've ever seen."

Labochev shrugged. He seemed to be losing some of his fear as the initial shock of his situation faded. He wasn't comfortable, not by a long shot, but he no longer seemed to be bordering on panic, either.

"There is no point in denying the truth if you have listened to my conversation with your Comrade Thornton. How is my old friend doing, by the way?"

"He's rotting in jail, which is better than he deserves. He'll spend the rest of his life doing hard time, but that's still a happier fate than the one you're facing."

"So," Labochev said. "You killed Comrade Speransky. Congratulations, that would not be an easy feat to accomplish."

"Speransky's not dead," Tracie said. "Not yet. But that's on the agenda for tomorrow, or whenever he drags his sorry ass to Leningrad."

"Ah, so you have *not* killed Piotr. Now this is beginning to make sense. You escaped death in the United States, only to come to Russia to die. I did not think you could defeat someone with Comrade Speransky's skills."

"I'm not worried about Speransky. I outwitted him so badly back in the states I had some extra time because he ended up so far behind me. I figured I might as well make good use of that time and kill you first, rather than hanging around this dump of a city one second longer than I have to."

"Again," Labochev said. "I must remind you, you are forgetting something."

"You think so?"

"I know so. I have a hostage, and thus I have the upper hand in this situation. You will not shoot the girl, and thus you cannot shoot me."

"There's a flaw in your logic."

"We already discussed the supposed flaw. I know you will not shoot an innocent girl."

Tracie shook her head. "That's not the flaw I was referring to."

Labochev's forehead furrowed and his eyes darkened. "What do you mean?"

"Well," Tracie said. "How do I put this politely? You're a… rather large man and your girlfriend is quite petite. Pretty, too, I might add. Too pretty for you. You're paying her to be here, aren't you?"

"That is none of your business," Labochev said archly, as if Tracie's judgment might be his biggest problem. "What does my personal life have to do with anything?"

"You're right. I apologize. But my point is, this young lady is quite a bit smaller than you."

"So? I like my women petite. Like you." Labochev grinned wickedly. He was gaining confidence, certain he held the upper hand.

"I'd rather feed myself to a hungry alligator than be touched by you. But back to my point. You think because you're hiding behind this little tiny girl, I'm helpless? That I'll wait until just before dawn and then flee the house because I'm afraid of getting caught?"

"That is exactly what I think. What choice do you have?"

"I don't know. I could always do this, I suppose." Tracie stepped into the middle of the hallway, her movement swift but measured.

A startled Vasily Labochev began swiveling his gun away from his hostage, panicked, desperately bringing it to bear on Tracie.

And Tracie shot him in the forehead.

33

Labochev dropped straight down and the girl in the nightgown screamed. She tried to back away from Tracie, tripped over her captor, and her head thunked against the hallway wall as she fell onto Labochev's dead or dying body.

And she never stopped screaming.

Tracie rushed forward, partly to reassure the girl she was safe but mostly to recover Labochev's gun. It had come to rest on the floor next to the girl's right hand, and Tracie had no desire to die in a hail of bullets in the unlikely event it occurred to the young woman to lift it and begin blasting away.

She knelt next to the two bodies, one with a single clean hole in the middle of his forehead, the other complaining loudly about her current situation. She swept the gun away from the girl and it skittered halfway down the hallway behind her.

That was good enough for now.

One look at Labochev's head wound was enough to convince Tracie the man was dead, but she was taking nothing for granted. She ignored the screaming banshee in front of her just long enough to ensure there was no pulse on the man she'd shot, that there was no way he could somehow awaken and threaten either of them.

No pulse. He was never going to threaten anyone again.

He immediately became a nonentity to Tracie and she turned her attention to the terrified woman screaming into her ear. "I'm not going to hurt you," she said, holding the woman's head between her hands and forcing her to look directly into Tracie's eyes. "I'm not going to hurt you."

Some of the goodwill behind the message was lost due to the fact Tracie practically had to scream to be heard. *She might be small but she has one impressive set of lungs,* Tracie thought, repeating her message over and over in Russian until it began to sink in.

The woman wasn't even a woman at all, Tracie realized. She was much younger than Tracie and probably not yet out of her teens.

She was obviously a prostitute, and likely thought she'd scored a plum gig spending the night with a guy like Labochev. Even if she were unaware of his status as a KGB bigshot—and that was probably the case—one look at his home and furnishings would have been enough to convince her he was a high roller of some sort.

Now her plum gig had turned into a nightmare: held at gunpoint by one lunatic and then shot at by someone she clearly thought was another.

The girl's screams finally died out and she lay panting and shaking in Tracie's arms.

"I'm not going to hurt you," Tracie repeated one more time, and the girl looked up at her with wide, still-frightened eyes.

"Who are you?" she whispered. "Are you the police?"

Tracie couldn't help smiling. "Something like that."

"How did you know Vasily was going to try to hurt me?"

"Because that's what Vasily does," Tracie said, realizing a lie wasn't even necessary, at least not as far as that one question was concerned. "Do you have somewhere to go tonight where you'll be safe?"

The girl thought for a long moment before finally nodding, and Tracie's heart broke. She was probably sixteen or seventeen years old, forced into prostitution by family or circumstances or both. Her idea of a safe place would be radically different than Tracie's: a pimp's stable where a half-dozen or more young girls were crammed into one tiny Leningrad apartment, in all likelihood.

But there was nothing she could do about that.

"Okay," Tracie said. "I want you to go straight there tonight. You do not need to go the police about this, because we're already here and we already know about what Vasily tried to do to you. We will want to interview you about what happened tonight, so you need to remain available, but it will probably be a few days before we get to it. We have a lot of investigating to do before we talk to you. Do you understand?"

The girl nodded solemnly. Apparently it didn't occur to her that the "police" had never asked her for her name or even why a clearly underaged young woman had been spending the night in the bed of a man old enough to be her grandfather.

"I understand," she said.

"Good." Tracie helped her to her feet. "Do you have clothes you can change into before you leave?"

The girl nodded and turned toward the bedroom she had exited just a few minutes ago with a gun to her head. She closed the door behind her modestly and Tracie shook her head grimly.

You can't save everyone," she reminded herself. *Hell, you couldn't even save your own father.*

While the girl was changing, Tracie backtracked down the hallway and picked up Labochev's gun. She glanced at it quickly and then jammed it into her jeans at the small of her back. Then she returned to Labochev's body, thinking about a teenaged girl with no future besides prostitution with a likely side order of drugs and abuse.

She knelt on the floor next to the KGB station chief. There was almost no blood coming out of the hole in his head, meaning he'd died instantly. It had been a hell of a shot under extreme circumstances, but rather than being proud, the only thing she felt was sadness for the girl changing clothes in the bedroom off her right.

Tracie placed her gun on the floor, close enough that she could retrieve it immediately even though she knew the threat had been eliminated. Then she began rifling through Labochev's pockets, looking for a wallet or any loose cash. While the prostitute had been wearing a gauzy, practically see-through nightgown, Labochev had come out of the bedroom still fully dressed. The upstairs smelled of vodka and it was clear the girl was not drunk, meaning Labochev had drunk himself into a near-stupor before falling fully dressed into his bed.

Good. That scenario seemed better for the girl than the alternative.

The bedroom door opened and out stepped the prostitute. She looked even younger fully dressed and Tracie revised her estimate of the girl's age down further.

The prostitute watched wordlessly as Tracie removed Labochev's wallet from a rear pocket and pulled out a thick wad of bills. Tracie counted the cash and did a little quick math in her head. There was over two hundred-fifty thousand rubles, or roughly five thousand American dollars, give or take.

Tracie looked up at the girl, who still hadn't said a word since exiting the bedroom. "Do you have somewhere you can safely keep this money?" she asked the girl quietly.

"Me?" the girl said as her eyes widened in surprise.

"Yes, you. Not your pimp. Not your father. Not your boyfriend. You."

"I-I think so," she said. "Yes, I have a place I can stash it."

"Good girl," Tracie said. She handed over the money and repeated, "This is for you, and no one else."

The girl nodded. She looked like she might be about to start crying again, and this time not from terror. "Thank you," she said.

Tracie smiled at her.

The girl blinked. "You are not the police, are you?"

"Why would you ask that?"

"Because if you were the police, this money—" she held up the wad of bills—"would be going into your pocket, not mine."

"Just remember I want that money in *your* pocket and not anyone else's."

"I will remember."

"Okay. It's time for you to go, so I can begin my investigation." Tracie led the girl down the hallway and through the house, careful to avoid the kitchen, where she'd left the three "security guards" trussed up. Any or all of them may have regained consciousness by now, and while they could not hurt the girl, they would probably frighten her much more than she needed to be frightened at the moment.

She escorted the girl out of Labochev's home and stood watching her walk away. Eventually she was swallowed up by the black Russian night and Tracie retraced her steps inside Labochev's home, closing and locking the door behind her.

There was no way of knowing how long it would take Labochev's security detail to be discovered or his dead body found. In all probability, both things would happen mere hours from now. But she knew the prostitute wouldn't be going to the police any time soon, and that was the best she could do under the circumstances.

In the meantime, she still had work to do. She needed to move the security guards to a more out-of-the-way location inside the house, and then double-check the entire scene to ensure she'd left no incriminating evidence.

She had expected to feel good at this point in the operation. She'd eliminated one of the two men responsible for her father's death, and if Aaron Stallings' assessment was correct, the only man in the Soviet Union besides Piotr Speransky who could identify her as an American intelligence operative. She was halfway to avenging her father and ensuring not just her mother's safety but the continuation of her CIA career as well.

She still didn't feel happy.

The reality was just the opposite. All she felt was gloom and a bleak sense of loneliness.

34

May 23, 1988
2:00 a.m.
Leningrad, Russia, USSR

Alexei Volkov was beginning to think his old colleague Piotr Speransky might just have lost his mind.

He knew Speransky had become involved in some nasty business with an American CIA agent, who'd kidnapped and tortured him until extracting vital intelligence that had led to the murder of a key researcher in the Soviet Union's chemical and biological weapons program.

Specifics were impossible to come by, of course, and that was as it should be. Alexei had no more right to know Piotr's KGB business than Piotr had to know his. But what he *did* know was that Piotr had fucked up badly, and that knowledge had led Alexei to the logical—indeed, the inescapable—conclusion that he would never see or hear from Piotr again, that his fellow KGB assassin was even now moldering in a shallow grave somewhere outside Moscow, victim of the most permanent form of punishment available to KGB officers who disgraced themselves and their country as badly as had Speransky.

So when he received a telephone call a couple of days ago, purportedly from Piotr Speransky himself, Alexei had almost refused it. He considered slamming the telephone receiver down into its cradle and forgetting all about the call, which was clearly some kind of bizarre prank.

But something had made him hold off on hanging up the phone, and that something was the voice of the KGB's Washington—as in the United States—Station Chief, Dmitri Smyrnovich. The call had come in on a secure line to the Moscow station. Smyrnovich had insisted Piotr Speransky, of all people, was seated in his office in Washington and desperately needed to speak with Alexei regarding a KGB operation.

Dmitri Smyrnovich, while being a smug, officious little prick, was not the sort of man who would waste his or anyone else's time with a pointless prank. If Smyrnovich said something was important, it was at the very least worth a little of Alexei's time.

So he had stayed on the line, stunned. Rather than being dead, the victim of two Makarov 9mm slugs delivered into the back of his skull, Speransky was alive. Not only was he alive, apparently he was already deeply involved in another KGB mission despite being just a few months removed from one of the most disgraceful failures in the history of Soviet intelligence.

Alexei would not have been more surprised had he learned United States President Ronald Reagan was secretly a KGB plant.

And the tale Speransky spun over the line had been spellbinding. A CIA covert agent was on her way—*her* way!—to Russia to destroy valuable intelligence being stored by Speransky in a Leningrad safe house. Piotr needed someone he could trust to watch over the safe house until he could return to Russia to deal with the agent himself.

Alexei listened mostly without speaking. He had never claimed to be as talented an operative as Speransky, but neither was he a complete idiot. He knew Speransky's failure had involved being tortured and interrogated inside Moscow's city limits by a female CIA agent, and now, here he was referencing *another* female CIA agent.

Women spies were not unheard of, of course. The Soviets had employed more than their share against the Untied States, often to great effect. But using women as spies was not exactly the same thing as sending women out to kidnap and torture KGB assassins, and Alexei had never heard of the United States employing a woman in such a dangerous capacity in his entire career.

So the likelihood the agent who had tortured Speransky a few months ago was a different woman than the agent he was referencing now was practically nil. It had to be the same person. Which meant the KGB—incredibly—had sent Speransky to exact vengeance on the very operative who'd gotten the better of him once already.

To say Alexei was shocked would be an understatement. But Piotr Speransky had long been valued more highly than any other operative by the powers-that-be inside Lubyanka, given his particular talents at torture and assassination. If anyone would be granted this nearly-unheard-of second chance, it would be Speransky.

But of one thing Alexei was certain: Speransky's claim to have valuable intelligence he needed safeguarded was a complete fabrication. His concern was for the extortion money he had set aside over the course of his career. All Soviet operatives employed the same retirement strategy, including Alexei, so it came as no surprise to think Speransky had squirreled away his own lucrative stash.

Somehow the American had become aware of Speransky's personal vault and was on her way to Russia to steal or destroy its contents, and Piotr was so far behind her he would be unable to return to his home base fast enough to stop her.

So much for Lubyanka's faith in their golden boy.

Alexei had never been one to shy away from helping out a fellow operative, but he was damned if he would allow himself to be played for a fool by the very man who had brought such recent shame to the KGB. He spelled out his theory regarding what was really happening quite succinctly to Piotr, who responded by admitting the truth.

Yes, the woman who had tortured him and the woman on her way to Russia were one and the same.

Yes, he had traveled to the United States on a mission of vengeance and had been outsmarted by the American again.

Yes, he stood to lose what was left of the wealth it had taken his entire career to build.

"I will pay you one million rubles to prevent the American from looting my safe house," Speransky had said, finally getting to the heart of the telephone call. "It is a fair offer, as it will require only the investment of a few days' time. In fact, it is more than fair, given the very small amount of work that will actually be required of you. Can I count on you, Alexei?"

He pretended to think about it, but he didn't really have to. One million rubles for a couple of days' surveillance and the capture of an unwitting foreign agent? It was no-brainer.

"There is something else I must ask of you, though," Speransky had said after Alexei's acceptance of his offer. "And this is a non-negotiable condition."

"What is it?"

"When you encounter the American CIA agent, you will detain her, only. You will not kill her unless it is absolutely necessary to defend your own life. I have some unfinished business with this woman and I intend to handle it myself."

Self defense? Against a woman? Alexei couldn't imagine what kind of woman could have gotten the great Piotr Speransky so spooked, but he readily agreed to the condition, knowing it would never be an issue.

"One last thing," Speransky had said after an awkward silence.

"What is it?"

"You sound…cavalier."

"It is an assignment, Piotr, one of hundreds we have both executed throughout the years."

"Do not take this woman lightly, Alexei. You will regret it if you do. Watch you step around her."

"Fine, Piotr. I understand. You do not have to worry, I will be careful."

Speransky had dithered a little longer before finally disconnecting. Alexei thought it might just have been the strangest telephone call he'd ever had.

And now, as he crouched in the shadows outside Vasily Labochev's home, Alexei had to seriously question Speransky's frame of mind, not to mention his professionalism. He had been watching the CIA woman for the better part of the day, picking up her trail this morning when she cased Speransky's personal safe house located inside the Druzhba Industrial Park on the outskirts of Leningrad.

And she was nothing.

She was less than nothing, a tiny wisp of a woman who would have trouble remaining upright against a stiff breeze.

Not only that, she had walked right past him to examine Speransky's safe house, utterly oblivious to his presence and to the fact he'd then begun following her around Leningrad. She seemed unaware of her surroundings, and if he hadn't been given a very specific description of his target, Alexei would have assumed she was a tourist, and not a very bright tourist at that.

This was the deadly CIA agent who had gotten the better of Speransky, and not once but twice?

Granted, with a gun in one's hand any person with a pulse could be considered dangerous, but this was ridiculous. If this woman weighed forty-five kilograms Alexei would be shocked. And her lack of situational awareness was stunning.

He had to give her credit for guts, if nothing else. Once arriving at Labochev's home, and after only a short time spent casing the property, she had taken down Labochev's security without breaking a sweat. Then she entered the house and apparently handled the KGB station chief as well.

But the security guard was nothing more than a hired goon, and if Labochev had ever spent time in the field, it was decades ago. He would have offered little in the way of real resistance.

It hadn't taken anything special to do what this petite woman had done here tonight.

She would find the going a little more difficult if she attempted to access Speransky's safe house while Alexei was holding down the fort. Now that he'd seen her in person, he almost wished she would try to access it before Speransky's return. It would be a fun little diversion.

Alexei leaned against a tree, keeping his eyes on Labochev's home, wondering what the hell had gotten into Piotr Speransky, and marveling at how quickly the great man had fallen.

He shook his head.

This girl was tiny.

She was nothing.

35

May 23, 1988
7:15 a.m.
Leningrad, Russia, USSR

Tracie had fully expected Speransky to call back to Russia for assistance once he broke into her D.C. apartment and found her note. And while the note was necessary to set up their final confrontation on Tracie's terms, it also presented a problem. Recognizing the enemy in a land where *everyone* was a potential enemy could be next to impossible, so how would she know who to defend herself against once Speransky had made that call and enlisted help?

But she had one trump card, and she decided to play it immediately: she knew exactly where the enemy would be waiting. Speransky would be desperate to protect his stolen wealth, so his KGB buddy would be camped out at the safe house. And since the nature of a safe house was to remain...well...*safe*...she guessed it would be located in a relatively secluded area, making the threat easier to spot.

She'd never spent much time in Leningrad, other than to skirt the city on her way to somewhere else, so her familiarity with the industrial park name Vasily Labochev had given the traitor Roger Thornton was nil. When she arrived at the park yesterday she had been surprised to discover it wasn't particularly isolated at all.

The "safe house" was actually a small, square concrete-block building, and the Druzhba Industrial Park's heyday, if there had ever been one, must have occurred during the reign of Vladimir Lenin. The building's original purpose most likely had been as a warehouse of some sort, or a transfer station used for shipping a product that had been manufactured somewhere else in the park.

A single entrance into and out of the facility was flanked in front by a pair of narrow windows, both fortified by iron bars that had clearly been retrofitted recently, obviously by Speransky, The door looked old but sturdy, and a series of heavy padlocks locks would slow down anyone intent upon accessing the safe house with anything smaller than a battering ram.

A small loading dock on the other side of the building had clearly not been used in decades. Its concrete slab was crumbling, and its iron latticework had rusted almost entirely away. The loading dock's garage door had been removed and the doorway bricked up tight.

She decided Speransky had made a decent choice if he wanted a secure building inside which to protect cash or other easily marketable liquid assets. The concrete construction offered a real challenge for any would-be thief, and the bars covering the dual windows appeared to be of the highest quality.

But Speransky's biggest advantage, and probably the reason he'd selected the building in the first place, was its apparent condition. It was entirely unmemorable, a rundown industrial building located in a cluster of rundown industrial buildings in a shabby neighborhood on the outskirts of the city. As much as she despised Piotr Speransky, Tracie had to give him credit: it was a good choice and had undoubtedly served his purposes well.

That was about to change.

She had observed the building from a distance for over an hour yesterday before ever approaching it. Despite the fact it was a weekday morning, activity inside the industrial park was minimal, and while she hadn't seen anyone who looked suspicious, she felt confident the threat would reveal itself as she approached the safe house.

So that was what she did. She knew she looked out of place in this grimy area, and that was intentional. She wanted to look out of place.

More importantly, since Speransky had paid Vasily Labochev to learn her identity, she knew that whoever Speransky had recruited to protect his safe house would have been given a precise description of her. Rather attempting to disguise her appearance, Tracie made certain her flame-red hair was plainly visible: no hat, no scarf, no high collar. Nothing that would cause Speransky's newly recruited partner to doubt that he'd gotten the right person in his sights.

She half expected to be assaulted before ever getting near the safe house and was a little surprised when it didn't happen. She made a show of emphasizing her interest in that particular building, ignoring all the others and circling the safe house several times.

She rattled the door.

She checked the bars on the windows.

She climbed onto the ancient loading dock and examined the brick work.

Before she'd completed her first circuit, Tracie had identified the KGB operative. It was a man standing in the shadows two buildings deeper inside the park. While he was dressed slightly more appropriate to the surroundings than Tracie—jeans and a light jacket—he wore no work boots, no hard hat, and seemed to have no purpose inside the industrial area other than to observe Tracie's activities.

She loitered around the building for a long time, drawing no attention from anyone besides the mysterious man lurking a couple hundred feet away. Then she left the industrial park and spent the rest of the day in preparation for her meeting with Vasily Labochev.

Three times over the next several hours Tracie caught a glimpse of her tracker, and while the KGB man did a better job at concealing himself than he had at the industrial park, she still felt he'd done a damned poor job overall. Even during the raid last night on Labochev's home, she thought she observed him skulking around the rear of the property as she was disabling the security guard prior to entering.

She'd again expected to be assaulted by the KGB man after leaving Labochev's home. The conditions were perfect for a kidnapping or attempted murder: a partly cloudy night obscuring the moon, and a distinct lack of potential witnesses because virtually everyone in Leningrad was fast asleep.

Again she had been surprised when he hung back. Apparently her escort had been given strict orders not to engage. He was to keep her under surveillance but leave her alone unless she made an assault on the safe house.

When Tracie thought about it, those orders made sense from Speransky's perspective. He had gone to a lot of trouble to ensure she knew exactly who was murdering her relatives and attempting to destroy her. He would not want someone else to end her life. It would be critical for his sense of self-regard—and maybe even his career—that he be the one to do it.

Tracie wondered if she could use that knowledge to her advantage. Piotr Speransky's single-minded obsession with revenge for the way she'd tortured and humiliated him had been fueling his every action since the day he'd escaped he CIA safe house.

That obsession would become his downfall.

She hadn't wasted a lot of time developing a strategy on her way to Russia because there had been far too many unknowns to develop anything. All she had really known was that she wanted to use Speransky's little piggybank as a lever to turn the tables on him, to let Tracie control the engagement and put her back in the position of hunter, rather than that of prey.

But now a plan was beginning to take shape. She thought she could use what she had learned at the industrial park—not just about the safe house, but about her opponent as well—to her advantage. It would not be easy, but she liked her chances.

Tracie had played sports in high school, and even as busy as her father was, he still managed to make it to almost all of her games. He'd drilled something into her head that she hadn't fully appreciated at the time, but that in the years since had played a significant role in the foundation of her career and, in fact, her life.

And it was something simple: *always respect your opponent. Don't fear them, don't be intimidated by them, but respect them.*

"They want to win every bit as much as you do," he'd said. "They're out there competing just as hard as you are. So give them credit, give them their due, but trust in your own practice and skill and preparation. And win or lose, do it with grace and compassion. Shake hands when it's over and move on, no matter the result."

She had approached every CIA assignment she'd ever been given with those words in the back of her mind. The enemy—in most cases, that meant the KGB—was every bit as dedicated to their mission as she, every bit as convinced they were fighting on the right side of history.

She would respect their training and abilities while trusting in her own. It meant never becoming *over*confident, never believing herself better prepared than the enemy, but also trusting that she was as prepared to face a challenge as she could possibly be.

Her father's words had served her well, and she had no doubt he'd intended them as a message that would be carried far beyond the soccer pitch or basketball court or softball diamond. And while she had no intention of ever shaking Piotr Speransky's hand—or the hand of the nameless KGB operative currently shadowing her for that matter—she would once again take his words to heart.

She would avenge her father's murder using his own advice against his killer.

36

The padlocks securing the single entrance to the concrete-block safe house were accessible not by key, but via combination tumblers. It was an arrangement that made sense, Tracie thought. Given the uncertainty and danger of his employment as a KGB assassin, Speransky could never be certain he would be carrying the proper keys if he needed to access the building in a hurry.

Tracie's first impression during yesterday's reconnaissance was that the locks represented a potential security weakness. Their size and quality—not to mention the fact they were on the door in the first place—would be a strong indication to any enterprising Russian burglar that the structure might be something other than it appeared.

Speransky had probably felt confident the safe house would never be disturbed, though, mostly because it was such an unlikely-looking repository for marketable liquid assets. From a distance and to the naked eye the building appeared decrepit, abandoned years ago and left to slowly crumble under the weight of inattention, much like the rest of the industrial park only at a slightly faster pace. An interested party would have to circle the building and approach it at the proper angle to see the combination locks at all.

For Tracie, the important question was whether Piotr Speransky would have trusted his KGB buddy with the combinations to all three locks. It would require a major leap of faith to assume from his location thousands of miles away in the United States that if he provided his comrade with access to the building, that man would not simply loot the safe house on his own and disappear.

She had slept inside her stolen car last night after leaving Labochev's home, and now she considered the issue on her way to the industrial park. There was no way to know the answer to that question, and while it would better suit her purposes if the KGB shadow had been given the combinations, she decided she could adjust her plan if necessary.

She had been sure to lose the man tailing her last night before finding a secluded area in which to catch a few hours of sleep, and hadn't seen any sign of him since. By now it had become apparent that Speransky had given strict orders to his KGB comrade that Tracie was not to be touched; that he was to protect the contents of the safe house but leave Tracie to him.

It was the only explanation for why the man wouldn't have tried to take Tracie down last night outside Labochev's home, when the conditions were as perfect for such an operation as they ever would be. He had tailed Tracie initially to become as familiar with her as he could, to get a feel for her habits and a sense of how dangerous an opponent she may or may not be, and then he had backed off to focus on his primary mission.

And she could use that knowledge to her benefit. If it came down to a confrontation—*when* it came down to a confrontation—the man's reactions would be a hair slow, because he would be worried about killing her and thus triggering the rage of one of the most deadly and unstable men Tracie had ever encountered.

That was her working theory, anyway.

She was about to test it.

She parked her stolen car an eighth of a mile from the industrial park and began walking. By now she was as certain as she could be that the KGB man had taken up a position in or around one of the abandoned industrial buildings surrounding the safe house. There were plenty of them to choose from.

In the event she was wrong, though, and Mr. KGB was still

tailing her but had gotten suddenly much better at it, she wanted to give him plenty of advance notice that she was making a move on Speransky's precious safe house. She wanted to provoke him, to make him commit to taking action against her, but at the same time not surprise him into a deadly *over*reaction.

She walked at a rapid pace, not quite trotting but almost, and in just a few minutes found herself at the entrance to the grimy industrial facility. There was still no sign of the man who'd followed her most of the day yesterday.

An ancient chain-link fence surrounded the park, topped with three parallel strands of barbed wire angled outward at roughly a forty-five degree angle, the universal security measure designed to protect against vandals or drunk kids looking to get into places they shouldn't. Any professional thief, or even a vandal who had planned ahead, would be able to circumvent the measure easily, and in a matter of seconds, by bringing along a set of bolt cutters and slicing through the fence.

Even that simple action was rendered moot, though, because the swinging gate located at the park's entrance had been standing open each time Tracie had been here. From the looks of the rust coating the hinges, it hadn't been years since anyone had closed the gate, it had been decades.

She turned left and walked straight through the gate and into the park. As was the case yesterday, the facility appeared mostly deserted, the majority of the structures standing empty and forlorn. The sound of work in progress somewhere deeper in the park echoed through the access roads and off the concrete and metal buildings, but mostly the place felt forgotten, a crumbling relic of a repressive political system that was finally beginning to topple under the weight of inevitability.

Tracie never slowed after entering the park. She turned immediately left and then right, moving between buildings like a woman on a mission, which, of course, she was. It just wasn't the mission she wanted KGB Man to think it was.

She moved straight to Speransky's entry door, the one protected by the series of combination locks. She bent and focused her attention on the locks, spinning the dials like she knew what she was doing, making it clear to KGB Man—wherever he was—that unlike yesterday, she was serious about accessing the building this morning. She'd purchased a hacksaw yesterday at a Leningrad hardware store, and if the business with the locks didn't get her shadow's attention, she would pull the tool out from under her jacket and begin slashing away at the bars covering the windows.

The damned hacksaw was so cheap she wasn't sure she would even make it through one bar before the teeth were so badly dulled the thing was rendered useless, but that was irrelevant. She hoped. The point wasn't to access the building by herself; the point was to convince KGB Man to do it for her.

She played with the locks and tried to use her body to block the view of her shadow, assuming he was watching from somewhere around the area she'd seen him yesterday. A minute went by, and then two, and she wondered how much longer the charade would remain believable, if it ever had been.

She sighed and was reaching for the hacksaw under her jacket—*Time for Plan B*—when she felt the heavy mass of a gun barrel being shoved into her back.

Finally.

From behind her, angled slightly off her right, a deep voice said, "Remove your hand from your weapon or die."

Despite the adrenaline racing through her system, or perhaps because of it, Tracie had to fight the urge to laugh. KGB Man was worried about her whipping out a semi-auto pistol when the only thing hidden beneath her jacket was a Russian handyman's tool she'd bought for the equivalent of seven U.S dollars.

She hadn't bothered wearing her shoulder-holstered Beretta because the whole point of this morning's exercise was to get herself captured. That being the case, it seemed like a poor strategy to bring a weapon that would only end up being confiscated, thus providing her captor one more tool to end her life than he'd started the day with.

"Okay," she said, speaking quietly and calmly. *Don't spook the Soviet spook.* She released her grip on the saw and began raising her hands slowly.

"*Nyet*," the Russian said. "Do not put your hands over your head, it is too conspicuous," and again Tracie almost laughed.

Conspicuous? Here? The place was so forlorn they could

probably fight a gun battle between two abandoned buildings and no one would notice.

"Spread your feet to at least shoulder width and place your hands flat against the door at shoulder height, and then remain still," the man said.

"And you think that's more subtle? A man holding a gun against a woman's back and forcing her to spread her legs? You don't go on many dates, do you?"

"Shut up," the man spat, "and just do it."

Tracie did it. The hacksaw fell out of her jacket and clattered to the rough pavement and the KGB agent flinched, and for one horrible moment Tracie thought he would squeeze his trigger just out of shock.

But to her surprise, not to mention her relief, he held his fire. For a moment nothing happened, and then he bent slowly, being sure to keep his gun pressed against her spine. He lifted the hacksaw and stared at is as though he'd never seen one before.

Then he chuckled. "You really thought this little blade would be sufficient to slice through these locks, or the bars on these windows?"

Tracie shrugged. "I don't know what you're talking about."

"Who are you?"

"Just an ordinary girl, out for a walk on a beautiful morning."

"With a hacksaw under your jacket."

She shrugged again. "You never know when one will come in handy. Like today, for example. I'm out, minding my own business, when I happen to stumble over this little shack. It's falling apart and yet it's got locks on the doors and bars on the windows, the whole thing sealed up tighter than Kresty Prison, and I think to myself, *I wonder why?* So I pull out my hacksaw and get to work. Or at least I would have, if you hadn't shown up and spoiled all my fun."

"You think you are quite clever, don't you?"

"Again, I don't know what you mean."

"I know what you are doing," the man said, shoving his gun harder against her spine.

"Really? And what's that?"

"You are trying to keep me talking out here, hoping someone will come along and see us and perhaps rescue you."

"Is that what I'm doing? I thought we were just having a little chat, you know, getting to know each other, now that you've forced me to spread my legs for you."

"Shut up," he said. "It will not work. The odds of anyone passing by are minimal, and the odds of anyone doing anything besides minding their own business even if they see us are even less. But still, we will continue this discussion out of sight, since you are so anxious to examine the interior of this building for yourself."

"That's very neighborly of you, and just as I was about to ask for my hacksaw back. Now I guess I won't need it."

"You will not need the gun you have beneath your jacket, either."

"Gun? I don't have any gun beneath my jacket."

"Of course you do."

"No, I'm pretty sure I don't. That seems like the sort of thing I'd remember. Would you like to reach in and check for yourself? Get a little free feel? Normally I wouldn't offer, but since we've already established you don't date much I thought you might appreciate it."

"Shut up!" he said again, this time emphasizing his demand by placing one hand against the back of her skull and shoving it against the door. She just managed to turn her head in time to avoid breaking her nose. Still, it was painful, and she blinked and shook her head but refused to give the man the satisfaction of taking her hands off the door to rub the bruise that was already beginning to swell.

"Does this mean you *don't* want to date me?" she said. "I'm getting mixed signals."

"Step aside," he said. "Move slowly and keep your hands against the door or the wall at all times."

Tracie did as he demanded, and when her body had cleared the locks he said, "That is far enough."

She stopped and he continued, "If you make one move I do not like you will suffer a very painful death. Do you understand?"

"I would say there is very little room for misunderstanding in that statement."

"Good. Do not forget." He held the gun in his left hand, keeping it pressed against her back, while he began manipulating the tumblers on the locks with his right.

At least you bothered to memorize the combinations, she thought, *and didn't have to pull a slip of paper out of your pocket.*

A moment later he had popped all three locks. He removed them, one by one, and tossed them onto the ground. Then he turned the handle and pushed open the door. "Get inside right now," he said.

That was easier than I expected it to be. She slipped past the KGB man and into Speransky's safe house.

37

The skies over Leningrad had dawned a slate-grey overcast, and the muted daylight struggled to clear the filthy windows. KGB Man stepped into the safe house behind Tracie and slammed the door closed and the little building's interior was plunged into a sort of murky semi-dusk.

Crates and boxes were stacked along three of the four walls, some of them two and three rows deep. In one corner, Speransky had set up a small table and a rickety chair, presumably to count and organize his loot.

Tracie assumed the crates and boxes were filled with cash and/or marketable assets such as bearer bonds, and if that were the case, it was no surprise Speransky was so desperate to protect this place. The potential value of the safe house's contents was staggering.

"You were so anxious to get inside this building," KGB Man said. "Now that you have done so, it hardly seems worth being held prisoner at gunpoint, wouldn't you agree?"

"I don't know about that," Tracie said. "From the outside, this place is a dump, but whoever redecorated has a real knack for interior design. The inside is just...wow!"

"I would not be so flippant if I were you," KGB Man said, annoyed. It was obvious he wanted Tracie to be cowed and intimidated, and her failure to cooperate was getting under his skin. "I am not sure you fully appreciate your situation. You will not survive this encounter. You are going to die inside this 'dump,' as you call it, and your body parts will be hacked off and scattered over the Russian countryside. You will never be seen or heard from again. No one will ever know what happened to you."

Tracie stood motionless, arms crossed and her chin resting in one hand as if deep in thought. "Huh. Well, thank you for the explanation, but that seems a little...I don't know...extreme. Is that how you deal with all curious Russian citizens?"

KGB Man laughed. "Russian citizens. That is a good one. I will admit your Russian is quite good for an American, but you cannot pass for a native of Russia, I assure you."

"American? I'm afraid you've lost me."

"I think it is time for us to place all our cards on the table, don't you?"

Tracie shrugged. "You're the one with the gun. And the saw. Feel free to place those bad boys anywhere you want."

He shook his head in disgust. "I know exactly who you are, Little Miss CIA operative."

He paused, apparently hoping for some kind of reaction. Shock, maybe, or fear. But Tracie simply stared at him, eyebrows raised.

After a moment he continued. "I know you are a covert agent of the United States of America, working for the CIA to destroy the Soviet Union, and I know also that your interest in this building was neither random nor harmless."

"Is that so?"

"Yes, it is so. I know you have come here to remove the fruit of my friend Piotr's labors from this storage area while he is away from Leningrad. But I will not allow that to happen, and you will not be breathing much longer, either."

Tracie had lowered her arms to her side, but now she raised them and began to clap softly. "You have it all figured out, don't you?"

"I have figured out enough to know you are a menace to my country. Enough to know you will never leave this place alive."

"And who's going to kill me? You?"

KGB Man smirked. "You should be a little less concerned about who is pulling the trigger and a little more concerned about the fact you are not long for this world."

"I only ask the question because it seems obvious to me that you're nothing more than Piotr Speransky's errand boy. While he's running around playing Soviet spy and defending the world from the menace of individual liberty, it's left to the likes of you to skulk around dirty little industrial parks, assaulting women and guarding the treasure of your betters."

Even through the murky half-light, Tracie could see KGB Man's face reddening as she spoke. "You should learn to choose your words more carefully," he said, his voice taut with fury.

"Or what? Your master gave you strict orders not to kill me, didn't he?"

"He is not my master," KGB Man spat. "We are equals. We are both men who have devoted our lives to protecting our country from the likes of you."

"And yet here you stand, doing exactly what your 'equal' demanded. You would like nothing better than to pull the trigger right now, I can see it in your eyes. But we both know you're not allowed to. Would you like to hear a secret?"

KGB Man stared wordlessly at Tracie, gun aimed center-mass, his angry eyes boring into hers.

"I actually feel sorry for you."

"You feel sorry for me? That is a good one. You are the one who will soon be dead."

"I really do," she insisted. "It must be horribly frustrating to be impotent, just another castrated calf, dominated by the bull."

With an inarticulate grunt, KGB Man charged her. He raised his gun and swiveled his wrist, aiming to pistol-whip her in the skull.

But Tracie was ready. She'd been pushing him to provoke exactly this reaction, betting her life on her theory that Speransky had insisted the redheaded CIA bitch be left alive for him to torture and kill.

She feinted right and ducked left, lowering her head while whipping out a sidekick. KGB Man's gun clipped her skull just above her ear, opening a gash but failing to knock her out as he'd intended.

Her kick connected solidly with KGB Man's knee, though, and he gasped in pain. He'd planted the leg in an attempt to slow his forward motion while pistol-whipping her, and with the kick Tracie heard the snap of bones breaking or ligaments tearing.

His momentum carried him past her, tumbling onto his side and crashing into some of the boxes stacked up against the side wall. He was screaming in anger and pain but he'd managed to maintain his grip on the gun and now he scrabbled to his knees and fired, Speransky's instructions forgotten in his unreasoning fury.

The slug whistled past Tracie's head as she was diving at KGB Man, not wanting to give him the opportunity to squeeze off a second round. Her small body crashed into his larger one and they tumbled to the floor. She brought her hands together and wrapped her left hand around her right fist, and rather than going for KGB Man's gun, she lifted her arms as high as she could and brought them down full-force onto KGB Man's injured knee.

He screamed in agony and reached instinctively for his knee and the gun fell out of his hand, thudding to the floor next to them. Tracie grabbed for it, but she had landed on the left side of KGB Man and the gun had fallen to the floor off his right and she couldn't quite reach it.

KGB Man stretched for the gun, grazing it with his hand and pushing it against his right hip. Tracie's feet scrabbled for purchase on the dirty floor as she tried to launch herself across KGB Man's body. She dropped onto his stomach and chest, forcing the air out of his lungs with an audible *oof*.

He could not breathe and his eyes were bugging out of his head, but KGB Man finally wrapped his fingers around his gun and he lifted it by the barrel. His left arm was trapped beneath Tracie's body and he worked desperately to spin the weapon in his right palm so he could pull the trigger and fire into Tracie's body.

Tracie was out of time. She swiped at the man's gun hand and missed, and as he settled the butt of the weapon into his palm she reached back with her right hand and straight up with her left. Then she hammered both hands into KGB Man, slugging him in the face with her right fist and assaulting his injured knee one more time with her left.

This time there was no scream of anguish. All the air had already been forced out of KGB man's lungs. But he thrashed beneath Tracie in pain and he again released his hold on the gun as he tried to cradle his knee.

Tracie ignored him, instead crawling over his body and falling on the gun, which had skittered maybe six feet away across the floor. She pushed to her knees and whirled, prepared to fire, but KGB man hadn't made a move to follow. He lay on his back, gasping like a fish out of water, his hands wrapped around his shattered knee.

She rose slowly, breathing heavily, adrenaline racing through her system, blood from the gash on her skull dribbling sluggishly down the side of her face. She walked to KGB man and stood over his prone body, training his own gun on him.

He raised his hands to cover his face, as though that would protect him if she decided to pull the trigger. "Please," he gasped. "Do not shoot."

"I'm not going to shoot you unless you give me a reason to," she said. "But you really need to learn not to be so sensitive. Why would you care what I think of you, anyway?"

38

Tracie walked to the corner of the one-room building and grabbed the chair Speransky had set up in front of his makeshift desk. She dragged it to the center of the room. Pointed KGB Man's gun at him and then flicked her wrist to indicate the chair.

"Get in it," she said.

KGB Man looked from Tracie to the chair and then back at her. "I cannot. You have destroyed my knee. I cannot walk."

"Then crawl," she said. "Or would you rather lie on the floor like a dying animal?"

"What difference does it make if you are only going to kill me anyway?"

"I told you, I'm not going to kill you. I've got no quarrel with you, aside from that business about kidnapping me and threatening me with violent death. Oh, yeah, and let's not forget opening up a gash in my head that's going to hurt like a bitch every time I wash my hair for the next two weeks. And the fact you're a KGB stooge. Other than those minor differences, though, we're practically besties."

KGB Man stared at her unblinkingly. It was clear he considered her a few bricks shy of a full load, and that was just fine with Tracie. Keeping him off-balance would make him that much easier to control, although if he were telling the truth about his knee he wouldn't represent much of a threat, anyway.

But she meant what she said about allowing him to live. This poor bastard was nothing more than a run-of-the-mill operative who had tried to do a favor for a comrade.

"The truth is," she said, "I prefer to leave you alive."

He gazed at her suspiciously, or perhaps that was just pain showing on his face. "Why?" he said.

"Because I have a little task for you to do once this is all over."

The suspicious look on KGB Man's face deepened.

"Well?" she said. "You going to lie there all day or are you going to get in the chair like I asked?"

He took a deep breath and started moving. It was unclear whether he believed her when she said she wasn't going to shoot him, but he seemed to have reached the conclusion there was nothing to lose by taking her at her word.

Tracie had placed the chair just a few feet from where KGB Man had fallen, but even traveling that short distance was a real struggle for him. He'd landed on his back, so his first order of business was to roll over onto his belly in order to have any chance of crawling.

He flopped onto his right side and then lifted his upper body with his arm until he was able to lean his weight on one elbow. Then he took a deep breath and pushed hard with his arm as he swiveled his hips, falling onto his chest and trying to stifle a groan prom the pain that was clearly blasting through his knee.

He struggled toward the chair, trying to pull himself along with his arms as he propelled his body forward with his good leg. Sweat covered his face and he gasped in pain every time his injured knee scraped along the floor, which was every time he moved.

He arrived at the chair in maybe ninety seconds, but Tracie had been in similar situations herself, trying to ignore the pain from an injury, and she knew the elapsed time had probably felt a lot longer to KGB Man.

"What now?" he said quietly. "There is no way I can lift myself into that chair." He was breathing heavily and she almost felt sorry for him.

"Do you regret doing a favor for your buddy yet?" she said.

"We are not friends. This was a contract job. He pays me, I do the job for him."

"How much is he paying you?" Tracie asked, curious.

"Not enough, it seems."

She smiled. As much as she wanted to hate this guy, she couldn't quite manage it. In fact, the reality was just the opposite.

"You know, I kind of like you," she said. "I truly hope I don't have to kill you."

"That makes two of us."

She gazed at him for a long moment. Dust and dirt from the filthy floor were smeared all over his clothing, and his left leg trailed helplessly behind him. Bruises from their desperate struggle over the gun were beginning to rise on his face and neck. He looked like a vagabond, and Tracie doubted her appearance was much better.

She said, "You know what will happen to you if you try anything stupid, correct?"

"My knee is on fire, what am I going to try?"

"Answer the question."

"Yes, I know what will happen if I try anything stupid. Contrary to how it must appear, I am not a complete idiot."

She smiled again, and then she moved out from behind the chair and walked the length of KGB Man's prone body. She knelt at his feet and pulled his right pant leg up toward his knee, exposing first his ankle and then his calf.

And his backup Makarov, nestled snug inside its leather ankle holster.

"Forget to mention something, Ivan?"

"My name is not Ivan. You can call me Alexei."

"And I'm Fiona. Did you forget to mention something, Alexei?"

"I do not recall you asking."

"I guess I can't argue the point," she said. She unsnapped the holster and removed the weapon, glancing at it before sliding it across the floor where it would be well out of Alexei's reach unless he suddenly turned into Carl Lewis. It was a transformation she considered unlikely.

She stood. "Any other weapons I need to know about, Alexei? Knives, brass knuckles, explosives?"

"No, there is nothing."

"You know what will happen if—"

"Yes," he interrupted. "I know what will happen if you find out I am lying."

"Good." She walked back to the chair and dropped into a crouch in front of the injured Soviet intelligence agent. "Lift your upper body."

"Why?"

"Just do it, Alexei. I'm in a good mood right now, don't wait too long or that might change."

He shrugged and placed his hands on the floor, palms down. Then he did a pushup, modified slightly by the fact his left leg was unable to support any weight. Tracie reached both arms under his, still holding the gun. She liked KGB Man, but that didn't mean she trusted him. She positioned her elbows under his armpits and then lifted the much larger man until he could grasp the seat.

"Now we're going to flip you over and slide you into the chair," she said.

"I don't think my knee can take the jostling." Sweat was pouring down his face, which was white as a bed sheet.

"Sure it can," she said. "You're almost there." She lifted again, as high as she could, her arms burning from the strain. Then Alexei removed his left hand from the seat and rotated his body while Tracie pulled him toward the chair back. He dropped into the seat and gasped in agony.

"This will not work," he said through clenched teeth. "My knee needs support."

"Jesus, Alexei," she answered. "You're a high maintenance guy, you know that?"

He tried to smile, but succeeded only in grimacing.

"Hang on a second." Tracie moved to the closest wall and dragged a wooden crate roughly the size of a seaman's trunk across the floor, stopping when the middle of the box was positioned next to the man's injured knee. She gauged the box's height and decided it would be almost but not quite sufficient for her purposes.

She returned to the wall and lifted a smaller box, placing it atop the larger crate and then once again gauging the height.

"Looks good," she said, and then told Alexei, "This might hurt a little."

"Might?" he answered. "Now who is lying to whom?"

"I never claimed to have a great bedside manner." She placed the gun on the floor next to Alexei's backup, not wanting to risk him making a play for it. Then she walked back to the injured man and lifted his leg, doing her best to support it under the knee. He screamed in pain as she used her hip to slide the crate and the smaller box into position.

Finally she lowered his leg onto the top of the makeshift table. His knee was lying flat, supported along the length of his leg and positioned slightly higher than the chair.

Tracie stepped back and picked up the gun. She eyed her work and said, "That's the best I can do, Alexei. Does it feel any better?"

He shot her a pained look. "It feels like a train ran over my leg, and then stopped and backed up just in case it didn't hurt enough."

"Sounds about right," she said. "I've been there."

"You had your knee shattered by a tiny woman?"

"I prefer the term 'petite,'" she said. "And to answer your question, no, not that specifically. But I did get shot in the shoulder by one of your KGB buddies, and still remember it felt like a flamethrower was burning through the bones."

"KGB?"

"That's right. Would you like to see the scars?"

"I'll pass," he said and fell silent. After a moment he said, "You know…"

"What?"

"You are not at all what I would have expected."

"What, that someone weighing one hundred-five pounds can kick like a mule? It's all in the technique. And practice, of course."

He chuckled. "That is not what I meant."

"What, then?"

"I have spent my entire career fighting against you, and against people like you."

"Americans."

"*Da.* Americans. And we have been taught to hate you, to fear you, that you wish to destroy our way of life. Destroy *us.*"

"We're just people, Alexei. Inside, we're no different than you. I believe in the rightness of my cause, believe that the citizens of Russia and of all the Soviet republics would benefit from the individual freedoms we enjoy in the United States. I admit I hate your system of government and everything it stands for. But I don't hate *you.* I don't hate any Russians, with the possible exception of the man you were trying to protect."

Alexei stared at her. "What happened between Piotr and you?"

"You don't know?"

He shrugged. "Why would I?"

"I thought he might have filled you in on why he needed you to protect his 'hard-earned' assets from me."

"I think you may misunderstand the nature of my relationship with the man known to you as Piotr Speranski."

"Why don't you fill me in, then?"

"There is not much filling in to do. We have worked together on a handful of assignments over the years. That is all. We are not friends. We are barely acquaintances. To be perfectly honest, I do not trust him and never have. I find him to be brutal, unstable and dangerous."

"Then why would you help him?"

A rueful smiled crossed Alexei's face and then vanished. "I do not know how well intelligence operatives are paid in your country, but in the Soviet Union it is never a good idea to turn away extra income. Piotr called me in a panic and offered to pay what I consider a large sum for just a few days work. And at the time, it seemed like a very simple assignment."

"Watch his safe house," Tracie said, "and if I showed up, kidnap me and keep me under wraps until he gets here."

"Exactly," Alexei agreed.

"And we see how well that turned out."

"To be fair, Piotr did warn me about you. He said you were extremely dangerous, but after following you for most of the day yesterday, including to Vasily Labochev's home, I concluded Piotr's skills must have begun to slip. You appeared..."

"Harmless?"

"*Da.*"

They lapsed into silence and Alexei began fussing with his leg. He was clearly in significant pain, but to his credit hadn't complained once, beyond answering Tracie's direct question.

"So I have described my relationship with Piotr Speranski," Alexei said. "Are you going to describe yours? I know you were the CIA agent who interrogated and humiliated him in Moscow, and my assumption would be that he was in the United States to hunt you down and kill you."

"Something like that," Tracie said.

"And yet, you are quite clearly still alive. What are you doing in Russia looting his safe house, while he is days behind you?"

"First of all," Tracie said, "I'm not looting his safe house. I don't give a damn about his money and, in fact, I wouldn't touch it with a ten-foot pole. It's blood money and I'd rather starve than take any of it.

"Secondly," she continued, "you're mostly right about everything. I was the operative who tortured Speransky and it's to my everlasting regret that I didn't put a bullet in his brain the second he spit out the intel I needed. But I spared his miserable life and he thanked me by coming to the United States to even the score. Instead of targeting me, though, he kidnapped and murdered someone extremely close to me. I won't say who the person was, because if you get out of this alive, I don't want you to be able to guess my identity. That's how this whole mess started."

Alexei's eyes were wide and shocked. "He...he killed an innocent?"

Tracie laughed bitterly. "He didn't just kill an innocent. He tortured the innocent for hours and *then* killed him. And please, don't pretend to be surprised. I've worked in and around the Soviet Union plenty long enough to know that targeting or killing family members to keep people in line is a specialty of the KGB.

Alexei looked away and Tracie continued. "Anyway, our friend Piotr Speransky isn't quite as clever as he thinks he is. I turned the tables on him and came here for one reason, and one reason only: I knew if I threatened his personal retirement account he would have no choice but to react, and that he would come straight to me. When he does, I'm going to finish him, like I should have done last winter."

"But he knows you will be waiting for him. He will be prepared."

"I don't care. One way or the other, this ends here."

"But..." Alexei shook his head, confused.

"What?"

"You have no idea how long it will take for him to track you here. You—we—could be stuck inside this little concrete building for days. Longer, perhaps." The KGB operative fussed with his leg and shook his head. "And I need medical attention. If you are going to allow me to live, as you claim, I would like to be able to walk again some day."

Tracie scoffed. "Come on, Alexei. You claim to know Speransky, do you really think it's in his nature to wait? He wants to protect his retirement fund at all costs. Hell, you're living proof of that fact, if he promised you a hefty payment just for keeping watch over this building for a couple of days. And he's so desperate to torture me, to pay me back for what I did to him in Moscow, that he can hardly contain himself.

"No," she continued. "He'll be here, and soon."

Alexei considered her words. "Alright," he said, and shrugged. "I will concede that point. But you have an obvious problem, which means I also have an obvious problem."

"Is that so? And what's our problem?"

"He knows you are here."

"Of course he knows I'm here. That's the whole point. Come on, Alexei, pay attention. I kicked you in the knee, not the head."

"No, you do not understand," Alexei said, exasperated. "If he knows you are here, inside this building, what is to stop him from simply waiting you out? Even if you purchase supplies before he arrives in Lenigrad, eventually those supplies will run out. Sooner or later you will have to expose yourself, and the moment you do, Piotr will have you right where he wants you.

"And, incidentally," Alexei continued. "Just because you are offering me the kindness of survival, that doesn't mean Piotr will. As I said, I have worked with him before and I know how he thinks. He will see my failure as a personal betrayal. Once he is finished with you, I will be next. We will both disappear and no one will ever know what happened to either of us."

"I see your point," Tracie said, "but there's a flaw in your reasoning."

"And what is that?"

"Only one of us is going to be inside this building: you."

"I will be the bait in your little trap."

"Exactly."

"And you will be waiting outside somewhere."

"Correct. And I've got another little surprise for him. By the time I'm done with him, he will be sorry he ever decided to renew acquaintances with me."

Again Alexei shook his head. "Another surprise? I do not understand. If you are outside and you see Piotr approaching the building, you must shoot immediately, and end this situation."

"I can't do that, my new friend."

"But you must! Why give the most unstable man I have ever met any opportunity to turn the tables on you, as you did on him back in your country?"

"He's not going to turn the tables on me, Alexei, don't worry. But I can't simply act as a sniper and cut him down the first opportunity I have."

"Why on earth not?"

"Because this is personal. He made it personal when he tortured and murdered someone I was extremely close to. He has to look into my face and know who is taking him down. He has to see it coming, even if only for a moment."

Alexei stared at Tracie in horror, his mouth half open. The pain from his injury had made his face pale and chalky before, but now it was ghostly.

"You told me you would allow me to live," he said, "but you lied. You are going to kill us both."

39

Sweat poured off Tracie as she moved crates and boxes around the inside of the building. Some were extremely light, almost as if they hadn't been filled yet, while others were so heavy she had to drag them across the floor because lifting them was out of the question.

There were only two windows in the entire one-room building, and they were narrow and covered with what Tracie assumed was several decades worth of grime. It was obvious Speransky had wanted them to be as difficult to see through as possible. She thought if she could line the wall beneath and around the windows with his boxes and crates so that they were not easily seen from the outside, she might buy herself a little time.

It wouldn't be much, but she wasn't going to need much.

Initially, Alexei had pleaded with her to reconsider her plan. He called it foolhardy and suicidal, and Tracie allowed for the fact he might be right. It would be far safer, he argued, to establish a position on the roof of one of the surrounding abandoned buildings and pick off Speransky the moment he came into view.

"It won't work, Alexei. In addition to what I already told you about wanting Speransky to know I'm the one who killed him, there's a practical consideration, as well."

"A practical consideration."

"Yes. I have two weapons: the Makarov I took off Vasily Labochev last night, and the handgun I took off you after you tried to cave my skull in with it, which is almost an identical model. Handguns, Alexei. Neither one would be accurate enough to hit Speransky from a distance. I have to be much closer than that."

He shook his head and mumbled under his breath and tried again a few minutes later. Tracie ignored him. She was too busy to waste her breath on the same argument over and over.

And besides, he had no say in the matter.

She had moved almost all the crates before finally stopping for a breather. There was no way to know how soon Speransky would appear, but her senses were telling her she was running out of time. And she trusted those senses implicitly. So she'd been working hard, torn between wishing Alexei was healthy enough to help and being glad he could barely move, because his injury rendered him effectively harmless.

She leaned against a tower of crates stacked one on top of the other and wiped a dirty sleeve across her face to clear the sweat from her eyes. The gash on her skull was throbbing with every beat of her heart and the headache she'd had since being clubbed with the butt of the gun had been gradually worsening.

She wondered whether she'd suffered a concussion and decided it was probably better not to know.

"What is the message?" Alexei hadn't said a word for the better part of the last forty-five minutes, apparently realizing—finally—that he would not be able to change Tracie's mind regarding her plan.

"Excuse me?" Tracie said.

"You told me you are allowing me to live because you want me to pass along a message to my superiors at Lubyanka. Since I very much doubt either of us will survive beyond the next few hours it is probably irrelevant, but in the unlikely event I do survive, I would like to know what that message is."

She had bent down, hands on her knees, in an effort to catch her breath, but now she stood and approached Alexei. "It is very a very simple message, and one I want you to repeat verbatim. You tell those sons of bitches that if anyone from your goddamned intelligence services ever comes within shouting distance of a member of my family again, I will return to this country and I will hunt him down, and when I'm finished with him he will wish he'd died quickly like Vasily Labochev did last night and like Piotr Speransky will when he shows up here.

"You tell them that I will then move on to the operative's family.

His parents, grandparents, wife and children. You tell your superiors that I will not stop until I've wiped that person's bloodline clear off the face of the earth."

Tracie realized she'd begun shaking with rage, and that her voice had increased in volume until it was nearly a shout.

She stopped speaking and walked back toward the boxes. Then she turned and faced him again. "Did you get all that, or would you like me to repeat it? I'll be happy to go over it as many times as it takes, because I want to make sure the message is clear. I truly feel sorry for whoever touches a member of my family again."

"You do not need to repeat yourself," Alexei said quietly. "I understand. And I believe you."

"Good. Because I told you I have no quarrel with you, Alexei, and I meant it. No matter what had happens inside this building today or tomorrow or whenever, even if one or both of us ends up dead, it is a fate we both signed up for. We understood going in it was always a possibility, understood the risks inherent in a career in covert intelligence. But the torture and murder of innocent family members is going too far. That's crossing a line I cannot tolerate. And I *will not* tolerate it."

Alexei said nothing this time; he simply gazed steadfastly at the filthy windows. Tracie assumed he was considering the likelihood he would die in a hail of bullets inside Piotr Speransky's safe house.

She didn't care. After a moment she turned and got back to work.

40

The prospect of spending at least one night inside a mostly abandoned industrial park in northwest Russia was singularly unappealing, but there was no way around it. This was where Speranksy
would come, so this was where she would stay until her showdown
with the man who'd killed her father was over.

Food and hydration could become an issue if Speransky dragged
things out, since she'd brought only a few bottles of water and
half-dozen or so protein bars. But she doubted that would happen,
because based on what she'd learned about Piotr Speransky, she
thought there was no way he could convince himself to delay
checking on what was left of his fortune, even if it would be the
tactically sound thing to do.

He would have to learn whether or not he'd been robbed blind
and left with nothing.

After concealing the crates and boxes as well as she could,
Tracie stepped out of the safe house and peered through each
of the windows to check her handiwork. The accumulated grime
on both sides of the glass, plus the fact that the iron bars would
prevent Speransky from pressing his face directly against the
window, combined to render a clear view of the building's interior
impossible.

She squinted and could just make out Alexei sitting in the rickety chair in the middle of the open room. His leg was stretched out
atop the two boxes Tracie had moved to support his injured knee,
and at first glance it appeared that the building had otherwise
been cleared out.

If she moved to the side of either window and gazed along the inside of the front wall, however, it was possible to see that some or all of the crates and boxes had been moved and stacked up more or less out of sight.

She shrugged. It was the best she could do, short of actually hauling all the crates out of the safe house and moving them elsewhere, and she had neither the time nor the means to do so.

Time was the real issue. She could feel it slipping away, could sense Piotr Speransky coming ever closer, and if her preparations were not complete upon his arrival in Leningrad, she would die; it was just that simple.

For all her hatred of Speransky—and of herself for that fateful decision to spare his life back in Moscow—she respected his abilities as an operative and an assassin. Her single advantage over him would be that of surprise: she knew where and roughly when he was going to appear. And if she weren't in position to take him down inside the industrial park, he would quickly gain the advantage.

Any extended conflict would spell doom for Tracie. She was alone and thousands of miles from home; he would be on familiar ground and could marshal significant tactical support if he managed to escape her ambush.

After satisfying herself that Speransky's crates were mostly invisible from outside the safe house, she returned inside the building for what she hoped would be the final time.

She eyed Alexei and said, "You remember the message I want you to pass along?"

"I remember."

Tracie nodded. "Good. Then I guess this is it. Goodbye Alexei. Hopefully our paths never cross again."

"No one wishes that more fervently that I," he said.

She stepped to the door and he said, "Wait."

She turned. "What is it?"

"If you are unsuccessful in killing Piotr…"

"I won't be."

"But if you are, he will not be kindly disposed toward me. He will be enraged at my failure and will almost certainly execute me where I sit."

"He's going to die, Alexei."

"But if he does not, I need a weapon with which to defend myself, or else I will be a sitting duck. I cannot possibly move quickly enough to fight him, or even to escape him. He will put two bullets into my skull and that will be that."

Tracie stared at him, unspeaking.

"I understand we are enemies. I understand we each work toward the destruction of the other. But if you refuse to provide me the means with which to defend myself, I will die helpless and alone. Can you live with that on your conscience?"

"I'll already be dead in your hypothetical scenario, remember?"

"You know what I mean."

She continued to gaze at the injured KGB operative, aware of the eerie similarity between the current situation and the one a few months ago with Piotr Speransky that had set this deadly confrontation in motion. The smart tactical move would be to kill Alexei, or at the very least to leave him unarmed so if she failed in her mission of vengeance, Speranksy would execute him and the KGB would find itself down one more operative.

But she simply didn't have it in her to abandon a helpless man, even one fighting for the wrong side.

She crossed the room in five strides and stopped next to Alexei. "Are you going to shoot me in the back if I return your weapon to you?"

"Why would I do that? Leaving you alive represents my best chance for survival, because even with a weapon I am likely a siting duck against a man like Piotr Speransky. Probably my only chance at living beyond the next few hours is for you to finish what you have started here."

A long moment passed, the two operatives regarding each other silently. Then she reached behind her back and removed Alexei's Makarov from the waistband of her jeans.

She handed it to him and said, "Goodbye, Alexei."

She turned her back on the KGB man and walked out of the safe house, pulling the door securely closed behind her.

41

May 23, 1988
9:35 p.m.
Druzhba Industrial Park
Leningrad, Russia, USSR

Think like a spy.

That had been Tracie's mantra from her earliest days in the field when dealing with Soviet operatives. She felt blessed to have been the recipient of the finest intelligence training in the world, but the KGB had been doing its thing for nearly seventy years, and they trained their people extensively as well.

Any operative to disregard that fact, or to underestimate the enemy, was risking violent death. Or worse, agonizing torture followed by violent death.

So after securing the three combination padlocks on the safe house door, she moved toward the industrial park entrance, rather than deeper into the park. Speransky's assumption would be that Alexei had by now neutralized Tracie, but still, he would take no chances.

It was inconceivable to think he would enter the park through the front gates.

A much more likely possibility was that he would cut through the chain link fence surrounding the park from somewhere in back, approaching the building from the rear. In fact, Tracie guessed, he had probably compromised the security fence somewhere back there shortly after establishing his safe house. As rundown as this industrial park was, the odds of anyone fixing a damaged fence—or even finding it, for that matter—were so slim as to be negligible.

Druzhba Industrial Park had long ago ceased to be a going concern, assuming it ever had been one. But what little activity remained was concentrated much deeper inside the park, meaning Tracie had her choice of every building surrounding Speransky's safe house when it came to taking cover and awaiting his arrival.

She selected a concrete-block structure similar in size and design to the safe house. She knew Speransky would come at night, under cover of darkness, so she needed to camp out as close to the target's building as she could manage and still remain out of sight.

The storage unit had once featured a pair of narrow windows like the ones in Speransky's safe house, but they had long ago been smashed out and never replaced. No iron bars covered the empty window frames, either.

Darkness was falling as Tracie pushed open the door and entered the abandoned building. She was tired but not sleepy, a seeming incongruity she'd encountered before, usually as a confrontation approached. Adrenaline raced through her but the tiredness prevented her from feeling jittery and allowed for a clarity of thought that went above and beyond what she felt at any other time.

And she would need that clarity. She would need every advantage she could muster. If she were to stand any chance against a man like Piotr Speransky she would have to be on top of her game.

She yawned and stretched and gazed out the empty window frame at the industrial park in the direction of Speransky's safe house. Darkness had fallen and the area was quiet and still.

From out of her pocket she removed the small gold cross she'd taken off Ryan Smith's corpse with the intention of returning it to the dead CIA operative's family. She'd been disappointed and angry when Aaron Stallings refused to consider her request, and while she understood his reasoning it seemed the sort of rule he could have bent, if only to bring some small measure of comfort to a dead hero's family.

But right now, at this moment, she was almost thankful for the way her request had turned out. The cross felt strong and inspirational in her hand, not for its religious connotations—Tracie didn't consider herself a particularly religious person—but because it served as a tangible reminder of the man who'd been captured and tortured by the Soviets and had faced the most horrible of fates with grace and dignity.

Tracie wondered whether she could have done the same.

She sat staring out the broken window and running her fingers over the cross, grateful for Ryan Smith's presence, remorseful that she'd failed him in her rescue attempt.

It was exactly how she'd failed her father.

* * *

May 23, 1988
3:05 a.m.
Druzhba Industrial Park
Leningrad, Russia, USSR

There was no security lighting inside the industrial park like there would have been inside a similar facility in the Unites States. No sodium vapor lights hanging from tall poles to aid Tracie in identifying approaching danger. Apparently the Soviets had decided that whatever was manufactured here when the buildings were all in use had been sufficiently protected by the chain-link fence topped with razor wire.

The good news—if there could be said to be any good news in this whole mess—was that the skies had cleared over the course of the day. The night was clear and the moon nearly full. It wasn't quite like the brightness of midday out there, but Tracie could see well enough from her vantage point to know when the KGB assassin was making his approach.

Hopefully.

The last of the few workers populating the park rolled along the main driveway and out the front gate just before six p.m., a parade of rust-bucket Ladas, Dacias and one East German Trabant. In the hours since, Tracie had seen no hint of activity from anywhere inside the park.

It was now after three a.m., and she knew if Speranksy were going to show tonight it would be soon. Even in such a secluded location, he would not want to risk torturing Tracie past six or seven a.m., when the workmen began showing up and one of them could potentially hear anguished screams and come to investigate.

And she knew Speransky would want several uninterrupted hours in which to play with her before ending her life. It was entirely possible he planned to transport her somewhere even more private to conduct his torture session, but before he did anything of the kind, Tracie knew he would want to reassure himself that his cache of money was safe and to—

From around the far corner of Speransky's safe house came a shadowy figure, moving with stealth but speed. The figure was dressed all in black, and appeared as nothing more than a vague, undefined shape, a suggestion of a person silhouetted briefly against the light-colored background of the building against which it flattened itself before continuing across the narrow alleyway.

It was Speransky.

It had to be.

Tracie watched as the figure moved directly to the first of the two narrow windows built into the safe house's front wall. She couldn't see whether Speransky had his gun out, but she didn't have to see it.

Of course he would have his gun out.

She began crawling through the empty window frame as quickly as possible but cognizant of the need for utter silence. Alerting Speransky to her presence while still this far away would not end well for her.

She dropped to the ground outside the building with a soft thump and then froze.

No reaction from the shadowy figure across the alleyway.

She began creeping across the pothole-strewn pavement as Speransky bent and peered through the grimy glass, exactly as she had hoped he would. The interior of the safe house would be bathed in shadows, but he should at least be able to make out the figure of the injured Alexei sitting in the middle of the room, leg elevated.

Speransky reached up with both hands—yes, he was holding a gun in his right hand—and grabbed hold of the iron bars as he forced his face closer to the window. Then he muttered a curse in Russian and bounded up to the locked front door.

Tracie had been moving steadily toward him, gun held in front of her in a two-handed shooter's grip just in case Speransky should hear her or detect movement in his peripheral vision and whirl around to shoot.

But her ruse had worked. She knew a man like Piotr Speransky wouldn't give a damn about the injury to his fellow operative; he would have only two concerns: checking the status of his money first, and determining the fate of Tracie Tanner second.

Those two concerns were overriding all else for Speransky at the moment. He'd thrown caution to the wind. As carefully as he'd approached the safe house a moment ago, he was now jabbing at the combination locks with shaking hands while muttering angry curses.

Tracie found herself maybe ten feet behind Speransky as he opened the first padlock. He removed it and tossed it to the side, immediately focusing on the second lock.

She had closed to within a half-dozen feet when he opened and discarded the second lock. He was lost in his task, panicked and worried that he'd lost everything.

But he had no idea what it was like to lose everything.

Tracie relished introducing him to the concept.

By the time the third lock clicked open, Tracie was close enough to reach out and touch the man who'd murdered her father. He never once considered checking his six to ensure he wasn't being ambushed, and now it was too late. She reached up and shoved the Makarov 9mm handgun against the side of Speransky's skull.

"Hello, Piotr," she said softly in Russian. "Move so much as an inch and you die."

Speransky froze, his left hand suspended eye height in front of the door, holding the lock. The gun he held in his right. Its barrel was pointing toward the sky.

"You should have let it go," she continued. "You could have lived to a ripe old age instead of dying in a graveyard of abandoned factory buildings."

"I could not let it go," he hissed. "When you walked out of that Moscow safe house you left me with nothing."

"I wouldn't say nothing. Some of those boxes in there are damned heavy. I know, because I moved them around. If they're all filled with cash, you could have disappeared and lived a pretty lavish lifestyle."

"I could not let it go," he repeated.

"But now," Tracie continued as if he hadn't spoken, "now you'll die exactly as you lived—violently and alone."

"Your father begged for his life before I killed him," Speranksy taunted. "He cried like a little child and pissed his pants like a baby."

"My father was ten times the man you'll ever be. Twenty times."

"Tell yourself that if you wish, but by the time I finished with him, he was begging for mercy, snot dripping from his nose and blood from everywhere else. He would have given you up to save himself if he could have. He would have—"

Without warning, the assassin stomped down on Tracie's foot with his boot as he spun and dropped into a crouch in a desperate effort to lower his head below the level of her gun.

But she was ready for him. She'd known exactly what he was doing, attempting to anger her and destroy her focus, and had known exactly what was coming when he felt the time was right. It was the only thing he could do if he wanted to live.

The pain exploded in her foot and she ignored it.

He fired his gun and she felt a 9mm slug whiz past her ear. She ignored that, too.

A preternatural sense of calm descended over her and everything slowed down and she lowered her gun in perfect timing with Speransky's body as he dropped into his crouch. It was as if she'd glued the weapon to his skull, and she squeezed the trigger and the gun roared and flame licked out of the barrel and Piotr Speransky's head exploded.

And as blood and gore and bone fragments flew, Tracie realized she was crying, and she was surprised by that fact because the last thing she could remember was responding calmly to the assassin's taunts and waiting for him to make his move.

She had known this was as close to a suicide mission as she

would likely ever undertake. Had known there was every possibility Speransky would get the better of her and he would be the one to survive this showdown. And now that it was over, somewhere in the dark recesses of her mind she wished he had.

Somewhere in the dark recesses of her mind she longed to join her father in darkness and peace.

And then everything resumed normal speed, and Speransky was falling to the ground, a large chunk of his skull blown off, and Tracie was standing in front of the door holding the gun she'd taken off Vasily Labochev and crying as the bloody mist continued to fall.

42

"I am armed," Alexei shouted from inside the safe house, and Tracie realized he'd heard the confrontation, had heard the gunshots, but had no idea who was still standing.

If anyone.

Tracie swiped an arm across her face to clear the blood and the tears, and bent over the crumpled body of the man who had tortured and murdered her father. She knew he was dead but checked for a pulse anyway. It was an action ingrained in her through years of training and experience.

She found no pulse and checked again.

When he remained dead, she pushed herself to her feet, suddenly exhausted. She forced her voice steady and called through the closed door, "That's a bad strategy."

"CIA?" Alexei answered. "You survived? I would not have predicted that," he said with a chuckle that revealed not amusement but pent-up fear and tension.

"Never bet against me," Tracie said, more to herself than to the injured KGB man. "You'll lose every time."

The safe house fell silent, both inside and out.

After a moment, Alexei said, "What do you mean about strategy?"

"I mean you had a bad one. In fact, it likely would have gotten you killed if things had gone the other way and Speransky was standing outside this door."

"I do not know what you are talking about."

"Of course you do. You just admitted you thought Speransky would kill me. By yelling, you were warning him not to come after you, letting him know he would face a hostile reception if he came charging through the door, gun blazing, as he tried to punish you for failing in your mission."

"So I should just have let him come in here and shoot me in the head?"

Tracie shook her head and tried to suppress a laugh. *I just put down one of the most dangerous men in the Soviet Union and now I'm discussing strategy with a KGB operative. I think I need a vacation.*

"Are you still there?" A nervous tinge had crept into Alexei's voice, as if he suspected Tracie might even now be finding a hidden entrance to the safe house and sneaking up behind him to put a bullet in his skull, exactly as she had done with Piotr Speransky.

"I'm still here."

"Then tell me what you would have done in my place, Miss Superstar CIA Operative."

"Well, I wouldn't have told my adversary I was holding a gun, that's for sure. I would have sat in the safe house and said nothing, put the pressure on Speransky to make a move. I would have bet on him being furious with me for failing and at the same time hopped up from a just-completed deadly confrontation, adrenaline racing through his system.

"I would have banked on him assuming my captor had confiscated my gun. I would have expected him to bull through the door bent on putting two 9mm slugs in my brain," she continued. "And when he charged mindlessly inside, I would have been waiting with my gun trained on the only entryway into the safe house. Then I would have started firing and I would have continued until my magazine was empty and he was lying fully ventilated on the concrete floor.

"That's what I would have done," she concluded. "Since you asked."

Another silence, this one longer than the first.

"So, what happens now?" Alexei said. "Am I next on your hit list?"

"I already told you, I have no reason to kill you. I certainly wouldn't have returned your gun to you if I were planning on eliminating you after I finished with Speransky. For that matter, if I was going to kill you I could have done it at any time today, before Speransky's arrival. You would have made just as effective bait dead as alive."

"It is silly to be having this discussion through a closed door," Alexei said. "Come inside and say goodbye before you leave the country."

This time, Tracie didn't bother to suppress her laugh. It sounded loud and long and foreign to her, almost like it was coming from someone else. Someone hollow and sad.

"What is funny?" Alexei called.

"I said I don't have any reason to kill you," Tracie answered. "But you have plenty of reasons to kill me. Why would I walk through the door and give you the opportunity?"

"I do not know what you mean."

"Come on, Alexei, of course you do. You needed me alive before, in order to protect you from Speransky. Now that he's dead, there is absolutely no reason for you to hold your fire."

"I do not know what you mean."

"You keep saying that when we both know it's not true," Tracie said with another laugh. "But that's fine, you can play devil's advocate if you want."

"What is…devil's advocate?"

"It means you advance an argument you know is not true, just to see how the other person will respond. Like, for example, claiming you would not fill me full of Russian lead the second I walked through that door."

Silence again. This one lasted longer than the first two put together.

"But that's fine," Tracie said. "I'll play your little game."

"Please," Alexei said. "Explain it to me."

"When I get far enough away from here, I'm going to drop a dime to the Leningrad police and tell them where to find you. About two hours after that happens, the fine folks at Lubyanka will be notified what went down here tonight. By midday tomorrow, you will find yourself answering a series of very pointed questions from your KGB superiors. Things would go much more smoothly for you if you were able to hand them the scalp of the

CIA operative who killed their best assassin and injured you in the process."

By now, Tracie knew exactly what to expect, and she allowed the ensuing silence to drag out. Alexei had nothing to say because there was no denying her point.

"I told you I liked you," she said with a tired smile she knew Alexei could not see. "But I don't like you enough to let you kill me to save your career."

"I hope you do not think less of me for trying," Alexei said, finally admitting the obvious.

"Not even a little bit. Like I said, I've been there. But the benefit I gain from leaving you alive is in knowing the message I want passed to Lubyanka will, in fact, be passed. You will pass it exactly as I told you?"

"*Da.*"

"Then there's nothing more to discuss, and I have a long journey ahead of me, not to mention a lot of work to do before I can relax. It's time for me to get started. Goodbye, KGB."

"Goodbye, CIA."

By now, Trace had backed away from the door and the dead body of Piotr Speransky, putting maybe eight feet of open space between herself and the safe house. She knelt and held the Makarov she'd taken off Vasily Labochev steadily on the closed safe house door, aiming low.

Alexei was injured and would be dragging himself across the floor in a crawl.

The door swung suddenly open and Tracie fired immediately, squeezing off a half dozen shots before Alexei could even pull his trigger.

The sound of the gunshots echoed off the surrounding buildings and faded slowly away and Tracie realized she'd begun crying again.

She hadn't lied to Alexei when she said she liked him.

She also hadn't lied when she'd told him her scalp would have made a tremendous trophy for the KGB, a fact that would not have been lost on any moderately talented intelligence operative. Alexei would have known handing over Tracie's dead body was likely the only thing that could save his career.

Maybe even his life.

Tracie had known what Alexei was pulling from the moment he began stalling, playing dumb about his situation and giving himself time to struggle off the chair she'd provided him and crawl across the safe house to the door. She had to give him credit, his voice had not revealed any of the pain he must have been feeling from his shattered knee as he struggled forward.

Once they'd said goodbye, she knew he would wait just long enough for her to turn her back on the safe house before pulling the door open and firing into her back.

One last time, she forced herself to stand. She approached the safe house carefully, gun trained unflinchingly on Alexei's motionless body, despite knowing—as she had known with Piotr Speransky—he was dead.

She knelt over him and verified what she already knew, and then shook her head. "You should have let me walk away," she whispered. "I really wanted you to pass that message."

She sighed and turned toward the front gate of Druzhba Industrial Park. One positive result of being forced to kill Alexei was that the local authorities would assume Alexei and Speransky had killed each other in some kind of dispute over the contents of Speransky's safe house. The confusion should allow Tracie the opportunity to get well clear of Leningrad before the truth came out.

Eventually, the KGB would become involved, either because Leningrad police would wise up and notify them of the strange killings at Druzhba or, more likely, the KGB would send someone to investigate before the police had the slightest notion what had actually happened. There was undoubtedly already a team of investigators from Lubyanka working just a few kilometers away in an attempt to get to the bottom of Vasily Labochev's death.

Tracie entered the narrow alleyway between the buildings. She looked back one last time at the bodies of the two dead Russians, one cooling on the ground outside the safe house, the other lying in the open doorway.

Then she kept walking as the tears continued to fall.

She cried for her father, who had deserved so much better than dying alone inside a wreck of a house after being tortured by a Soviet spy.

And she cried for herself and for what she had become.

By the time she reached the industrial park's front gate, Tracie had dried her tears and was refocused on slipping out of the Soviet Union and returning to the United States.

She was highly motivated.

She needed to see her mother.

She needed to see Marshall Fulton.

She especially needed to visit her father's grave, partly to let him know he could now rest in peace, but mostly so she could finally say goodbye to the best man she'd ever known without the bitter weight of vengeance hanging over her.

And she needed sleep. She was so damned tired.

She hiked southeast along the deserted road, reaching her stolen Russian car quickly despite walking at a relatively unhurried pace. It wasn't like the dead men were going to spring to life and chase after her. They would never chase anyone again.

Tracie slipped into the front seat and turned the key and the engine started on the first try. It was a minor miracle given the vehicle's age and pedigree.

She executed a neat K-turn and accelerated away, anxious to leave Leningrad behind for good.

She watched in the rear view mirror as the front gate of Druzhba Industrial Park shrank into the distance. Eventually she rounded a corner and it disappeared entirely.

And Tracie shifted her attention forward, settling in for the long trip home.

––––––––––

Tracie Tanner returns soon in her eighth action-packed thriller. In the meantime, if you'd like to read the series in order from the beginning, please visit Amazon's *Parallax View* page. Happy reading!

To be the first to learn about new releases, and for the opportunity to win free ebooks, signed copies of print books, and other swag, take a moment to sign up for Allan Leverone's email newsletter at AllanLeverone.com.

Reader reviews are hugely important to authors looking to set their work apart from the competition. If you have a moment to spare, please consider taking a moment to leave a brief, honest review of *The Soviet Assassin* at Amazon's *The Soviet Assassin* page, at Goodreads, or at your favorite review site, and thank you.

––––––––––

About the Author

Allan Leverone is the *New York Times* and *USA Today* bestselling author of more than twenty novels and four novellas, as well as a 2012 Derringer Award winner for excellence in short mystery fiction and a 2011 Pushcart Prize nominee. He lives in Londonderry, New Hampshire with his wife Sue, and has three grown children and three beautiful grandchildren. He loves to hear from readers and other authors; connect on Facebook, Twitter @AllanLeverone, and at AllanLeverone.com.

Also from Allan Leverone

Thrillers

Parallax View: A Tracie Tanner Thriller
All Enemies: A Tracie Tanner Thriller
The Omega Connection: A Tracie Tanner Thriller
The Hitler Deception: A Tracie Tanner Thriller
The Kremlyov Infection: A Tracie Tanner Thriller
The Bashkir Extraction: A Tracie Tanner Thriller
The Lonely Mile
Final Vector
The Organization: A Jack Sheridan Pulp Thriller
Trigger Warning: A Jack Sheridan Pulp Thriller
Death Perception: A Jack Sheridan Pulp Thriller

Dark Fiction

Mr. Midnight
After Midnight
The Lupin Project
Paskagankee
Revenant
Wellspring
Grimoire
Covenant
Linger: Mark of the Beast (Co-written with Edward Fallon)

Novellas

The Becoming
Flight 12: A Kristin Cunningham Thriller

Story Collections

Postcards from the Apocalypse
Letters from the Asylum
Uncle Brick and the Four Novelettes
The Tracie Tanner Collection: Three Complete Thriller Novels

www.ingramcontent.com/pod-product-compliance
Lightning Source LLC
Chambersburg PA
CBHW060536260626
47161CB00003B/931